THE PATH OF THE WICKED

A Liberty Lane Mystery

Gillian Linscott
writing as

Caro Peacock

CRÈME de la CRIME

This first world edition published 2013
in Great Britain and the USA by
SEVERN HOUSE PUBLISHERS LTD of
19 Cedar Road, Sutton, Surrey, England, SM2 5DA

Trade paperback edition first published 2018
In Great Britain and the USA by
SEVERN HOUSE PUBLISHERS LTD
Eardley House, 4 Uxbridge Street, London W8 7SY

British Library Cataloguing in Publication Data
A CIP catalogue record for this title is available from the British Library.

ISBN-13: 978-1-78029-041-6 (cased)
ISBN-13: 978-1-84751-901-6 (trade paper)
ISBN-13: 978-1-78010-396-9 (e-book)

ONE

'The problem is, I'm a coward.'

The gentleman sitting in my clients' chair made the confession as simply as a person might admit to short sight or a dislike of marmalade. No drama about it and a tone that came closer to mild regret than self-reproach. Mildness seemed to be his chief characteristic. His height was moderate, his figure rounded but not corpulent, his face clean-shaven with the lightly sunburnt complexion of a man who spent most of his time in the country. A pate that was almost completely bald, apart from a trim fringe of brown hair round the circumference, and arched brows over mild grey eyes gave him the face that a child might draw on a hard-boiled egg. A pleasant-natured child, though, who'd made a likeable face. His eyes stared across the table into mine, as if I'd understand everything from that one admission. I waited.

'I'm a magistrate. It's expected of one, living in a small community. I can't say I enjoy it, but it's my duty and it doesn't usually involve much unpleasantness. Fines for being drunk, a few months for poaching or stealing a chicken and so on – everybody knowing everybody else and not much resentment on the whole. We sit as a bench of three, and usually I agree with the other two. Now and again, if I think they're being too severe, I might tell them so. Sometimes it makes a difference and sometimes it doesn't. I think Penbrake thinks I'm by way of being a nuisance now and then, but—'

'Penbrake?'

'Chairman of the bench. A very just gentleman, very able. I fear I annoy him, but he doesn't usually show it. Which is why all this is so very disagreeable. It was a man's life, I told him. It was our duty to give him a chance to produce evidence. He thought I was making some reflection on his character, which was not what I had in mind at all.'

Again, that grey-eyed stare, begging me to understand. I felt tired. It was late July, the tail-end of the social season, when the air in London feels as if too many people have been breathing it, the grass

in the park is trodden and yellowish, thin layers of dried horse dung
coat the streets. I was sleeping badly, aware of the workhouse clock
across the way striking the hours through the night, the smell of
the cesspit, which the landlord would never empty when he was
supposed to, wafting through the open window on the first breeze
of morning. I could smell it now, in the small upstairs room I use
as an office, and I assumed my potential client could, too. The first
I'd known about him was when a note was delivered to my quarters
in Abel Yard, Mayfair, the day before.

> Dear Miss Lane,
>   I hope you will excuse this note from a person who has not
> had the pleasure of being introduced to you. I live in a village
> near Cheltenham in Gloucestershire and am in London on
> family business. While talking with my solicitor about it, I
> took the opportunity to raise another matter which was causing
> deep concern to me. He suggested that I should consult you.
> If, therefore, you find it possible to favour me with an appoint-
> ment tomorrow, before I return home, you would be doing a
> great service to the man who respectfully subscribes himself
> Stephen Godwit.

The address for reply was a Piccadilly hotel. The note was enclosed
in a covering letter from the solicitor in question, an honest man
who had been involved in several of my cases. I'd suggested an
appointment at eleven next morning, and Mr Godwit had arrived at
the bottom of my staircase on the first stroke of the hour.

I was inclined from first acquaintance to like him, because he did
not seem disconcerted by either Abel Yard or me. Respectable visitors
tended to raise eyebrows at a place so at odds with a Mayfair address,
surprised at chickens in the yard, the smell of cows from the byre at
the end, sounds of hammering from the carriage repair shop by the
gate. When I'd gone down to open the door to him, he was bending
and gently ruffling a hen's neck feathers just the way she liked it.
The bird was already swaying on its legs in a pleasant trance. It nearly
fell over when he straightened up and gave a little bow.

'Miss Lane. So very kind of you to see me.'

Just a hint of surprise in his eyes. Perhaps he'd expected somebody
older. But he'd made no comment, as some people annoyingly did,
on the oddness of finding a woman in my profession. He had stepped

up the stairs in his neatly shod feet, sat in the chair I offered him and come out with his story. It was simple enough in its way. A young man was likely to be sentenced to death by hanging in a few weeks' time and Mr Godwit could not rid himself of the idea that it would be partly his fault.

'I should have persisted, I can see that now. But Penbrake is a chop-chop kind of chairman – have done with it, then on to the next thing. And he was right in many ways. The evidence against young Picton is pretty strong and he didn't help himself with the attitude he took. He denied the charge, but refused to answer most of the questions that were put to him. He claimed the landowners were determined to see him hanged no matter what he said and as good as accused Penbrake of being in their pockets. He said he'd been elsewhere on the night in question, but not very convincingly, and wouldn't give names of anybody who might support him. I tried to argue for an adjournment to give Picton time to produce a witness to his whereabouts, if he had one, but Penbrake wouldn't have it. He said that could wait till the assizes, that all we had to do was decide whether there was a *prima facie* case against Picton, and there was, so we had no choice.'

'What about the third magistrate?' I said.

'He's seventy years old and more than half deaf, poor man. He just goes along with Penbrake.'

'Wasn't it a fair point that Mr Penbrake made?' I said. 'It will be the jury at the assizes who decide whether the man is guilty or not.'

He shook his head.

'That's the worst of it. The jury will have made their mind up before young Picton even steps into the dock.'

'He has a bad reputation?'

'I fear so.'

I waited, imagining some rural thug with a record of violence. Mr Godwit's enlargement of the point, given with some regret, came as a surprise.

'The fact is, I'm afraid young Picton is by way of being a revolutionary.'

He looked at me, waiting to see disapproval on my face.

'What kind of revolutionary?' I said.

It was a nervous time, with dark warnings from some political quarters of an English revolution brewing.

'A trade unionist,' Mr Godwit said sadly. It was, after all, only a few years since six Dorset farm workers had been transported to Australia for trying to form a trade union. Then, seeing that I hadn't immediately reacted with horror, he added: 'A Chartist, too.'

'Quite a lot of people are,' I said.

More than a million people had signed the petition calling for votes for working men. From Mr Godwit's face, there was worse to come.

'The fact is, Picton was almost certainly involved in that unpleasantness at Newport last November.'

This was more serious. The night of rioting, when thousands of men marched on Newport prison to try to free one of the Chartist leaders, had ended in soldiers opening fire and men dying. The rising had failed and the Welsh Bastille hadn't fallen, but it left the comfortable classes badly shaken, fearing rocks through their windows and peasants with pikes in their drawing rooms. Mr Godwit was probably right about the opinion of the jury. Jurors are property-owning men.

'Was Picton convicted of taking part in the riot?' I said.

'No. But nobody saw him for quite a long time afterwards. A lot of them went into hiding.'

'So whom is he accused of murdering?' I said.

'A young woman named Mary Marsh. She was governess to the Kemble family. That's all part of it. There was bad blood between young Picton and the Kembles.'

'The Kembles being local landowners?'

'Yes. Colonel Kemble owns about eight hundred acres. He's retired from the army. His wife died last year. His son, Rodney, runs the estate farm and they keep a few racehorses. Young Picton's father used to work for them, until he had an accident. He was killed falling off a ladder in a barn, leaving the wife with three young children to bring up. They say he was drunk at the time. I believe Colonel Kemble behaved decently enough, paid a pension to the widow and so on, but young Picton harboured a grudge.'

'Was that common knowledge?'

'Very much so. Last year Kemble cut off the pension, because of all the talk about young Picton and so on. Picton threatened Rodney Kemble in pretty violent terms – said in front of a dozen witnesses that the Kembles' time was coming and they shouldn't expect to be landowners for ever.'

'And yet it was the governess who was murdered. Is Picton

supposed to have hated the Kembles so much that he'd kill anybody from the household?'

Mr Godwit looked ill at ease. 'Rather the reverse. There seems to be some evidence that Picton and Miss Marsh were on . . . conversational terms, so to speak.'

'More than conversational, you mean?'

A reluctant nod. 'So it's said.'

'Is it likely – the governess in a landowner's family and the local revolutionary?'

'Surprising, I grant you. But Picton was a good-looking fellow, and quite the orator.'

I noted the use of the past tense, but mainly I was wondering how such an unlikely pair could have met. But then there were sometimes hidden depths in governesses. I knew. I'd once been one myself.

'So why did he kill her?'

He wriggled in the chair. 'It's supposed that he . . . made advances to her and she resisted.'

'Where was the body found?'

'In a copse, on the Kembles' land. Young Kemble was walking with the keeper early one morning and they found her lying in a clearing. She was quite cold and her clothes were soaked with dew. It seems certain she'd been there since the night before.'

'How had she been killed?'

'With a blow to the head from an iron bar. It was found in the nettles not far from the body, with traces of blood and some of her hairs on it.'

'How long ago did this happen?'

'Eleven days ago.'

'Was Picton arrested immediately?'

'No. He disappeared again. He was found hiding in a barn some miles away, five days later.'

'And charged with the murder?'

'Yes. They arrested him on the Wednesday and he was brought before the bench last Friday.'

'Did he deny knowing Miss Marsh?'

'No. He admitted meeting her from time to time, in that very copse where the body was discovered.'

'Wasn't that foolish of him?'

'There's evidence that a housemaid had spotted them there once.

He must have known that would come out at the assizes. But it was all part of the man's attitude. He was treating the magistrates with contempt, as if we didn't matter.'

'And where was he on the night Miss Marsh was killed?'

'He was seen by a reliable witness earlier in the evening on a road not far from the Kembles' estate. He says he was on his way somewhere else, but wouldn't say where. It was put to him repeatedly that it would damage his position.'

'Was he asked why he'd disappeared after the murder?'

'Yes. He said that since he hadn't committed a crime, he didn't have to account for his movements.'

I'd been taking notes as we were talking, but now I put down my pencil, feeling oppressed by his story. Unless young Picton had amazing luck or a much better lawyer than anyone likely to be available to a farm labourer's widow, yes, he would hang and there was probably precious little I could do about it.

'So Picton denies killing Miss Marsh, but admits to meetings with her. He was seen not far away near the time she was killed and won't say where he went after that. Then he went into hiding. In spite of all this, you think he's innocent?'

'No.' Mr Godwit said it forcefully. Then, seeing the surprise on my face: 'I'm not a fool. In the face of all this, I can't claim he's innocent. And yet, I'm not totally convinced he's guilty. As a private gentleman, that wouldn't matter one way or the other. But I'm a magistrate, with a sworn duty to justice, and rather than annoy my friends and neighbours I've sent that young man on the road to the gallows when there's a doubt in my mind whether he's guilty or not. Should I really be shrugging off the responsibility?'

You could tell he wasn't a man accustomed to making speeches. His eyes were distressed, his face red.

'I wish I could help,' I said.

'Meaning that you can't?'

'It would take some time, getting to know the place and the people. I suppose it's not long to the next assizes.'

'Three and a half weeks. They open on the fifteenth of August.'

'I can't simply leave my cases here.'

'Of course, I see that.'

He dropped his eyes, apologetic. That made me feel shabby. The fact was, I had only one minor case on hand, which I could probably have seen to its end in a day or so, leaving me free to travel to Cheltenham. There were two other reasons, which I could not give to Mr Godwit.

'Even if I were free, it's not certain that I could help you,' I said. 'Suppose whatever I found only confirmed Picton's guilt?'

'I'd accept that. At least I'd feel that I'd done whatever was possible.'

His humility made me feel worse. I sighed.

'I'm sorry. I don't think I can do it. But if you'd care to leave your country address with me, I'll write to you if things change.'

He took the pencil I offered him and wrote the address in a neat round hand. I went downstairs and to the gateway with him.

'Perhaps the best you could do is to see that he has a lawyer,' I said.

'Would that be proper, for a magistrate?'

I was on the point of saying that people needn't know, but guessed Mr Godwit would be as innocent as the egg he resembled when it came to subterfuge. Which meant young Picton was as good as hanged. Cravenly, I hoped he were guilty.

Back upstairs, I put his address away in a drawer and picked up the rectangle of card that was the real reason for my reluctance to go out of town: an invitation to an evening of Italian operatic arias in the garden of a house in Kensington, inside if wet. I enjoy Italian arias, but that did not account for the spark of excitement in my mind when the invitation had been delivered the day before. Since I was unknown to the aristocratic person hosting the event, the only reason for it was that Mr Disraeli had a case for me and – according to the custom of the unusual relationship between us – this was where he'd tell me about it. Over the few years since I'd adopted my profession, some high affairs of diplomacy and government had come my way. At first it hadn't been of my seeking, but the truth was I'd come to enjoy my privileged and occasionally dangerous glimpses behind the scenes. The very things that had seemed to my disadvantage as an inquiry agent – my gender and comparative youth – sometimes gave me access to places where heavy boots could not tread. That ambitious young MP, Mr Benjamin Disraeli, was not a government minister, much to his disappointment, but he had a finger in many pies. The authorities knew of our friendship – if it could be called that – and had several times used him as the means of sounding me out for commissions. Since care for my reputation and his meant we could not meet in private, the first indications I'd have were invitations like this one.

In the evening, I put on my printed glazed cotton with guipure lace at bodice and sleeves, fastened my lucky dragonfly in my hair and told my housekeeper, Mrs Martley, not to wait up. Treading carefully to the gateway in new satin pumps, I gave one of the boys from the mews a few pennies to find a cab for me. Normally, I should have asked my unpredictable assistant, Tabby, to do it, but she'd gone wandering again. A case a few months before had strained our relationship badly and the damage was by no means healed.

The house was in Kensington Gore, practically out in the country and an expensive cab ride. On the way, we passed a town house with the shutters up. Nothing unusual in itself, at a time when the fashionable world was beginning its migrations to spas or grouse moors, but this house was part of the reason why I did not want to exile myself to Cheltenham. It belonged to a man named Stephen Brinkburn. His father had died recently, so he was now Lord Brinkburn. His half-brother Robert and I were . . . well, what were we? Not engaged officially. Not even unofficially. We had cared very much for each other, but he had chosen to go travelling and I had encouraged him. Six months ago he had set off with a friend on a leisurely journey to Athens and probably beyond, which would take them away for a year or more. At first his letters had been warm and frequent, but now I hadn't heard from him for months. Lord Brinkburn owed me a favour, and I'd fought a battle with my pride and decided at last to ask if he'd heard from his half-brother, but by the time I brought myself to that point, he'd shut the town house and gone to his country estate. I'd resolved to ask as soon as he got back. If the answer was yes, he heard from him regularly, then whatever had been between Robert and me did not exist any more. I sighed. With one thing and another, I needed whatever task Mr Disraeli was going to offer to divert me. I hoped it might be some scandal at the Foreign Office.

At Kensington Gore, clouds were threatening showers, so the recital took place in the huge conservatory, with tropical birds fluttering free through swathes of palms and lianas. Seated behind a frangipane, I looked around for Mr Disraeli and caught sight of his wife, Mary Anne, at the end of a row near the front. Since she seldom left his side in public, that guaranteed his presence at least. She was wearing carnation-coloured silk and what looked like a matching turban, with fringes. On a stage between tubs of orange trees, Lucia di Lammermoor went decorously mad in white satin, her cadenzas competing with screeches from the macaws. At the interval, I collected a cup of coffee and walked into the garden. The showers had kept off and a smudgy sunset was staining clouds to the west. I waited on a stone bench by a pool where goldfish flickered, knowing he'd find me when he wanted.

'Miss Lane, how nice to see you here.'

His affectation of surprise was one of the customs of our meetings. I said nothing, trying to resist the feeling that with his presence the world became instantly a more exciting place, though not necessarily more dependable.

'May I join you?'

I nodded. There were enough people strolling in the garden to make our tête-à-tête acceptable. He sat down on the other end of the bench. He was wearing two or three gold chains and a brocade waistcoat that matched Mary Anne's dress. Goodness knows how he'd managed to escape her.

'What did you think of the soprano?' he said.

The hitch of an elegant eyebrow gave his own opinion. I couldn't help smiling.

'A very tasteful madness,' I said.

He laughed. 'Yes, for a young lady who's just stabbed her bridegroom, she was commendably restrained.'

We sipped coffee and watched the goldfish.

'The Home Secretary's very worried,' he said.

Down to business. So no scandalous foreigners this time.

'He has plenty to be worried about,' I said.

'The demands of the Chartists are very reasonable in many ways,' Disraeli said.

He knew my views and I didn't try to hide them.

'In every way,' I said.

'The problem is, the manner of asking.'

'Isn't signing a petition one of an Englishman's rights?'

'Indeed, but it doesn't stop at the great petition, does it? There's the question of riotous assembly.'

'If peaceful marches turn into riots, it's usually because the authorities are heavy-handed,' I said. 'If you call out the dragoons every time men are asking for food and employment, of course there's trouble.'

'Yes, you're quite right,' he said.

It should have been a danger signal when he agreed with my opinion so easily, but I was too heated to catch it. He went on talking, eyes on the fish, voice serious.

'The problem for the authorities is how to know in advance which marches and meetings are intended to be peaceful and which have been subverted by agitators who want to overturn everything in society. If the Home Secretary knew, for instance, more about the people who are involved in planning these demonstrations, he'd be in a much stronger position to decide which ones needed serious steps and which didn't.'

A cold feeling came over me as he was speaking.

'So what has this got to do with me?' I said.

'You're something of a radical; you can't deny it.'

'I've never tried to.'

It was in my bloodline. My late father had been threatened with prison for openly supporting the French Revolution.

'You have contacts among pamphleteers and so forth.'

'Has somebody been spying on me?'

'Of course not. The point is that you are in a good position to get to know some of the men involved and, from time to time, report on what they're planning.'

'How dare you!'

The clattering of coffee cup on saucer warned me that I was literally shaking with anger. I clinked them down on the bench. Disraeli stared at me, seeming honestly surprised.

'You'd be doing the honest men among them a favour,' he said. 'It would make it more likely that the genuinely peaceful gatherings wouldn't be broken up by the police or army. Surely that would be worthwhile.'

I stood up, dazed with anger.

'So you're asking me to be a government spy on the Chartists. I won't say I'm sorry you hold such a low opinion of me, because after this your opinion doesn't matter one way or the other. Goodnight.'

As I turned away, I had a glimpse of his annoyed and puzzled face. In my anger, I lost my way in the rambling garden, stumbling over box hedges, my sleeves torn at by rose briars. By the time I found my way to a side gate, everybody else had gone in and the tenor's voice in 'Una furtiva lagrima' came faintly from the conservatory. There were no cabs to be had as far out as Kensington Gore and by the time I'd marched all the way to Knightsbridge my satin shoes were shredded beyond repair. When I got home, I used them to stir up the ashes of the parlour fire, found pen and ink and wrote a note.

Dear Mr Godwit,
Since our meeting, I find myself unexpectedly free of my obligations in London. If you still require them, you may call on the services of Liberty Lane.

TWO

'Lively sort of place, Cheltenham,' Amos said. 'I was there when they burned down the grandstand.'

My friend Amos Legge and I were taking our usual early-morning ride in the park, I on my thoroughbred mare, Rancie, he on a bad-tempered roan from the livery stables where he worked as a groom. I'd told him about Mr Godwit, but not about the meeting with Disraeli.

'Grandstand?'

'On the racecourse. Ten years ago, that was. Local preacher went around stirring people up about all the devilment that went on every July at the Gold Cup meeting.'

'So did burning down the grandstand get rid of the devilment?'

He grinned. 'What do you think? They just moved the racing to another course not far off, and the devilment went on as usual. Still does, I daresay.'

There was a faintly wistful sound to the last words.

'I didn't know you knew Cheltenham.'

'Place where I grew up was less than fifty miles away to the west. I worked for a while for a man who kept a racehorse or two. We used to lead them over.'

Amos came from Herefordshire and talked about it sometimes as if it were the Garden of Eden – with cider. In spite of that, he hadn't gone home for more than three years, since he set out with an employer to deliver a pedigree bull to a breeder near Paris. That was partly my fault. In Paris, our fortunes had come together and never quite parted. He was now the most fashionable groom in Hyde Park, with some high-class horse dealing on the side, and seemed in no hurry to return to a rustic life.

'About time I went back for a visit, though,' he said. 'Business has gone quiet enough for them to spare me for a week or two. I could lead her down with me and drop her off at Cheltenham if you liked.'

He nodded towards Rancie.

'I'll be working,' I said. 'What would I do with a horse?'

'How are you going to get around without one?'

It was a fair point. I was thinking too much like a Londoner, with cabs or hired carriages always to hand. Also, the prospect of country rides on Rancie was the first cheerful thing that occurred to me since the quarrel with Disraeli.

'It's a long way for you to ride and lead a horse,' I said.

'Hundred miles or so. Five or six days. Of course, it would be quicker if I wasn't leading her.'

'Then go by yourself and don't worry.' My voice sounded pettish from disappointment.

'Quicker with you riding her, I mean. Probably do it in four days in that case.'

As opposed to around half a day by fast stagecoach. But a long ride through summer countryside was a more pleasant prospect than being cooped up in a rattling vehicle with strangers.

'Start the day after tomorrow, if you like,' Amos said.

I could tell from his voice that he'd picked up my thoughts and knew he'd won.

'Amos, that's far too early. I have things to do here.'

But had I really? A few hours' work would wrap up my current case. All I'd be doing in London was watching to see when the shutters came down on the Brinkburns' house. Better altogether to get away.

'You can send Tabby in the coach with the heavy luggage,' Amos said.

'I haven't seen her for days. I'm not even sure she'd come.' A sad admission since she was supposed to be my apprentice.

'She'll come if you tell her to,' Amos said. 'A bit of country air will do her good.'

I was certain that Tabby wouldn't see it that way, having no enthusiasm for life outside London. Still, by the time Amos and I parted at the gateway to Abel Yard it had been agreed that we should ride to Cheltenham together. The only change was that we should leave in four days' time instead of two, leaving early on the following Sunday. I had preparations to make and another letter to write to Mr Godwit.

By the magic of our new penny post, his reply arrived the day before we were due to leave.

Dear Miss Lane,

I am happy to agree to your terms as stated, including expenses, and look forward to your arrival, which, according to my best

calculations, is likely to be in the middle of next week. You ask
if I can recommend a nearby inn for yourself and your maid, with
stabling for your mare. Since our local hostelry would hardly be
fit accommodation and the hotels of Cheltenham are a good three
miles away, I hope you may find it convenient to lodge in my
bachelor establishment. My housekeeper heartily welcomes
visitors, having so few, and is even now shaking the lavender out
of her best sheets. My stables are modest and my groom fulfils
a dual role as gardener, but I am sure we can accommodate your
mare suitably and offer our own oats, hay and good grazing. If
your maid would consent to share with our girl, Suzie, I am sure
we could provide for her equally comfortably.

I entirely understand your warning that you are not able to
guarantee success. I assure you that even in agreeing so kindly
to take up the case you are contributing very greatly to the
peace of mind of Stephen Godwit.

I liked the tactful mention of a housekeeper, giving respectability
to the proposed arrangement. As for my maid, I'd mentioned in my
letter that she would bring my heavy luggage by stagecoach, but
Tabby had not reappeared. Tabby had been my assistant and apprentice, willing to be called my maid on occasion – though incapable
of behaving like one – but in the last few weeks she seemed to have
reverted to her street-urchin way of life. I'd seen her now and then
in Abel Yard but could only get a word or two out of her before
she disappeared again. I was worried, but knew that while she was
in her present mood it would be no good trying to chase after her.
I finished packing my small trunk with clothes, sketching materials
and a few books, wrapped it in hessian, roped and labelled it with
Mrs Martley's help and then went down to the mews to find two
lads to carry it to the alcove under the stairs, ready for the carter.
There, sitting on a mounting block, looking every bit as disreputable
as the ragged lads around her, was Tabby. Her eyes were sunken,
cheeks pinched and pale. She didn't look particularly pleased to see
me, so I just said hello to her and offered twopence each to the two
biggest lads. When they and I came back down with the trunk,
Tabby was waiting in the alcove. She watched impassively as they
set it down and were given their pay.

'You didn't need to have paid them that much,' she said. 'Penny
was enough.'

I sat on a step of our staircase and signed to her to join me. From the smell, she'd given up washing. I resisted the temptation to move up several steps.

'I'm going away for a while,' I said. 'Not long, probably.'

'Oh, you are, are you?'

'I thought you might like to come with me.'

She considered.

'D'you need me?'

'I might. For one thing, I need somebody to see that trunk to a village near Cheltenham.'

'Where's that?'

'Quite a long way.'

She knew London down to the darkest basements and alleyways. Further than that was either not far or a long way.

'What are you going for?'

'A case. There's a man accused of murder.'

'Did the one he murdered deserve it?'

Tabby's and the law's idea of justice seldom coincided. That was part of the problem between us.

'It was a woman, a governess, so probably not. And I don't know if he did the murder. That's what we're supposed to find out.'

More consideration, then a grudging concession.

'If you want me to, I'll come.'

Details were settled through the rest of the day. I booked a place for her, travelling outside, on the Berkeley Hunt stage from London to Cheltenham, leaving three days after Amos and I started, so that we should arrive at approximately the same time. She listened impassively to instructions from me about visiting the bath house round the corner, washing her hair in anti-lice tincture and getting out her respectable grey dress from wherever she'd stored it or pawned it. I gave her three sovereigns, broken into silver and copper coins, for the expenses of the journey and wrote Mr Godwit's address on a piece of card so that she could show it to people when she arrived in Cheltenham. It was a risk, sending her on her own so far from her usual haunts, but perhaps it would lift her out of her sullen mood. Amos came round in the evening to bring a couple of saddle bags for the things I'd need on our journey and to ask what we should do about Rancie's cat, Lucy. It was a problem that hadn't occurred to me until then.

'We can't take the cat with us, but will Rancie settle without her?'

'Need be, I could put her in one of my saddle bags,' Amos said.
'But the cat's happy where she is. Rancie should settle, long as
you're there.'

I was worried that the cat might pine without her companion,
but Amos said she was on friendly terms with the little hackney in
the next box, so we decided that Lucy could stay in Bayswater.
When Amos had gone, I packed a few necessities into the saddle
bags and reread a hurried letter from my brother Tom, sent from
Cairo. He'd be at sea again now, on his way back to Bombay. I
missed him dreadfully – another reason for wanting to be away
from London.

As agreed, Amos was down in the yard at first light on Sunday
morning, holding Rancie and a dark bay charger I hadn't seen before.
It was a great heavy-headed beast, over seventeen hands high, and
the first thing he did as soon as we'd mounted and were moving
along the mews was snort in terror and perform a four-footed sideways leap at the sight of a small stray dog. Amos urged him on as
if nothing had happened.

'Does he often do that?' I said.

'Only two or three times a minute.'

It turned out that the animal, named Senator, was a reject from
the cavalry, with the looks of a war horse and the nerves of a white
mouse. He'd have had a bullet through the brain by now if Amos
hadn't bought him at a knock-down price and determined to cure
him of shying. He thought a journey of several days cross-country,
with the start of it being along some of the busiest roads in the
kingdom, was just the prescription. By the time he reached his home
county, he reckoned he'd have taught Senator enough manners to
make a gentleman's hunter out of him and would sell him to pay
his expenses for the journey. This made for a lively first day, first
along the familiar main road route over Hounslow Heath, then
turning north-westwards and stopping for the first night at an inn
near the Thames at Cookham. When we arrived there, as always on
our travels, Amos switched from friend to groom. As I followed the
maid upstairs to my room, it was a respectful 'Early start tomorrow,
then, Miss Lane' from Amos down in the hall. It had worried me
in the past, but I knew now that he preferred it that way. In any
stable yard in the country, Amos was guaranteed to meet an old
friend or find a new one among the grooms and ostlers and join
that network of gossip from the horse world that was so much part

of his life. There was another woman staying at the inn, which meant ladies and gentlemen could all, with propriety, dine together at the parlour table.

We were on the road early, after a breakfast of good coffee and yesterday's bread. The horses were fresh and rested. Senator was already responding to Amos's firm but gentle treatment and managed to react to oncoming carriages with no more than a rolling eye and an attempt to sidestep. This meant that Amos and I were able to talk about my latest case.

'There were a lot of questions I didn't ask Mr Godwit,' I said.

'Not usual, for you.'

Amos couldn't know that when I'd talked to Mr Godwit I thought I wouldn't be taking up his case.

'As far as I can gather, the accused man, Picton, is claiming he was somewhere else when she was killed, but won't say where,' I said. 'Two things could follow from that. One is that he's lying.'

'And the other is that he was somewhere else, but it would be awkward for another party if he talked about it,' Amos said.

'Exactly.'

'Which usually means there's a woman in the case.'

'There is anyway – the poor governess. There's gossip that she and Picton were meeting in secret. Or are you suggesting there's another woman?'

'If a man won't talk about where he was, often enough it's because he was somewhere he shouldn't be, doing something he shouldn't do,' Amos said.

'Not necessarily with a woman. He might have been committing some other crime,' I said.

But that wasn't logical because – unless the other crime had been a murder too – a man would surely prefer to be sentenced for the lesser one.

'Any road, he'll have to talk about it come the assizes,' Amos said. 'That's unless he thinks it's worth getting hanged for.'

Which was as far as we could get on the few facts as I knew them. The long day's journey was uneventful and we spent the night on the outskirts of Abingdon. The next day, by bridleways up the eastern slopes of the Cotswolds, was pure pleasure. The hills were patched green and gold, sheep pasture alternating with fields of ripe or ripening grain under a blue sky. It had been a good summer, with just enough rain to bring on the crops, and the farmers had started harvesting the barley. Lines of men with scythes moved forward in such regular rhythm that, from a distance, they looked like one great munching animal, laying swathes of gold smoothly behind them. I almost forgot why we were travelling, and what I was travelling from, in the sheer enjoyment of being back in the country. Even Senator relaxed and only tried to shy a couple of times a mile.

'Country horse,' Amos said. 'By the time I get him to Hereford, a lady could ride him in a silk bridle.'

The horse showed a fair turn of speed when we cantered, but had nothing like Rancie's stamina.

We came to Northleach as the sun was low and red in the sky and the air hazed golden with dust from the harvest. Here we were on the crest of the Cotswolds, with an easy ride down to Cheltenham next day.

'What's that building?' I said.

It rose stark and black against the western sky, like a barracks. Amos asked a lad sitting on the gate.

'House of correction, that is.'

I didn't know where Jack Picton had been sent, but it was probably some larger prison. Still, my good mood sank. Tiredness, perhaps.

The inn was surprisingly busy. I was lucky to get a room, Amos had to share with three other grooms, and the stables were so crowded that Rancie and Senator had to make do with stalls instead of loose boxes. It turned out that some grooms and jockeys, along with their horses, were making their way home from the Cheltenham race meeting that had taken place the week before. This time there were no other ladies present, so I had to eat my chop and drink my glass of wine at an unsteady table in my attic room, with the window open to let out the day's heat. The clink of glasses, male talk and laughter came up from the public bar. Outside in the yard, a dozen or so tobacco pipes glowed in the dusk. I guessed that one of them belonged to Amos and that he was in his element, getting the latest racing gossip. As we rode out next morning, I had some of the fruits of it.

'Odd business they were talking about.'

'Oh?'

'Gentleman and his horse disappeared clean off the face of the earth.'

'Snatched up to heaven?'

He laughed. 'Not unless Saint Peter likes long odds.'

I waited while he persuaded Senator to walk quietly past a rattling harvest cart. Then he told the story.

'Two local sporting gentlemen dropped more than they could afford on the Derby this year – that and a few other races. They'd pretty well got to the end of their credit and the legs were pressing them to pay up.'

'Legs?'

'Short for blacklegs. The bookmakers.'

'How much did they owe these legs?'

'Depends who you ask, but not much less than ten thousand apiece.'

'Ye gods! Ten thousand?' A family might live very comfortably for ten years on that sum.

'From what I was told, they could hardly drum up enough credit between them for a bottle to drown their sorrows in,' Amos said. 'But they manage it somehow, and they're sitting in their club, drinking and complaining about their bad luck. One of the gentlemen takes his last sovereign out of his pocket and says to his friend, "Double or quits." Meaning they should toss the coin and the one who wins'll take on the debts of the other as well as his own.'

'I'd guess they'd drunk more than the bottle of wine by then.'

'You might be right. Well, their cronies are egging them on and telling the other man he's got to accept. Then somebody comes up with a better idea. You see, both of the men had been nattering on about how good their horses were, and what a loss it would be if they had to sell them. So somebody says that first thing next morning they should all go up on the racecourse and the two men should race their horses one against the other – the gentlemen themselves up, no jockeys – and the one that loses takes on both lots of debts. So it's decided, the two men shake hands on it, and first thing next morning they're up on the racecourse, ready for the off.'

We rode on for a while without saying anything. I'd seen a lot of the casual attitude of the upper classes to debt, but something about the brutality of this affair sickened me.

'Whoever won, they could hardly remain friends with that between them,' I said.

Amos had been watching me sidelong, waiting for me to plead for the rest of the story.

'You might be right. Any road, looks as if we'll never know.'

I gave in. 'So what happened?'

'It's just after sun-up, still mist down in the valley and dew on the grass. So the course is hard-going but a touch slippery – not ideal but good enough. This time of the morning there's nobody there but the gentlemen themselves, their friends and the grooms – not above three dozen people and their horses all told. The two gentlemen strip down to their shirts and breeches and shake hands as if they were going to fight a duel, and I daresay it didn't seem much different. The two of them look a bit green about the gills and they'd probably have backed out of it if they could have done, but with the bet taken before witnesses, there was no way out.'

'Of course there was, if they'd had a tenth of the brain of their horses.'

'That'd be asking a lot. Funny thing, if a man drinks too much. Come morning, you wake up with a sick and guilty feeling, as if you've done something wrong and the consequences of it are going to catch up with you any moment. I reckon that's how those two gentlemen must have felt. Any road, they get up on their horses and come under starter's orders. I should have mentioned before that it was a fair race as it went, horses pretty well matched and both of them useful enough riders. So the friend who's acting as starter gives the word and off they go.'

By then we'd come to a good level stretch, so off we went ourselves into a mile of easy canter. When we reined in at the end of it, Amos didn't need any urging to go on with the story. I guessed that one of the grooms at the inn last night must have been among the spectators.

'The bet was for two circuits of the course. First circuit, they were pretty well up together, neither of them wanting to draw ahead too soon. Halfway round the second circuit, one of them pulls ahead; then the other one comes up beside him, spurring and whipping for all he's worth, and overtakes. By this time most of the other gentlemen are at the finishing post, cheering them on. The other one makes up ground, so a furlong out they're pretty well neck and neck and it looks as if it's going to be a dead heat. No more than three strides out, one of them stumbles. Might have been tiredness, sheer bad luck or maybe the whip once too often. He recovers but not quickly enough, so the other one wins clear enough by a length. Of course, there's a lot of cheering and to-do, and the gentlemen crowd round, congratulating the one who's won. For a while, nobody gives much thought to the other gentleman. Then somebody spots him on the far side of the course, still going. They all start laughing and hallooing, pretending he's got it wrong and thinks its three circuits, not two, only they know he hasn't. After all, in a couple of strides he's just doubled the debts he can't pay anyway, so naturally he has to work off his bad temper on himself and his horse before he comes back and takes it like a sportsman.'

'Only he doesn't?'

'Only he doesn't. A shout goes up. Out in the country he suddenly veers off the course and jumps a hedge into a field, all the world as if he was out hunting. And that's the last any of them sees of him.'

'Didn't they try to follow him?'

'No. They decide he was in an even worse temper than they supposed and couldn't face them, and he'd be back in his own good time with his tail between his legs. So they spend the day drinking and celebrating with the one who won, and it's not until the next morning, when the man's groom comes to one of the other gentlemen, looking for his master, that they realize he's properly gone.'

'Then they start looking for him?'

Amos nodded. 'Fairness to them, they made a thorough job of it, riding round the country, checking with all his friends, even the livery stables. Not hide nor hair of him or the horse.'

'Nobody saw him after he jumped the hedge?'

'A couple of reapers about half a mile from the racecourse say they saw a man on a horse galloping across a stubble field not long after they started work, but it was in the distance so they couldn't describe the man or horse, except it wasn't a grey.'

'And the man's horse wasn't?'

'No, a bay.'

'Then it quite possibly was him.'

'More than likely.'

'And that's the last anyone saw of him?'

'Yes.'

'How long ago was this?'

'About ten days before the Cheltenham races. Makes it getting on for three weeks ago.'

By now Cheltenham was in sight in the distance. It's a pretty spa town, nestled in the hills, like a smaller version of Bath with its fine terraces and squares. In spite of that, my heart sank. This side of the town was Mr Godwit's village and the start of a probably hopeless case that I'd taken on for the wrong reasons. Also, Amos's story had depressed me. He hadn't meant that it should. To him, it was no more than a tale of the turf, where a gentleman's ruin was as common as a jockey's broken bones and to be taken with the same stoicism. But the despair of that lone rider had got into my mind and somehow mingled with the bleakness of the prison against the sunset the evening before. More was to come. Towards midday we watched a column of smoke rising near a farmhouse on a hill about a mile away. The smell of burning hay and shouts of men fighting the fire travelled across to us.

'Somebody's rick,' Amos said. 'Leave him short for winter, that will.'

He thought it probably came from careless stacking of the hay. If it were piled in the rick with any damp in it, it would gradually ferment and heat up from the centre. Then, with full summer sun, the whole thing would suddenly burst into flame.

Soon after that we came to a rough inn at a crossroads. Both we and the horses were thirsty, so we dismounted and I held the reins while Amos ducked under the low doorway of the inn's one room to arrange refreshment. A lad came out from the back with two buckets of water and then Amos emerged, holding two rough pottery mugs.

'Just home-brewed ale. Will it do?'

It did very well, though Amos reckoned it was thin stuff. He emptied his mug at two gulps and nodded over his shoulder towards the column of smoke, now no more than a wavering line.

'Some people talking about it inside there. Reckon it wasn't an accident.'

'Oh?'

'Farmer's got a bad name for laying off men and cutting wages. They say he got the warning last week and, sure enough, his rick's gone up.'

'Warning?'

'Dead thorn bush tied to his gate one night. Seems there's a gang of troublemakers round here, and if they don't like what a farmer's doing, they give him the thorn bush, and if he doesn't mend his ways, they set fire to his ricks or barns.'

More bad news for Mr Godwit, I thought. Rick burning was scaring farmers all over the country as labourers reacted to lost jobs and low wages. If it was breaking out round here, a jury certainly wouldn't look tolerantly on a known agitator. We remounted and rode on downhill into the afternoon sun. After an hour or so, we stopped to ask directions from farm workers at a crossroads near Mr Godwit's village and were advised to head for a church spire about a mile away. His was the second biggest house in the village, opposite the vicarage, they said; couldn't miss it. It was a small village and the second biggest house was no more than medium-sized – three storeys of honey-coloured Cotswold stone, with a short gravel driveway leading to a blue front door between rather stunted Doric columns. The first thing we noticed wasn't the house but a small figure under a horse chestnut tree some yards away from the gate: Tabby, sitting on my trunk, peaceful as a pigeon on a branch. She stood up when she saw us.

'Thought you weren't coming today, after all.'

'How long have you been sitting there?' I said.

She shrugged. Hours didn't mean much to her.

'Dunno. A boy came out of the house and asked what was I doing and then an old man came out and said was I your maid and why didn't I come in and get comfortable? I said I supposed I was, more or less, but I'd wait till you got here.'

I sighed, any hope of presenting Tabby as a proper maid destroyed again. Mr Godwit was clearly a man sensitive to public opinion and this changeling camped at his gates couldn't have helped matters.

'Well, you'd better come in with us now. Leave the trunk. They'll send somebody out for it.'

We went up the drive in procession, Rancie and I first, Amos and Senator at groom's distance, Tabby trudging along in the rear. Mr Godwit must have been watching from a window because he opened the front door in person, his smile of welcome so determinedly fixed that it looked painful. I guessed he already regretted that I'd accepted his invitation, and I entirely agreed with him.

THREE

'The fact is . . .' Mr Godwit said and then hesitated. 'I hope you won't be offended, but I thought it might be best in the circumstances and there was no time to consult you . . .'

His voice trailed away. He looked out over his orchard, where hens were scratching under apples already well formed on the branches. It was the day following our arrival and he'd proposed a little stroll after breakfast. I'd been shown his kitchen garden, his henhouse, his pond with six white ducks, the three beehives next to an herbaceous border vibrant with hollyhocks, penstemons, dahlias, his south facing wall with the espaliered apricots and pears. We were now sitting on a bench beside the hazel copse, his spaniel at our feet.

'Consult about what?' I said, when it looked as if the pause might go on for ever.

'The fact is I've let it be known that you're . . . that you're by way of being a member of the family. A very distant member, of course. That is to say, I shouldn't want you to be distant if you really were, but . . .' Another pause, then, in a rush: 'It seemed best to avoid embarrassment.'

I felt like saying that it certainly wasn't succeeding as far as he was concerned, but took pity on him.

'Oh, really? How are we related?'

'I've said something on the lines that you're the daughter of my mother's niece by marriage. When I say I've let it be known that we're related, I mean that's what I told my housekeeper, but in a village naturally word gets round.'

He looked so ill at ease with his deception that it was hard to be angry.

'Won't there be talk in the village anyway, when people notice that your distant relative is going around asking questions about a murder?' I said.

He blinked. 'You'll have to do that, you think?'

'There's no point in my being here otherwise. I can hardly sit in your garden and pluck evidence out of the air.'

'No, I suppose not.'

He looked so doleful that I decided to get down to business before he changed his mind about the whole thing.

'Since we happen to be sitting in your garden anyway, we might as well start here. The more you can tell me, the less I'll have to find out from other people. Did you ever meet Mary Marsh?'

'Not to speak to. I've seen her once or twice at lectures or concerts in Cheltenham, with Colonel Kemble's daughter. The daughter's eighteen now and out in society, too old to need a governess, but I suppose they kept Miss Marsh on as a chaperone.'

'What did she look like?'

'Respectable-looking, dark hair, quite tall as far as I remember and carried herself well. She was twenty-nine years old, but looked younger. Pleasant face.'

The face of a young woman who'd risk position and reputation for love of a rebel? No use asking that. 'What was the gossip, after she was killed?'

'People were shocked, of course.'

'But not too shocked to talk about it, I'm sure. Were there any theories on who killed her?'

'I think they all assumed it was Picton.'

'Why? Was it common knowledge that she and Picton had been meeting?'

'No. That only came out after she was dead.'

'From that one housemaid who's supposed to have seen them together?'

'I suppose so. I heard it from Penbrake. I don't know who he heard it from.'

So the chairman of the magistrates had been picking up gossip about the accused. Probably only to be expected in a community where everybody knew each other.

'When was Miss Marsh last seen alive?'

'The evening before she died, by the daughter, Barbara. She spoke to her in the garden after dinner.'

'And I suppose Miss Marsh said nothing to her about intending to meet somebody in the copse?'

'Well, she wouldn't, would she?'

'So there's no evidence she'd gone there to meet Picton?'

'No.'

'And no evidence whether she went there of her own accord or was taken against her will. Was she killed where they found her?'

'I assume so. Nobody said otherwise.'

'What about the piece of iron they think was used to kill her? Did anybody identify it?'

'No. It was a piece of rusty iron such as you might pick up in any farmyard. It looked as if it might have been part of a cart or plough.'

'Was it produced in the magistrates' court?'

'Yes. Young Picton was asked if he recognized it.'

'What did he say?'

'That he wouldn't know it from any other bit of old iron. That was all of a piece with his regrettably arrogant attitude. He seemed to regard the whole proceedings with contempt.'

'Unwise, with an accusation of murder.'

Mr Godwit looked even more ill at ease. 'The fact is, he claimed he didn't know he'd been arrested on a murder charge until the clerk read him the accusation in court.'

I stared. 'Surely they'd have told him when he was arrested.'

'They should have told him, I'm quite aware of that. In fact, that was one of the points I put to Penbrake. It surely didn't accord with justice to have a man brought before us thinking he was facing an accusation of rick burning and then have a capital charge sprung on him.'

'Rick burning?'

I think he noticed the change in my face. 'Ah, you've heard about it?'

'As we came down from Northleach, we saw a fire. They said at the inn that the farmer had been given the thorn bush warning.'

'Raddlebush.' He said the word almost under his breath. 'That's what they call it. A dead thorn bush dipped in the red raddle dye they use on sheep, with strips of black fabric dangling from it. The Raddlebush Brotherhood.'

'And Picton was suspected of being one of the brotherhood?'

'Everybody is well-nigh certain he's the leader of it. Only they couldn't prove it. They say those brotherhood fellows swear a secret oath in blood not to betray each other. I think that's why Picton took such a high hand with us. He walked into the dock seeing himself as the hero who wouldn't name his friends. When he found out that the charge was murder, he practically sneered at us. He

claimed he didn't know Miss Marsh was dead, and yet he didn't
react as if it surprised him.'

'Was it possible he really didn't know?'

'Possible, I suppose. It depends where he was and what he was
doing in the five days between the body being discovered and his
arrest.'

'Does an innocent man go into hiding for five days?' I said.

'Hiding's pretty well a way of life with Picton. He's guilty of
something.'

'Where's his home?'

'On the outskirts of the village, half a mile down the road towards
Cheltenham.'

'I'll have to speak to somebody in the family. Are his mother
and sisters in the village?'

He looked unhappy at that. 'The mother and one sister. I don't
think you'll get much sense out of the mother. I hear she's been
driven half mad by it all. A respectable person she was, too.'

'Was?'

'Well, it reflects on her, the son being an agitator and all the
other business. It's all such an unnecessary tragedy, all of it. Why
is there so much discontent around these days?'

If I'd even tried to answer his question, he'd have thought he'd
taken a dangerous radical under his roof and my small chances of
doing anything for Picton would be non-existent. I tried to concentrate
on practicalities.

'Still, I must try to speak to the mother and sister. And I shall
need to see Picton himself. As a magistrate, I suppose you can
arrange a visiting order.'

His grey eyes went round as marbles. 'You surely can't propose
going into prison to talk to him?'

'I can't see how I'm going to talk to him any other way.'

'But it would be entirely inappropriate. What possible reason
could I give?'

I made myself take long, deep breaths, trying to keep my temper.
He'd warned me, after all, that he was a coward. Letting me into
his well-ordered life was probably the bravest thing he'd ever done.

'Well, since you've been kind enough to recruit me as a member
of your family, you'd better give me some virtues to deserve it.
Suppose I'm a pious lady, concerned for his spiritual welfare.'

The panic on his face faded a little.

'I suppose it might be possible, but . . .'

'Please try, and as soon as you can. I'll go and see Picton's mother this afternoon and spend tomorrow talking to people, trying to get my bearings.'

'What people?'

'Anybody who'll talk to me.'

'But you can't just go up to people and ask them about a . . . a murder.' The panic was back in full force.

'Not at first, no. Remember, I know nothing about people here. It's a matter of seeing a background to fit things into.'

'But how will you know who to talk to?'

'I won't, but people will talk to me. I have a magic power.'

'Magic?'

'You buy it from a stationer's shop for a shilling. It's called a sketchpad.'

To calm him, I explained what a resource that is for a woman. If she wanders around the country on her own, she attracts attention and even disapproval. Equipped with pencil, sketchbook and small folding stool – all of them in my trunk – she becomes a familiar feature of the countryside. Better still, any idler, from child to oldest inhabitant, will come sidling up to see what she's drawing. By the end of it, he was even smiling. Sad that I had to spoil it.

'And I need to speak to Colonel Kemble and his son,' I said.

'Oh no.'

'Why not?'

'The colonel's quite convinced Picton killed Miss Marsh. He'd be annoyed if he thought I was questioning it.'

'Would that matter?'

'One doesn't want to be on bad terms with a close neighbour.'

'How close?'

'His house is in the village, about half a mile away.'

It was no use pressing the point. I'd already given him enough to worry about. After a while he went back into the house and I wandered through the orchard to the paddock to see Rancie. Amos had left the previous evening on Senator, intending to spend the night in Cheltenham before riding on towards Herefordshire. Before he left he'd instructed Mr Godwit's groom-cum-gardener on how to care for Rancie. She looked at ease, munching grass that seemed surprisingly good for this late in the summer. Mr Godwit's cob was grazing in another corner of the paddock and it seemed the two of them had decided to tolerate each other. She raised her head when she saw me and came walking over, not hurrying. When I ran my hand along her neck, her coat was fine and glossy, no sign of distress at her new surroundings. It would do her good to have a country holiday and I decided not to ride her that day, to give her time to recover from the journey. After that, we'd explore the area and find out where the good canters were.

Mr Godwit must have been giving some thought to my need to meet Jack Picton's mother, because after lunch the housekeeper, Mrs Wood, appeared in the dining room with a round wicker basket and an expression that said this wasn't her idea, so not to blame her. She was a tall, craggy-faced woman with a clump of hairs growing from a large mole beside her nose. I had the impression that Mr Godwit was a little scared of her.

'I asked Mrs Wood to put up a few things for you to take to Mrs Picton,' he said.

So this was to be dressed up as a charitable errand. At this rate, I'd be a candidate for sainthood before the case was over.

'We'll want the basket back,' Mrs Wood said.

It had been clear from the start that my status as a remote relative by marriage had failed to impress her or, probably, even convince her. Still, she'd made a good job of the basket: half a dozen eggs nesting in straw, the remains of a ham, a wedge of cheese, potatoes and a cabbage from the garden.

'I suppose your girl will be carrying it,' she said, as I went to take it.

Definite disapproval in her voice. I'd last seen Tabby apparently usefully employed picking things in the vegetable garden along with the household's plump little maid. Had she managed to cause trouble already?

'She won't lower herself to sleep in our good bed,' Mrs Wood said.

'Won't lower herself?' Tabby had slept in gutters.

'I put her in to share with Suzie. A good big bed with a goose feather eiderdown, big enough for four girls, let alone two. Suzie says your girl spent the night on the floor, rolled up in her coat.'

I took the matter up with Tabby as she and I were walking along the road with the basket.

'I won't be in the same bed with anyone,' Tabby said.

'But it's quite usual for maids to be asked to share a bed.' No answer. If she kept on swinging the basket like that, the eggs would fly out. 'Did the maid annoy you in some way?'

'Nah. She's all right, once you can understand what she's talking about. I just don't do it, that's all.'

I sighed. 'I'll tell Mrs Wood that you get nightmares. Perhaps she can find you a pallet and a blanket.'

Goodness knows, there'd been enough in Tabby's fifteen years or so of life to give her nightmares. Still, that was another untruth I'd be forced to commit. It was time Tabby made herself useful for something besides carrying groceries.

'I'm glad you haven't made an enemy of Suzie. Get her to talk to you as much as you can about the people in the village, especially what they're saying about the murder.'

Tabby nodded. This was familiar territory.

The Pictons' cottage stood on its own some two hundred yards from its nearest neighbour, where a narrow lane joined the road. The patch of unkempt garden that surrounded it had neither hedge nor walls. An ash tree, leaves already yellowing, stood at the junction of the road and the lane. It was leaning sideways, as if the next winter gale would bring it crashing down on the cottage. By the look of the stone-tiled roof, it had already suffered damage from some of the branches. Tiles had slid off and broken on the ground, long enough ago for weeds to grow round them. They'd been replaced by thin planks of wood, roughly nailed to the roof timbers. The front door had once been painted green, but only faded streaks of colour were left, alternating with sun-bleached wood. Brambles grew across the step. The two front windows were curtainless and most of their small panes cracked.

'Nobody there,' Tabby said.

A face appeared at one of the windows. The panes were so dirty that it looked no more than a pale blob and then it went away. I walked up the overgrown path and rapped with my knuckles on the door. The face appeared again, and a hand pointing round to the back.

Tabby and I picked our way over the weeds and broken tiles. At the back, things were slightly more orderly: a half row of onions in an otherwise bare vegetable patch, a spade and a small pair of boots by the porch, a window with a rag of curtain across it on a wire. A girl came out of the open door. She looked not much older than Tabby, maybe seventeen or eighteen at most, and was as thin and pale as a peeled willow twig.

'Yes?' she said.

Her stare wasn't quite hostile, but not welcoming either.

'We've come to bring some things for Mrs Picton,' I said, indicating the basket. 'They're from Mr Godwit.'

'Ma's not well.'

'Does she need a doctor?'

'Doctor.' It wasn't scorn in the girl's voice, just a statement that she and her mother weren't in a world where doctors called. She looked at the basket. 'What's in it?'

'Food.'

'You'd better come in.'

We followed her into a room that seemed almost dark after the sunlight outside. It was quite large, probably taking up most of the ground floor of the cottage, but the ceiling beams sagged so low that you could only just stand upright. Bluebottles buzzed against the window pane. The place smelled of cabbage water, old bacon fat and defeat. A stone fireplace with a bake oven alongside took up one wall, the ashes in it cold and unraked. Beside the fireplace a woman huddled in shawls creaked backwards and forwards in a rocking chair. All you could see of her under the shawls were a pair of boots with holes cut out of them for her bunions and a twist of lank grey hair.

'Visitors, Ma.'

The only response was a creak. I moved so that I was facing the woman in the chair.

'Mrs Picton? Mr Godwit has sent some provisions.'

One bleary grey eye opened and then the other one as she tried to get me into focus.

'Are you ill? Can we help at all?'

'She won't be helped,' the girl said. 'She just sits there, morning and night.'

'Since your brother Jack was arrested?' I said.

It felt brutal to launch into it like that, but I could see no way of breaking through to them.

'Before that.'

The mother went on rocking, but her eyes stayed open and on me. Impossible to guess if she knew what was being said. The girl put the basket on the table and started unpacking it, handling the eggs like precious things. When she lifted out the wedge of cheese, a large crumb of it fell off. It was fine-looking cheese, orange as marigold petals. Instinctively, the girl picked up the crumb and put it in her mouth. For just a moment her eyes flashed with pure childish pleasure; then a guilty look came on her face and she glanced at me as if expecting criticism.

'Why don't you cut yourself a proper slice?' I said.

She wouldn't. Moving carefully round us, she fetched dishes from the dresser, arranged the food on them and shut it away behind the zinc screen of a meat safe in the corner. The old woman stopped rocking. Her eyes were following the girl and the plates.

'You're both hungry,' I said.

Starving, more like. The meat safe had been as bare as Mother Hubbard's cupboard.

'We do all right,' the girl said. I thought the obvious untruth came from pride, until she added, 'Better than being taken off to the workhouse at any rate.'

She went back to the basket and began sifting through the straw that had protected the eggs. Nothing else there, I thought, until she found a screw of blue paper. She unwrapped it. Two ounces or so of tea, with something gold gleaming in it. A sovereign. Typical of Mr Godwit's cautious kindness. The girl froze with surprise and then looked at me.

'He must mean you to have it,' I said.

Slowly, her hand went to it. She picked it up and slid it in her pocket.

'What's that, Sal?'

The old woman, speaking for the first time, her voice grating like flint on slate. She'd sensed something.

'Tea, Ma. He's sent tea.'

A grunt that might have been satisfaction; then the rocking resumed. The girl gave me the empty basket. I handed it to Tabby.

'Thank him,' she said. 'Thank him from Ma.'

She came with us, round the side of the cottage and back to the road.

'I heard your father's dead,' I said.

'Long time ago.'

'And Colonel Kemble had been paying a pension to your mother?'

An intrusive question, the sort the workhouse board of guardians would ask people. She answered reluctantly, eyes lowered.

'Shilling a week, it was. Only he stopped it, with all the trouble.'

'Trouble? Because your brother had been in the riots or because of the rick burning?'

A long silence, then: 'Everything.'

'When did Colonel Kemble stop the pension?'

'Last back-end.'

'So you've had nothing to live on since last autumn? Have you seen your brother in all that time?'

'Sometimes.'

'Recently? I mean, near the time when he was arrested.'

'No.'

She had her arms crossed on her chest and was looking down. I thought she might be lying, but I couldn't bully her.

'Does your brother have any particular friends?'

'Friends?'

Her head came up, alarmed.

'Just somebody who liked him, somebody I could talk to about him?'

She thought about it. 'There was Will Smithies.'

'Is he in the village?'

'He works at the wheelwright's.'

A small enough scrap, but all we were likely to get. I tried a last question.

'Do you think your brother killed Miss Marsh?'

She looked me in the face.

'He couldn't kill a chicken. When we kept chickens, it was me had to wring their necks.'

I said goodbye. She turned back towards the cottage and we started walking along the road. Then there were footsteps running behind us.

'Miss.'

The girl, Sal. We waited until she came up to us, breathless.

'Miss, can you tell me something?'

'If I can.'

'When are they going to hang him?'

I'd expected some question about food or money. This staggered me.

'He's not even been found guilty yet. He won't be tried till the assizes.'

'So when after that?'

There was a world of sorrow in her voice, all the worse for being so trodden-down that she hadn't let it show till now. The settled hopelessness of it was worse than fear or anger.

'He may not be hanged,' I said.

But she only shook her head, not believing me. It would have been cruelty to raise her hopes by talking about inquiries and evidence.

'I'd like to see him before they do,' she said. 'Will they let me see him?'

I think I said yes, I thought they would, accepting her hopelessness. Whatever I said, it seemed to give her some bleak comfort because she thanked me and went back towards the cottage. Tabby and I walked on.

'I want you to go there every day,' I said. 'Walk past slowly and make sure Sal sees you. Get her to talk to you if you can – not about the murder, just anything.'

'All right. I'm getting used to the way they talk here.'

To a born and bred Londoner like Tabby, a Gloucestershire accent was practically a foreign language, but she had a quick ear and even quicker understanding.

'You think she knows more about her brother's friends than she lets on?'

'Sure of it,' I said. 'You saw how she looked. I think he'd have impressed on her that she wasn't to talk to anybody about them.'

'Except Will Smithies.'

'Yes. I think she gave us that name because Smithies is nothing to do with the Raddlebush Brotherhood. Still, it will be useful to speak to him.'

Above all, I wanted to build up a picture of Jack Picton. All I knew so far was that he was probably a rioter, almost certainly a rick burner, not especially kind to his old mother and . . .

'It's the way they look at you,' Tabby said.

'What look at you?'

'Chickens, when you're killing them. They turn their heads round and there's those little round eyes staring straight at you.'

I tried to put the picture out of my head.

'Sal thinks if he couldn't kill a chicken, he couldn't kill a woman,' I said. 'Do you think that follows?'

'Nah. Course not.'

The way she said it put the matter beyond argument, but I agreed with her in any case. We walked most of the rest of the way in silence. One of the things that puzzled me was how the mother and daughter had come to be so close to starvation. In country areas, when people fell on hard times, there was usually enough kindness among neighbours to send round a few pounds of potatoes or the remains of a pie. It looked as if the village had deliberately turned its back on the Pictons, long before the murder. Was that entirely because of the son's activities? A smaller puzzle was that Mr Godwit, in his first consultation with me, had said the widow had been left with three children, yet there was only Sal at home. Presumably, the third child had either moved away or died and Sal was having to cope on her own.

'So, are we going to help her?' Tabby said, as we went in at the orchard gate.

'I'm sure I can get Mr Godwit to send more food. It will be a good excuse for you to see her again,' I said.

That hadn't been what she meant and she knew I was avoiding the real question, but had the sense not to press it. Not for now, at any rate.

FOUR

Mr Godwit agreed that Tabby should carry food to the Pictons every other day, but his attitude seemed guarded, as if it embarrassed him to be their benefactor. He'd seen the magistrates' clerk and asked him to try to arrange an order for me to visit Jack Picton in prison, though he still disliked the idea. He thought the order might come through the next day or the day after that. By then it was dinner time, as Mr Godwit dined at an unfashionably early country hour, and he was adamant that what he called 'this unhappy business' should not be discussed at table. Once that was decided, he was an agreeable host. We dined, just the two of us, at a pearwood table overlooking the garden, with late roses twining round the open window. The food was all from his own modest estate or from local farms and streams, and his housekeeper was a talented cook. She gave us trout fillets in watercress sauce, lamb chops with beans, carrots and glazed potatoes, raspberries and cream, accompanied by good claret from Mr Godwit's wine merchant in Cheltenham. He turned out to be a devoted amateur naturalist, with observations on the comings and goings of swifts and swallows, wild orchids, badger setts, as if he knew every flower and creature on his acres. He was the third generation of his family to live there, so he knew the history of everybody in the village back to their grandfathers and was happy to talk about them, as long as we didn't venture on to the big subject.

Once I'd established, with a discreet question or two, that he wasn't conscientiously opposed to horse racing, I told him Amos's story of the two gamblers.

'Did it really happen like that, or was it grooms' gossip?' I asked.

'Much as you heard the story. As far as I can gather, at any rate. The whole of Cheltenham has been talking about it since it happened.'

'Do you know the two men?'

'I know something of Peter Paley, the one who disappeared. His father, Colum Paley, is very well known round here. The winning man is the younger son of Lord Ivebury. I've met the father – a decent enough man – but not the son.'

'And young Paley hasn't reappeared?'

'No. That sighting by the reapers seems to have been the last anybody saw of him.'

'Or written to let his family know he's still alive?'

'No.'

'His father must be dreadfully worried.'

Mr Godwit sipped thoughtfully at his claret. 'They're a strange family. New money. The word is that the grandfather was a butcher who made his fortune supplying meat to the army in the wars against Napoleon. Bad meat, some people said, though that's probably malicious gossip. Some of the young bloods at assemblies in Cheltenham used to call Colum 'Stinker Paley' and hold their noses, behind his back. That was until he caught one of them at it and thrashed him senseless on the pavement under the canopy of the assembly room. They're pretty well accepted in the neighbourhood now.'

'Well enough accepted for his son to run up tens of thousands in debts.'

'Certainly. Nobody doubts that Paley has sackfuls of money and he's always been generous to young Peter, perhaps too much so. There have been signs that his patience has been wearing thin. He put a notice in the paper quite recently, saying he wouldn't be responsible for his son's debts. When Peter was engaged to Kemble's daughter, I think his father hoped it might make him behave better. It probably did for a while, but then the engagement was broken off and the boy went back to his old gambling ways.'

'The man who disappeared was engaged to Miss Kemble?'

I was surprised to see the story coming so near home. Mr Godwit looked uneasy at being close to the forbidden subject.

'The engagement was broken off two years ago. It had nothing to do with young Paley's disappearance.'

'Did she break it, or did he?'

'I gather that the young lady did. Or at least her father and brother did it for her. She was only sixteen at the time.'

'Was it broken because of his reputation?'

'There'd been a quarrel between Peter Paley and Rodney Kemble. I don't know the cause, but it was clearly a serious one. In the circumstances, the engagement could hardly stand.'

I wondered if that had been young Miss Kemble's opinion, too. Since she was too young to consent to marriage on her own account, she'd have been given no choice in the matter. Mr Godwit was probably right that the broken engagement had nothing to do with young Paley's spectacular disappearance. He didn't sound like the kind of man who'd nurse a broken heart for two years.

'Has Colum Paley been trying to find his son?' I said.

'If so, there's not much sign of it. When somebody asked if he'd heard from him, he said the young hound would come home when he was hungry.'

'You'd have thought he'd be hungry by now.'

'Yes. It will be three weeks this Saturday.'

He suggested that we should drink our coffee in the summer house on the lawn. As we watched the swallows looping low over the grass to catch flies, I was doing sums in my head.

'You said it will be three weeks this Saturday since Peter Paley disappeared. Isn't that about the same time that Mary Marsh was killed?'

'The day after she was found.'

I stared at him. He was still watching the swallows.

'What? Didn't anybody make a connection?'

He looked at me, seeming genuinely puzzled.

'A young woman dies and the day afterwards a young man gallops off and hasn't been seen since,' I said. 'Hasn't anybody suggested the two might be linked?'

'Why should they have been? Young Paley took up that ridiculous gamble out of the blue. Besides, I don't think there's any real harm in him. He's like a lot of young men these days – not enough brains for the law or morals for the church, so they have to find something to do with themselves.'

'Did he know Miss Marsh?'

'I suppose he must have seen her sometimes when he was engaged to Miss Kemble. No more than that.'

We finished our coffee. The swallows went to roost. Mr Godwit asked what I'd like to do tomorrow, as if I really were that remote relative on a pleasure visit.

'I think I might take a ride on my mare in the morning.' His smile of approval disappeared when I added, 'And make a call on the wheelwright. You know him?'

'I know the Smithies, father and son. Decent craftsman; nobody denies it.'

'But?'

'Chartists. They make no secret of it, attend meetings and so on.'

'Is Will Smithies the father or the son?'

'Son.'

'Picton's sister says Smithies and her brother are friends.'

'It wouldn't surprise me. Birds of a feather. What are you hoping to find out from him?'

'At present I'm trying to build up a picture of Jack Picton. It's just possible that a friend might know why Picton won't give an alibi.'

Although not likely that he'd talk about it to a complete stranger.

Dusk was coming down, so we went inside and, at Mr Godwit's request, I played the piano for him. He listened with the closed eyes and gentle wafting of the hand that denote the entirely unmusical, but he seemed soothed. That was something I could do for him at least.

It was a slow start next morning. Mr Godwit's gardener acted as driver for their placid cob but, in his own words, came over all of a dothering when faced with an equine aristocrat like Rancie. She picked up his unease and I had to calm the pair of them as best I could, doing most of the grooming and tacking up myself. For an hour or so I behaved like any visitor, riding Rancie round the lanes, enjoying the late-summer sunshine. The village was near the top of the hill, looking down on the roofs of Cheltenham. The land was a mixture of stubble fields, pasture and coppices. I glimpsed what looked like a large manor house in a dip in the land about half a mile away and guessed it belonged to the Kembles. Mr Godwit had given me directions to the wheelwright's yard, about a mile north of the village. It looked a moderately prosperous place as I rode up to it: a solid house of the local limestone, facing on to a yard with open barns on two sides of it. The gate to the road was open, so I rode straight in. A man with a square greying beard and thatch of grey hair, a cap perched on top, was working with a lad who looked young enough to be an apprentice, fitting a curved section of outer rim on to the spokes of a wheel. The lad looked up as I rode in, but the older man told him to keep his mind on his work. I slid off Rancie and stood watching. If you want something from a person, it's not a tactful start to ask it from horseback. The curved section slid sweetly on to the two spokes and the man tapped it home with a few hammer blows. Only then did he turn.

'Good day, miss.'

There was no surliness in making me wait, or the lack of apology for it. Mr Smithies was a man on his own land, master of a craft that wouldn't be hurried. The way he was looking at me was neither hostile nor especially welcoming, just an invitation to state my business. I'd not worked out my approach in advance, but decided to be straightforward. I introduced myself and told him that I was staying with Mr Godwit.

'If possible, I'd like to speak to William Smithies,' I said. 'Sal Picton says he's her brother's friend.'

Behind us, in the open barn, a young man was working at a treadle-operated lathe.

'What's your business with the Picton family?' Mr Smithies said.

'If Jack Picton isn't a murderer, I'd like to prove it.'

'Does Godwit think he isn't?'

'He's a magistrate. He can't have an opinion either way.'

The wheelwright considered that and me and came to an unhurried decision.

'William, a lady to talk to you.'

He led the way towards the shed. I looped Rancie's rein over a hurdle and followed. The young man who'd been working at the lathe was on his feet, holding out his hand. The father introduced us and went back to the work he'd been doing, without any further explanation.

The son was less solidly built than his father, with a pale complexion and light brown hair, but he had the same level-eyed look. I repeated what I'd said to the older man.

'You think you can help Jack, then?' He spoke with the Gloucestershire accent.

'I'd like to, if I can.'

'How?'

'I don't know. I was hoping you might be able to tell me.'

'I'll say to you what I've said to everybody: if Jack Picton says he didn't kill the young lady, then he didn't.'

'Did you know that he was seeing Miss Marsh?'

'I don't know that he was.'

'Did he ever mention her?'

'No.'

'Did you know there was gossip about them?'

'I've got no time to listen to gossip.'

'If Jack Picton didn't kill her, why won't he say where he was that night?'

'He'll have his reasons.'

'He was seen near the Kembles' house.'

'It's a free country for walking in – or so they say.'

'Do you know what he was doing that evening and night?'

'No.'

I thought I believed him. There was a shade of regret in the way he said it.

'Is there anyone who might know?'

Before he shook his head, there was the slightest of hesitations. Then he said something in a lower voice, as if worried his father might overhear.

'I might have tried telling the magistrates we were together, only I'm a poor liar and I'd have been found out.'

'Can you tell me anything at all that might help?'

'What sort of thing?'

'What kind of man he was. Who his other friends were. Anything.'

'For a start, he's the stubbornest man on God's earth. Once he's made up his mind to something, he's as hard to shift as that block there. Always was.'

He pointed to a squared-off oak block that must have come from a giant of a tree.

'You knew him from a long way back, then?'

'Nearly as long as I can remember. We were at school together.' He glanced at me, then at the lathe. It had a thick piece of elm wood, pale as cream, clamped into it. Judging by the shape, it was being rounded into a hub for the centre of a wheel. 'I'll talk about him as much as you like if it's any use to you, only it'll have to be while I'm shaping it. We've got as much work on as we can handle.'

He brushed wood chips and bird droppings off the oak block for me to sit down and took his place at the lathe. It whirred quietly nearly all the time he was talking and he kept the blade of his chisel against the turning hub, so delicately that the wood seemed to change shape of its own accord.

'He was always in trouble at school for being impudent; ruler across his knuckles more times than you could count. He didn't mean to be impudent, just he was always asking questions about things – the Bible, history, anything. Tell him two times two made four and he'd ask why. But then he could never show respect. I reckon that's what most schools are for, as far as working men are concerned – teaching them respect for their betters. He wouldn't "sir" or "madam" anybody. Jack's as good as his master; that was what he lived by.'

'Don't you think so too?'

'I do. "When Adam delved and Eve span, Who was then the gentleman?" My dad brought me up on that one, but he taught me a bit of sense, too. You can't go fighting everybody all your life. You have to be patient and choose your time.'

'You're Chartists, you and your father?'

He looked up briefly from the lathe. 'We are. A vote for all men, a confidential ballot and wages for Members of Parliament so that workers can have a voice.' His eyes met mine, looking for disapproval but not finding it.

'And Jack's a Chartist, too?'

'Oh, he signed the Charter, all right. But he thought we were being too cautious, relying on petitioning Parliament. All for action, Jack was.'

'Like joining in the riot at Newport?'

He glanced up at me again, then away, not confirming or denying it.

'A fat lot of good that did them. If Jack had his way, he'd have had all the farmworkers marching out to join them with their pikels and ploughshares. Only farmworkers aren't easy to organize; that was part of Jack's trouble. It's all very well getting a crowd together in towns, but when you've got men scattered all round the countryside, depending on the farmer for the roof over their heads and every mouthful they eat, it's slow going getting politics into their heads.'

'But some farmworkers must be political,' I said. 'What about the Raddlebush Brotherhood?'

The rhythm of the lathe didn't change. 'Political! A gang of grudge-bearers without an idea about anything except destruction.'

'And yet your friend Jack was part of it, wasn't he?'

'I'm not saying so.'

'If he was out with the brotherhood the night Miss Marsh was killed, that might be why he's not saying anything. He wouldn't want to get the other men into trouble.'

'I'm not talking about it.'

The hub was almost finished. He gave it a few more caresses with the chisel and then stopped the lathe and unclamped it, rubbing the palm of his hand along it. The wood looked smooth as velvet.

'I hope to be seeing Jack,' I said.

His head came up, surprised. 'In prison?'

'Yes.'

'Can you do that?'

'Is there any message you'd like me to give him?'

He thought about it. 'Tell him we're doing what we can for her, me and dad.'

'For his mother?'

That was a puzzle. From what I'd seen of the Picton household, nobody was doing anything.

'Just tell him what I said. Say we'll get her back if we can. He'll understand.'

He walked with me to where Rancie was standing patiently and rolled a log of wood over for a mounting block.

'Will you come back and tell me, if you see him?'

I said I would. His father, still busy fitting spokes, raised his hand to us as we went. He looked concerned. I guessed he didn't approve of the friendship with Jack Picton, but he had at least allowed his son to talk to me without interfering.

Back at Mr Godwit's, I untacked Rancie and let her out to graze in the paddock. At luncheon, I gave my host a brief account of the talk with William Smithies, but admitted it didn't take us much further. He had good news for me – although that wasn't how he saw it.

'Our clerk is arranging the visiting order. He's bringing it this afternoon.'

'Excellent. That means I can go and see Jack Picton tomorrow.'

'If you really think it's necessary. But there'll be no date on the order. You could keep it by you and use it later if everything else failed.'

'Tomorrow. Where's the prison?'

'Gloucester. That's where the assizes will be held.'

That was no more than half a day's ride away. I thought I could get there and back on Rancie, but once he saw I couldn't be dissuaded, Mr Godwit offered me the use of the cob and gig, with the gardener as driver. There was something else on his mind.

'I think when you do see Picton, it might be best not to mention me at all.'

Seeing he was so concerned about it, I agreed. It was settled that I should leave in the gig about eleven and visit the prison in the afternoon, a Saturday. It would suit me well, because that would give me time to exercise Rancie first, provided I rode out early. A good idea, Mr Godwit thought, pleased that I should be doing something so harmless. If he'd known the true reason, he'd have been horrified, so I didn't tell him. Instead, I inquired about sending letters to London. A great improvement since the new post, he told me, glowing with local pride. The vicar's lad rode down into Cheltenham every afternoon with mail from the village, in time to catch the evening post from Cheltenham. Letters would be delivered in London the following morning and, if the correspondent was efficient, an answer received next day. After lunch I wrote a note to a political friend in London and took it over to the vicarage, with a penny for the post and another for the vicar's lad for his trouble.

Back in Mr Godwit's garden, I found Tabby picking beans, along with the maid, Suzie. She seemed surprisingly cheerful, but more than willing to put aside her basket and accompany me on a sketching trip.

'So what are we really doing?' she asked, as soon as we were out of the gate.

'Sketching. I want somewhere with a good view.'

She gave me a disbelieving look, but stepped out briskly beside me, carrying my block and pencil case.

'No word from Sal Picton, I suppose,' I said.

'Nah. I'm supposed to be taking some food there tomorrow. Are you coming?'

'I'll be doing something else. You seem to be getting on well enough with Suzie.'

'She's all right. We have a laugh at Mrs Wood. We were digging up carrots and there was one such a rude shape that we were both creased up with laughing. So Mrs Wood came out and asked what was so funny, and—'

'Did you get any gossip from Suzie about what local people think of the Picton case?'

'She said most people think the family's no good. Her young man – well, she thinks he's her young man – works at the stone quarries and he says they'll all go into Gloucester to see him hanged.'

'Charming. So what does she think herself?'

'She says she'll be sorry if they hang him. He was the best-looking man in the village and always spoke to her civil enough.'

That seemed to be the closest thing Jack Picton would get to a character reference. We walked up the hill to where a grassy bank by a signpost gave a fine panorama round the hills. I spread my cloak, avoiding an ants' nest, and started sketching while Tabby wandered up and down, scowling at the scenery.

I'd done no more than rough in the outlines of the hills when a plump man with a collie came slowly uphill from the direction of the village. He stopped beside me, raising his low-crowned hat, and remarked that it was a fine day for views. I agreed.

'You'll be the young lady staying with Mr Godwit. Fond of drawing, are you?'

I said it was such beautiful countryside. That was all it needed to make him a stationary guide to the locality. That hill over there was where the Romans camped; there was the quarry where they got the stone to build the town.

'And that one over there?' I asked, pointing north.

'That's Cleeve Hill, the racecourse. Pity you've missed the races.'

'I daresay men still exercise horses there, even when the races aren't on.'

'Indeed they do. You'll see strings of horses out there most mornings.'

'Very early in the morning, I suppose.'

'Very early for the grooms, a bit later for the gentlemen. You're wanting to put some horses into your drawing?'

'It might make it livelier.'

'If you came up here straight after breakfast – around nine o'clock, say – you might see them. Have to draw fast, mind, to get racehorses in.'

He laughed at his own joke till he ran out of breath, raised his hat again and walked back downhill. I waited until he was out of sight and then put away my pencils.

'So, are we coming all the way up here tomorrow to draw horses?' Tabby said. She'd been listening as usual.

'No, we've got other plans and we'll have to be up earlier.'

I told her as we walked back downhill. She said it seemed a roundabout way of going about things. I said that sometimes the only way was roundabout.

FIVE

Tabby met me by the paddock at daylight next morning and helped me bring in and tack up Rancie. Although beyond hope as a lady's maid, she had the makings of a useful groom. Before we parted, I asked her to unpack my plain blue cotton dress from my trunk and have it ready for a quick change out of my riding habit when I arrived back. As Rancie and I went at a walk along lanes and byways, the sun rose in a clear sky and the only people we passed were a few farm labourers on the way to work. We got to the foot of Cleeve Hill just as the distant clocks of the town were striking nine. A broad track ran up the flank of the hill, marked with many hoofprints. Rancie's head came up, sensing a gallop.

'Not yet.'

I kept her at a walk, up a side track alongside some bushes. It was a noble sweep of hill, and although the summer had been dry, the turf was still green and yielding. About halfway up I glimpsed horses and riders coming up a broad track from the town, at right angles to our own. There were a dozen or so of them, loosely grouped together and keeping to a walking pace. Rancie and I came to the crest of the hill before them. This was clearly the racecourse, with a rough grandstand and a finishing post at one end, though no rails. Rancie was thoroughly strung-up by now, but I calmed her with voice and hands and made her wait, in the shelter of some bushes.

The sun was behind us, in the eyes of the riders on the other path, so they didn't see us. When they came to the top of the hill, they grouped together a couple of furlongs away from us, the first ones circling their horses and waiting for the others to catch up. They were a mixture of gentleman riders in top hats and grooms in caps, all mounted on useful-looking thoroughbreds. Then four of them were bounding forward, covering the ground in long galloping strides. Two more followed, one horse rearing in its eagerness, then the rest in a loose group. As far as I could see, they weren't galloping all out as they might in a race. This was a regular training session.

Once they were on the way, I let Rancie follow on our separate track, keeping her with some difficulty to a canter and stopping well short of the point near the grandstand where the other riders had drawn up. They walked their horses in circles to cool them and there was some swapping around, with the gentlemen taking over their second horses from the grooms. I'd have liked to have gone closer and seen faces, certain that these would be men from the same set as the missing young Paley, but there was no point in going to all this trouble and spoiling it by impatience.

The men were settled in their saddles, getting ready to race back. I gathered up Rancie's rein, feeling her energy like an arrow in a taut bow the moment before you release it. As the group of riders galloped past us, I gave her the slightest sign with my heel and let her go. Divots of turf flew round us as she galloped after the other horses in a long curve that took us on to the same track. A groom on one of the back horses glanced round when he heard us, and his mouth opened in surprise. We went past him and two or three others without even trying. Not surprising, as Rancie was fresher than they were and raring to go. We came alongside the first of the top hats. A long pale face, also open-mouthed, turned towards us as we overtook him. It wasn't my intention to get to the front, even if we could have managed it, and the leaders were pretty fast. I contented myself with overtaking another pair of top hats and then gave Rancie the signal to turn off to the left, towards the track we'd come up on. As we went, I raised my riding crop in a goodbye salute, quite sure that some of the horsemen would be watching us. I hoped nobody would follow us – not today. Nobody did. The other riders thundered on their usual track. As the ground fell away, I slowed Rancie to a canter, then a walk, and went downhill on our path beside the bushes. On the long ride home, walking most of the way to let Rancie cool down, I imagined the conversation of the racing men as they rode home to their stables. *Nice-looking horse – woman riding, definitely sidesaddle. So where had they sprung from? Not seen them before. Anybody recognize them?* Sporting men have limited topics of conversation and it was certain that our appearance out of the blue would be discussed wherever they gathered to drink. Next time they'd be looking out for us.

We arrived back with only just time to change. The cob was already harnessed to the gig and Mr Godwit was looking anxious. I apologized and said my ride had lasted longer than expected. Like everything connected with my host's little estate, the cob was a good one, the gig well maintained and beautifully sprung, so the ride to Gloucester was uneventful. The gardener drove well enough, but with great concentration and he was not inclined to talk. That suited me, because now that I was about to come face to face with Jack Picton, I had some hard thinking to do. I'd insisted on meeting him because I wanted to know what kind of man he was. Some of the answers I had already: political, argumentative, impatient – and, so it was said, handsome. But it was a wasted opportunity unless I could find out something about the killing of Mary Marsh that I didn't know already and the prospects of that weren't good. It was unlikely that the arrival of a woman he hadn't met before would change Jack Picton's attitude. I was still without inspiration, so I asked the driver to put me down near the cathedral and come back in an hour, hoping he'd have the sense to find beer for himself and water for the cob.

I had directions from Mr Godwit and knew that the prison was downhill from the cathedral, near the river and the docks. I walked slowly, still thinking, but it wasn't long before I found myself facing a red brick wall about thirty feet high, closing off one side of a narrow street. I knew that Gloucester prison was no more than fifty years old, regarded as a model of its kind for the humane housing of inmates. Still, it looked grim enough from the outside. When I stood back, I could see over the wall to raw slabs of red brick buildings with small square windows. I walked round, looking for a way in. The river tide was high, seagulls swooping over it with a freedom that must have been taunting to the men and women inside the walls. I turned away from the river and came to a gatehouse. It seemed at odds with the rest of the design, shaped more like the gate lodge to a country estate than a prison, built of sandstone blocks, quite low, with a flat roof. I found out later that the roof was flat for a purpose. It was where they hanged people. The big gates were shut, with no sign of a bell or knocker. There were two ordinary doors on either side of them. I rapped with my knuckles on the left door. After a while a man's face appeared at the barred window alongside it. I held my visiting order to the window. The face disappeared and the door was opened by a pale and poorly shaved warder in a dark uniform. He let me inside, told me to wait and carried the order off to a side room. The temperature felt several degrees colder inside. Another warder came out, better shaven and completely bald, and told me to follow him. His manner was polite enough, so obviously a magistrate's influence had smoothed the way.

We went across a yard, into one of the slab-like buildings and up a staircase. Even in a hot summer, the air was damp, probably from being so near the river. A smell of drains and something half-remembered hung in the air. A rhythmic thumping and clacking came from a room below us and set the whole staircase vibrating.

'Treadmill?' I asked.

'Looms,' the warder said. 'We teach them weaving – stuff for mailbags mostly.'

The smell was damp hessian. We went along a corridor. Apart from the thumping looms, the place seemed quieter than a cathedral, with not even a whisper of a human voice. The bald man opened the door to a small windowless room, told me to wait and went out, closing the door behind him. Some minutes later, two sets of footsteps came along the corridor, so briskly they were practically marching. The door opened and I had my first look at Jack Picton. It wasn't reassuring. He was glaring at me and, if he'd happened to be holding a piece of iron in his hand, I'd probably have ducked. As a man on remand, not yet sentenced, he wasn't manacled or wearing prison uniform, but his clothes were rough: canvas trousers, an old jacket and waistcoat in dark wool, a dirty shirt open at the neck, labourer's boots. They were probably the clothes he was wearing when arrested more than two weeks before. They looked too small for him. Everything looked too small – the room, his escort, my reason for being there.

After the first glance, I realized it wasn't simply a matter of size. He was tall certainly, probably six foot or more, and broad-shouldered, but what filled the room was the anger radiating off him. He'd marched in like a busy man sparing minutes he couldn't afford for an annoying client, leaving the warder trailing in his footsteps like a clerk. Even without the glare, it would have been a forceful-looking face, with a square brow and large but well-shaped nose, dark brows over eyes the colour of oak bark. It wasn't difficult to imagine him as an orator. He could have modelled as a general addressing his troops or Danton at the barricades. His hair was cut brutally short, his scalp stained brownish from some rinse, probably to kill head lice. His smell was frowsty.

'So, you're doing me the kindness to worry about the state of my soul,' he said. 'I thought they left that to the clergyman at the foot of the gallows.'

The bald warder said something about showing respect for a lady and then sat down on one of the chairs with his back against the door. This was disconcerting. I'd assumed that the prisoner would be allowed to take the second chair, but this arrangement left me seated and Jack Picton glaring down at me. I stood up and said the first thing that came into my head.

'I'm not in the least concerned about your soul, but I'll have some clean linen sent in to you, if you like.'

He blinked, surprise in his face, then annoyance at being caught off balance. Then just a glimmer of amusement. It didn't last for long, but was just enough to show why women might think him a good-looking man.

'They have charitable funds for that, do they? So that the smell of me doesn't offend the judges?'

He had the Gloucestershire accent, but spoke with sharpness and precision. His eyes were sharp, too. At first he'd been too angry to look at me properly; now he was taking stock.

'Did you kill Mary Marsh?' I said.

Surprise again, and then a droll look came over his face. He spoke past me, to the warder sitting by the door.

'I'm being given the quality, aren't I? I thought it was other prisoners you use if you want to get people to confess when their guard's down. I get pretty young ladies offering clean shirts.'

The way he said 'pretty', rolling it around on his tongue, was so insulting that I felt like getting up and walking out.

'Well, did you?'

I let my anger sound in my voice. That surprised him.

'No, I did not.' That to me; then to the warder: 'So that's that. Do we go now?'

The warder wasn't a quick-thinking man. He was staring from the prisoner to me, bewildered. I wondered if it was within his power to end the interview and hustle Picton back to his cell. Probably, yes. In that case, there wasn't much time.

'So, who did kill her?' I said.

'Somebody who wanted to keep her quiet, I'd say.'

'Quiet about what?'

'If you really want to know, you could try asking people about what happened at the race fair.'

'Race fair?' I stared at him. 'What race fair?'

'Cheltenham races, of course.' He said it as if there could be no other.

'But Mary Marsh was dead already,' I said. 'She was dead before the races.'

He looked at me, grinning like a chess player who knew his opponent was cornered.

'Have you any evidence against anybody?' I said.

'The magistrates didn't seem too concerned about evidence. There's one kind of evidence for men like me and another kind for the quality.'

I repeated the question, though I knew it was a waste of breath.

'Supposing I had, what would you do about it?' he said. 'Tell the police or the magistrates?'

'Yes.'

'So that by the time I come up for trial, they'd have torn my evidence to pieces and used it against me? Picton accusing anybody and everybody, trying to save his neck? The jury would love that, wouldn't they?'

'If you have evidence and you're not using it until the trial, you're playing a dangerous game,' I said.

'Really? I hadn't thought of that. How kind of you to warn me.'

The smile that went with his words might have made it look as if he meant them, if it hadn't been for the coldness in his eyes. I changed tack.

'I saw your friend William Smithies yesterday,' I said. 'He gave me a message for you.' He waited, expressionless. 'He said, "We're doing what we can for her, me and dad. We'll get her back if we can."'

That surprised him. Not the message itself but the fact that it came through me. His expression turned blank and guarded, and when he spoke it was in a normal voice with no anger in it.

'If you see him again, thank him from me.'

'I'll see him. Is there anything else you want me to say to him?'

A shake of the head. He still didn't trust me.

'Or to your sister?'

Another head shake. From somewhere below us a handbell clanged. The sound of many feet shuffling on stone flags came up to us. The warder got to his feet.

'Time to go.'

The room seemed very crowded with the three of us standing up. I tried a question at random.

'Did you know that Peter Paley has disappeared?' I said. 'He galloped off the day after Miss Marsh was found dead and hasn't been seen since.'

Surprisingly, that brought a flicker of interest to his face. It looked almost like concern but was soon suppressed. 'What's that to me – unless I'm supposed to have killed him too?'

The bell was still clanging. He turned towards the door and gestured to the warder to open it. Time for one last throw.

'What were you doing near the house on the night she died?' I said.

Picton turned back, a grin on his face but not a nice one. When he raised his arms, the warder took a step towards him, but all he did was put his hands on top of his head, palms outwards, fingers fully extended, and waggle them at me.

'Hopping into a trap, like a good little bunny rabbit.'

The warder opened the door and they were gone.

After a while the bald warder came back and escorted me to the doors. Mr Godwit's gardener was waiting with the gig by the cathedral. He was impatient to get back to the village, but I made him drive round the city until we found a men's outfitter that was open. My business didn't take long: two large cotton shirts and a set of flannel unmentionables to be sent to J. Picton at Her Majesty's prison. Yes, Monday morning would do.

It took all of the drive back through lanes of honeysuckle and meadowsweet to get the smell of drains and damp sacking out of my nostrils.

SIX

'I can't think of any reason why Picton should be concerned about young Paley,' Mr Godwit said.

Sunday morning at breakfast, sun streaming in through the window and ducks quacking from the pond. Our return the evening before had been late, well after dinner time, and although Mr Godwit was obviously brimming with curiosity, he'd played the good host and insisted I should eat and sleep.

'They'd know each other by sight, I suppose,' I said.

'Not necessarily. The Paleys live just outside Cheltenham. I can't think of any circumstances in which Picton and young Paley might have met.'

He pushed the honeypot towards me. I shook my head. I'd already had two slices of bread and honey. Delicious.

'So, what did you make of Picton?' he said.

It was a fair question and I'd been puzzling half the night on how to answer it. Mr Godwit set such store by my opinion that he'd probably hoped I'd spend an hour with Picton and come back with a verdict: he's the murderer or he isn't. If I'd told him about the impression of anger and violence burning off the man, as well as the cold-eyed sarcasm, he'd have concluded that Picton was guilty as charged and would have been, I was sure, very relieved.

'My problem was much the same as yours,' I said. 'I couldn't find a way to break through that arrogance.'

There'd been his quiet acceptance of the message from William Smithies, but I'd decided not to tell Mr Godwit about that, for the moment at least. The Smithies, father and son, had to make their living in the community. Mr Godwit already had a black mark against them as Chartists and remaining on friendly terms with a possible murderer would have brought another.

'He still claims to have been somewhere else?'

'Not even that. Right at the end he talked about a trap, but there was no time to ask him what he meant. I had the impression that he thinks he has some trump card of evidence that he'll produce at the trial.'

'But he gave no idea as to what it was?'

'I asked him who killed Miss Marsh and he said somebody who wanted to keep her quiet. Quiet about what, I asked, and he said I should try asking people about what happened at Cheltenham race fair.'

A wasp was buzzing round the honeypot. Mr Godwit flicked it deftly away with a spoon and replaced the lid.

'It makes no sense,' I said. 'The races were going on when you came to see me in London. By that time, Mary Marsh was dead and Picton in prison.'

The wasp was making another circuit. Mr Godwit watched it with too much attention, spoon poised.

'Did anything happen at the races?' I said. I remembered Amos's story about the time people burned down the grandstand.

'As far as I know, nothing,' Mr Godwit said. 'They seem to have been remarkably quiet this year.'

He made another swipe with the spoon. The wasp was yards away.

'And other years?'

'There was some serious trouble a couple of years ago,' he admitted.

'What sort of trouble?'

'Illegal gambling – mostly rogues up from London. Excessive drunkenness and so on. The constabulary and the magistrates had to intervene. There was some violence.'

'Were you there?'

'No. As it happened, I was visiting a sick friend in Bristol. I heard about it on my return and some of the perpetrators came up in court.'

'Was Jack Picton among them?'

'No.'

'And was there anything at all relating to Mary Marsh?'

'Of course not. What would a governess be doing at the race fair?'

'So you have no idea of what Picton meant, telling me to ask people about it?'

'None in the world. I suspect the man is trying to create as much confusion as possible.'

He asked me to excuse him, saying he must go and change for church. Naturally, the entire household would be attending.

'Will the Kembles be at church?' I said.

'Of course.' Then, sensing something in my voice: 'You aren't going to ask them questions, are you?'

'I shall have to at some point. Mary Marsh lived under their roof. Miss Kemble may have been the last person to see her alive, apart from the murderer. Rodney Kemble found her body.'

'Colonel Kemble won't like it.'

'Won't he? If one of your household had been found dead on your land, wouldn't you want to know what happened?'

He shuddered. 'You can't go up to a man you've never met in church and talk about murder.'

'I was thinking of the churchyard outside,' I said, only half seriously but it caused another shudder. 'Very well, I won't try to talk to them today, but at least it will give you a chance to introduce me to them. I'm sure you'd do that with a visiting relative.'

Unarguable. He gave in, but still unhappily.

Churchgoing had strict patterns in the village. At half past ten, the bells started ringing. At a quarter to eleven, the children from the Sunday school marched in a double line from the parish hall, across the road and in at the church porch. Various gigs and carts dropped off families from outlying farms – little boys in stiff collars, girls in white pinafores, farmers clutching prayer books in gloved square hands that would have been happier round a spade. By that time our party was assembling on the garden path – Mr Godwit formal in tail coat and top hat, Mrs Wood in navy-blue wool and bonnet with restrained bows, myself in the plain blue cotton and a bonnet that might be a shade frivolous but would have to do. Suzie and Tabby appeared suddenly on the path behind us, pink-faced as if they'd been up to something. For a mercy, Tabby was wearing her grey dress and bonnet and looked halfway respectable, though she was gloveless and wearing scuffed boots. The look Mrs Wood gave her didn't miss a detail. The peals from the church tower gave way to a single summoning bell. Mr Godwit offered me his arm politely and we all went along the road and through the gate to the churchyard. The vicar was standing at the porch, welcoming the congregation. This caused something of a queue and Tabby took advantage of it to come alongside me.

'What am I supposed to be doing?'

I asked Mr Godwit to excuse me and took her to one side.

'You're going to church. You've done it before, haven't you?'

The look on her face told me no, she hadn't. By now the queue was moving forward and Mr Godwit was looking over his shoulder for me.

'Just watch Suzie and do what she does,' I said hastily. 'Only don't try to sing.'

I knew something about her song repertoire. Goodness knows what she might come out with. She didn't look reassured, but I had to leave her to her own devices, because once we were inside the church, it was clear that seating was by long-established order. A pew opener held back the flap to let Mr Godwit, Mrs Wood and me into a row on our own near the front, while Suzie dragged Tabby into one near the back with other servants. The service began.

It went on for some time, with three hymns and a twenty-minute sermon, which gave me time for a discreet look around. It was a large church, built long ago when wool prices were high, and half full, with the congregation arranged in three slices like a layer cake. At the back, household servants and labourers. In the middle, farm families and tradespeople. I looked for the Smithies father and son but didn't find them. The important ones of the village, including ourselves, were at the front. The very front pew to the right of the altar had six people in it and I was certain that three of them were Kembles. A tall elderly man, sitting so upright that his back made no contact with the pew, must be Colonel Kemble. The high dome of his head was almost completely bald when seen from the back, apart from a band of close-cropped grey hair. His coat was black and well cut. When it was time for prayers, he took some time to get to his knees, suggesting arthritis, and bowed his head in a soldierly way, enough for convention but without extravagant humility. The younger man beside him looked a couple of inches shorter but broader across the shoulders. His hair was an unremarkable light brown, worn long enough to hide the fact that his ears stuck out, unless you were looking at him a long time from the back, which I was. He must be Rodney Kemble. I noticed that when his father had trouble getting up from his knees, the son made no attempt to help and didn't look at him.

It was the same with the person on his other side – no turning towards her or sharing his hymn book – but then brothers don't always pay sisters much attention. I didn't even know Miss Kemble's first name, only that she was eighteen, had suffered a broken engagement, and three weeks and a few days ago she'd have woken to the news that her governess and chaperone had been found murdered. If she was grieving for her, there was no sign of it in her dress. Jade-green corded cotton with lace at the neck is not mourning wear, nor are bonnets with frilled green ribbons. She fidgeted during the sermon and turned round a couple of times. Under the bonnet were a round chin and ringlets of hair just bright enough to be called golden by men who wanted to pay compliments. The other three people in the Kemble pew were sitting at some distance from the family members and looked like upper servants – probably steward, butler and housekeeper.

The service came to an end at last and we walked out into the sunlight. Annoyingly, people stood back to let the Kembles go first, so they were halfway down the path on the way to a waiting carriage before we were out of the porch. I practically dragged Mr Godwit at a quick march between the gravestones to get to the lychgate before them and he did his duty.

'Good morning, colonel. Miss Lane, may I introduce Colonel Kemble, his son Rodney and Miss . . .'

But Miss Kemble had already disappeared into the coach with a flutter of green ribbons. The elder Kemble touched my hand and said he was delighted to make my acquaintance, without any flicker of curiosity in his eyes. He stood very upright but looked like a man who'd been bearing illness for some time. The contours of his face were sharp, his eyes bright but sunken, lips thin under a neat iron-grey moustache. Rodney Kemble was delighted to make my acquaintance too, or so he said. He didn't look or sound as if he'd ever been delighted about anything, although he wasn't a bad-looking man apart from those ears, with regular features and hazel eyes. Dull hazel. Hazelnuts that had been buried in the soil by a squirrel and forgotten during a long winter. I had clockwork automata in my nursery toybox that looked livelier than the young Mr Kemble. When the courtesies were over and father and son moved to their carriage, he even walked like an automaton, a few paces behind his father in regular steps, arms clamped to his sides as if moulded there. The coach drove away and the line of gigs and carts that had been waiting politely behind it began edging towards the gate to pick up their passengers.

'Is Rodney Kemble always like that?' I said to Mr Godwit as we walked back.

'Like what?'

'A man who expects the sky to fall on him if he makes a move out of place.'

'I don't know him well enough to judge. He's always had a reputation as a serious young man and I gather he makes a good job of running the estate.'

'It must have shocked him, finding her,' I said.

But did that account for his dazed look? A man who runs a country estate is used to dealing with death, from slaughtered pheasants to unfortunate horses. Wouldn't the shock be wearing off by now?

After lunch, I went in search of Tabby and found her helping Suzie with the washing-up. The broken halves of a plate, partly concealed by cabbage scrapings in the pig bin, showed that I was doing Mr Godwit's crockery a favour when I took her away for a talk in the garden.

'Did you take food to the Pictons yesterday?'

'Loaf of bread, more cheese, two cold lamb chops.'

'And did you get Sal to talk at all?'

'Nah. Nothing useful at any rate. She's hiding something, I know that.'

'About her brother?'

'S'pose so. Couple of times I caught her looking at me sideways, as if I was trying to find something she didn't want me to.'

'You didn't tell her I was going to see her brother, I hope.'

'Nah. Are you going to tell her?'

'I can't see it would serve any purpose. Goodness knows, there's nothing cheerful to report. He didn't even ask after his mother.'

I was beginning to feel worn down because everybody in this case was suspicious of us. We walked up and down the border for a while, Tabby scowling at the flowers. I asked what she'd made of the church service.

'Not bad. We had a good laugh, Suzie and me.'

I'd been faintly aware of giggling and rustling from the back pews and had tried to ignore them.

'What at?'

'The man in the big white smock doing the talking . . .'

'The vicar.'

'Whatever his name was, he had this piece of lint stuck to his lip, just here. Must have cut himself while he was shaving. It was going up and down all the time he was talking. Suzie and me had a bet of a halfpenny whether it would fall off before he finished. It didn't, so she won.'

That ended the hope that the morning might at least have started Tabby's religious education. It had only been a faint one in any case. She rattled on.

'Suzie was telling me about some of the people in church. She knows all about everybody.'

'Including the Kembles?'

'Mostly about the girl, the one with the green ribbons. Her name's Barbara. Suzie knows her maid. The maid says she's a right little madam.'

'I rather thought she might be.'

'Suzie says she threw a scent bottle at the maid when she was in a bad temper because her engagement had been broken off. Cut her forehead.'

'Do you think Suzie could get her friend to meet us?'

'Don't see why not. I'll ask her.'

I took Tabby out for a stroll, leaving my sketchpad at home because the village seemed to have a fairly strict attitude to Sundays. For the same reason I resisted the urge to call on William Smithies. The place was as quiet as a sitting hen, our stroll unproductive. Before abandoning Tabby to whatever tasks Mrs Wood could find for her, I asked her to meet me at daylight at the paddock again. I was becoming desperate to find somebody – almost anybody – prepared to talk to me.

The long ride to the racecourse was becoming familiar. It was another fine day, with a light breeze bringing a few clouds in from the west. We followed the same plan as before, going up the path by the trees and waiting until the gentlemen and grooms appeared from the town. This time they were watching out for us. Heads turned and it looked as if a couple of the gentlemen were going to satisfy their curiosity by cantering straight over to us, but the others went off along the course at a gallop and they followed. When they were a furlong or so ahead, I loosed the rein and let Rancie follow. I managed to bring her back to a walk before we reached the finishing post. The line of gentlemen and grooms had turned to watch us.

'Left you at the start, did we?' one of the gentlemen called, in a voice that would probably carry over several fields when out hunting.

I said nothing, just patted Rancie and smiled. The man with the hunting-horn voice and two others rode over.

'Nice mare you've got there,' one of them said.

I agreed and answered several questions about her age, her pedigree and so on. Rancie had become a stalking horse for their curiosity about me. Eventually, one of them came out with it.

'Are you here to take the waters, Miss . . .?'

I gave them my name; they gave me theirs. No, I wasn't taking the spa waters, I said. I was visiting a friend in the area. Such an informal introduction would have been out of the question if we were all on foot. Being on horseback excused some familiarity, but by riding out alone and entering into conversation with strange men I was pushing convention pretty far. They were aware of that and making assumptions from it. I saw it in their eyes as I looked from one face to another, coming to a decision. The one with the voice was a few years older than the rest and the most forward of them, with hard and cynical eyes. A younger one on a big chestnut went red in the face and giggled when I looked at him. He was not much more than a schoolboy. The third, on a dark bay, was somewhere between them in age, with a good-natured round face but no great air of intelligence. He'd introduced himself as Henry Littlecombe. I gave him a smile.

'You've got a good horse there,' I said.

He smiled back.

'A youngster, but he's coming on. Would you care for a little race, Miss Lane, if your mare's breathed?'

I let him win by a head, making a mental apology to Rancie. The other men galloped up to join us, horses surging round in an excited group. I raised my riding switch to Mr Littlecombe in fare-well and began to walk Rancie away. He was beside me in a couple of strides.

'I wonder if I might be permitted to escort you home, Miss Lane.'

'I couldn't possibly trespass on your kindness so far. But if you'd care to give us your company as far as the bottom of the hill, I'd be very grateful.'

His obvious pleasure made me feel a little guilty, but I consoled myself with the certainty that the other gentlemen were watching us as we rode off side by side. Mr Littlecombe had successfully cut out all of them and would probably live on that triumph for a day or two. Providing me with some information seemed a fair price for him to pay. It wasn't difficult to turn the conversation to gambling by way of the recent Cheltenham meeting. He was all too willing to analyze the performance of every horse in every race.

'I suppose a lot of gambling goes on,' I said.

'I should say so. The sportsmen and the legs come up from London. A good few thousands change hands, I can tell you.'

'Not just at the race meeting, so I've heard. I gather there was quite an expensive two-horse race about ten days beforehand.'

His cheerful face clouded. If he hadn't been so eager to keep up his reputation as a good sporting man, he'd have preferred not to talk about it.

'The business of Peter Paley and Teddy Ivedon, you mean?'

'Teddy Ivedon – is that Lord Ivebury's son?'

'That's right. He's a particular friend of mine. He's pretty cut-up about it now Paley's disappeared, but we keep telling him he shouldn't blame himself. It was all Paley's idea.'

'Really? The way I heard the story, they just agreed double or quits.'

'Teddy had to agree in the end, because Paley as good as accused him of hanging back if he didn't.'

'Were you there, the night they made the agreement?'

'Yes, a lot of us were. I was trying to persuade Teddy to walk away from it. His debts were bad enough in all conscience, without risking doubling them.'

I doubted that. He'd probably been as drunk as the rest of them.

'I daresay both of them had taken a drink or two by then,' I said.

'That's the odd thing. Paley was more or less sober as a judge. That's to say, he'd had his couple of bottles and a brandy or two, but nothing out of the ordinary. But he was hell-bent . . . excuse me . . . he was dead-set on that race. And it turned into a disaster for him.'

'It could have been a disaster for your friend Teddy.'

'Yes, we all think he'd have been pipped at the post if it hadn't been for Paley's horse stumbling on the run in. Bad luck, too. That horse is usually as sure-footed as a stag.'

'Even a sure-footed horse can stumble if a rider shifts his weight suddenly,' I said.

'Paley's as good a jockey as any in the county,' Littlecombe said, but there was a touch of uncertainty in his voice. We'd come to the bottom of the hill by now and turned on to my road home, but he showed no intention of leaving me. 'Anyway, it's not as if poor old Teddy got any advantage from it. No chance of Paley taking on his debts now.'

'Why?' I said. 'Do you think Mr Paley's dead?'

Henry Littlecombe blinked, as if that hadn't occurred to him.

'Oh, I wouldn't say dead, exactly. But he's not in a hurry to come back, is he?'

'So what do you think's happened to him?'

'Some people say he's gone abroad or joined the army.'

'But even abroad you need money to live on. And if he tried to join the army as an officer, they'd want to know something about him.'

'Maybe he's gone into a cavalry regiment as a ranker. He had the horse, after all. It was about all he did have.'

We rode on for a while together, without my gathering anything more to the purpose. When we came to crossroads with a signpost pointing back towards Cheltenham, I thanked him and said I'd ride on alone from there because some friends were coming to meet me. He was reluctant to part at first, but was flattered when I said that it might harm my reputation if friends saw me riding with a hand-some young gentleman.

'You'll come to the racecourse again, Miss Lane? Tomorrow?'

I said no, not tomorrow, but sometime perhaps, and gave him a wave as I turned in the other direction towards the village. For the rest of the ride back, I thought about what I'd learned. Far from being egged on by his friends, Peter Paley had been determined to bring about the race that had ended so disastrously for him. More than likely, he'd engineered his own defeat by causing his horse to stumble. And the whole sequence of events had happened a few hours after Mary Marsh had been killed. The problem with making a connection between them was that there was no evidence that the sporting man and the governess had as much as set eyes on each other. All the way back, I wondered how to find out if they had – and didn't come up with an answer.

SEVEN

Tabby was waiting to help me untack Rancie. We gave her a quick brush down and let her out in the paddock. She rolled over in the grass from one side to the other and then scrambled up, shook herself and made the 'hrrrr' sound that is the nearest a horse gets to a purr. Rather to my relief, Mr Godwit was out. Mrs Wood told me he'd gone in the gig to a meeting of the board of guardians in town. This was the body that ran the parish workhouse and administered the Poor Law, and I gathered he served on it reluctantly as a public duty, like his magistrate's work. At least that meant I didn't have to satisfy his curiosity about where I'd been riding for so long. In the afternoon Tabby and I went for a stroll with my sketching materials, mainly to give me an excuse for another call on William Smithies. He was at his lathe again, but this time stopped working when he saw me.

'I gave Jack Picton your message,' I said. 'He asked me to thank you.'

He nodded. 'How was he?'

'Angry.'

Another nod, as if that was only to be expected. I'd hoped William Smithies' gratitude might run to giving me some idea of what the message meant, but he saw his father looking at us and started the lathe again, so that was that. Mr Godwit returned in time for dinner, bringing with him the mail he'd collected from the office in town. One of the letters was a reply from my radical printer friend.

Dear Liberty,
   You might try asking for Barty Jones at the Mechanics' Institute. By all means mention my name, but you may find him not very informative, for the usual reasons. Yours in haste,
   Tom Huckerby

At dinner I broke the news to Mr Godwit that I intended to spend a day and night in Cheltenham. As expected, he was alarmed.

'I'm sure we could take you in the gig, whenever you wanted.

Whom do you need to see? Do you know anybody there? Where will you stay?'

I answered, more or less truthfully, that I was by no means sure whom I needed to see, but my inquiries in the village weren't getting far, so I should fish in a wider pool. No, I knew nobody there, but I had a couple of lines of inquiry which I would let him know more about if they were successful. As for where I'd stay, I supposed that a spa town would not be short of hotels. That, at least, provided a distraction. Over coffee he pondered the rival merits of hotels: the Royal or the Imperial were the choice for many visitors, but the Plough and the Belle Vue were thoroughly respectable. On reflection, though, it should be the Queen's. He knew the manager there – a very decent man. He'd have a word with him to see that I was looked after and made comfortable. I would have preferred to do without such attention, but it made him feel better. He insisted that he'd drive me in himself next morning in the gig.

I went to find Tabby. She was by the gates, looking out at the road and probably pining for London. Her mood wasn't improved by the news that I was going away and leaving her behind.

'I'm fed up with shelling peas and Mrs Wood looking at me sideways. And what if you get in trouble and I'm not there?'

'I'm not intending to get into trouble. You've got work to do for me here. You know I'm relying on you to find out what you can from Sal Picton.'

'I'm getting nowhere with that.'

'You've only just started. You can't expect her to tell you the family secrets in two visits. Then there are the Kembles. Speak to the maid if you get a chance, even if I'm not there. What we want is to find out anything we can about Miss Marsh, the governess.' I hesitated, wondering whether to share the thought with her. 'Especially whether there's been any gossip at all about her and Rodney Kemble.'

She gave me a sideways look. 'You reckon?'

'I don't know one way or the other. But it wouldn't be the first time the son of the house had taken advantage of the governess.'

'Then knocked her on the head to stop her telling anyone?'

'There's not a shred of evidence for that, so don't think about it. Just pick up what you can and let me know. I'll be back by Thursday at the latest. Give Rancie her morning carrot and talk to her now and then.'

Because Mr Godwit dined so early, there was plenty of daylight left. I walked to the road and found the village sunk in summer-evening peace, not even a dog moving. I strolled with no clear sense of direction, thinking that there was a great gap in my investigations. The name of that gap was Mary Marsh. Usually, if you're investigating a murder, the victim is where you start. What were her habits? Who were her friends or enemies? Did she meet her killer at home? Go willingly or unwillingly to the place where she was killed? I'd started from the opposite side, with the presumed killer, so had asked none of these questions. Asking them now, I found no answers. Nobody had said anything about the dead woman's family or friends. That went with her occupation. Usually an educated woman would go into service as a governess because she had no relatives or close friends to help her. It was the loneliest of positions – above the other servants but below the family. When not with her pupils, she'd be left very much on her own, closed in by the respectability of being a lady, without any of the advantages. It would have been even worse in Miss Marsh's case because she'd had only one pupil, and Barbara Kemble was now almost too old to need her. After a mile or so of this, I realized that I had a direction, after all. My feet were taking me towards the Kembles' house, the red-tiled roof in the woods I'd seen from the hill. Without thinking much about it, I'd decided I needed to find the place where Mary Marsh died.

Pasture stretched downhill on my right, golden in the light from the setting sun. On the left hand, woods of ash and oak crowded close to the path and were already smudged by dusk. They were well-kept woods, the trees straight and even. I guessed I was already at the boundaries of the Kembles' estate. After another half mile or so, a narrow gate led into the woods. Its latch and hinges were so well balanced that it opened at a touch. I took that for an invitation and walked through it into a woodland ride, at right angles to the road. It seemed darker under the trees, the ground deeply rutted, probably from where timber had been dragged out. Rabbits scuttered across and a tawny owl scooped the air with a whisper of wings just above my head. When the track came to a crossroads, I took a right turn, judging that was in the direction of the house. I was guessing that if Mary Marsh had gone to meet somebody by appoint-ment, it wouldn't have involved a long walk. After a few hundred yards, the track broadened out into a clearing. Trees must have been thinned there quite recently, because the only ones left standing were tall young ashes as straight as pencils. The trunks were silver columns, the tops feathery silhouettes shifting in the after-sunset breeze against a white sky. I stopped suddenly, sure beyond all doubt that this was the place where Mary Marsh had died.

There was no logical reason for it. After twenty-five days there'd be no lingering smell of blood. If the tramplings of people who'd taken the body away were still there on the hard earth, they wouldn't show in the dusk. The nettles beside the track might have been crushed down for a while when a piece of iron matted with blood and hair was thrown into them, but nettles grow quickly at this time of year and they showed no sign of it. So I couldn't explain it logically, beyond the thought that if somebody wanted a secluded meeting place not too far from the house, this would do very well. I stood in the clearing, feeling cold enough to wish I'd brought a shawl, and imagined Mary Marsh waiting there, hearing footsteps that surely weren't coming for the reason she expected. She'd have heard, as I heard, the leaves shifting in the breeze, the low of a cow from a distant field, a fox rustling through the under-growth. Then footsteps on the hard earth, just as I was hearing them now. I was so absorbed in Mary Marsh that it took me a few seconds to realize that these weren't in my thoughts of her; they were happening here and now, coming not towards her but towards me. My heart started racing and for a few moments of confusion I couldn't move. Male steps, certainly. Not hurrying, but not slow either; confident, as if the man planting his bootsoles down knew the ground and had a right to be there. I turned, intending to go back along the track. I managed maybe twenty yards before I knew it was useless. The male steps had stopped. Instead, there was a presence in the clearing and the feeling of eyes watching my back. It was all I could do to turn round and look at him. A young man, quite tall, in jacket and breeches. A shotgun, broken, in the crook of his arm. A face that was no more than a pale mask in the dusk, with dark ovals for eyes. I knew from my sight of them in the churchyard the day before that the eyes were the colour of buried hazelnuts. I was looking at Rodney Kemble and he was looking at me.

I spoke first. I had nothing to lose.

'It was here, wasn't it?' I said.

I thought he wasn't going to say anything. I waited, alert for the movement of lifting the shotgun and snapping its two halves together. I'd run into the woods and dodge, not a great hope but the best. The shotgun stayed where it was, angled over his arm.

'Who are you? What do you want?'

He sounded as alarmed as I was. Obviously, any memory of meeting me the day before had gone.

'It was here?' I asked again.

The mask-like face dipped briefly and rose again.

'What do you want?'

This time there was something close to panic in his voice. I wondered if he'd taken me for the ghost of Miss Marsh.

'To know who killed her,' I said.

'Do you know?' There was something like appeal in his voice.

'I don't know. I'd like to know,' I said.

A fox or something moved to the side of us. His hand went to the shotgun, then away again. If I stayed any longer with that pale face looking at me, I'd scream or babble.

'I'm going now,' I said.

I turned and started walking back along the track, which looked much darker than a few minutes ago, trying not to hurry or stumble. I expected shotgun pellets to come at any moment, exploding through the leaves into my back. Then, when the explosion didn't come, I listened for footsteps running behind me, even imagined I heard them. But they didn't come either. More by luck than anything, I found the track back to the gate. When it closed behind me and I was standing on the road, with no footsteps following me out of the wood, I leaned on the top bar, gasping and sobbing as if I'd been running a mile. Eventually, I got myself back to the house. The lamps were lit and Mr Godwit mildly concerned. I'd gone for a stroll and got lost, I said. I was sorry he'd been worried.

In the morning we went to town and Mr Godwit made a great production of seeing me comfortably settled at the Queen's. We drank coffee together; then he went off to do various errands, promising to come and collect me around noon the next day. I unpacked my travelling bag in my room and then strolled out to take a measure of the town. Like spas everywhere, it moved to the quiet rhythms of people not quite ill but not exactly well. A stream of elderly people in bath chairs pushed by maids or valets rolled along the wide Promenade. The people in the chairs were swathed in rugs, although the day was hot enough for ladies to need sunshades. Among pedestrians, white-haired men with a military look still managed something like a marching step by precise placing of their walking canes. Many of them had sunburned faces that suggested long service in the Indian army, or yellowish complexions from troubled livers. Somebody told me later that people from the Indian service liked Cheltenham for retirement because it reminded them of their summer hill stations in the Himalayan foothills. The public buildings were grand and mostly quite new, designed for people with cultivated tastes and time on their hands. There were the assembly rooms, a Literary and Philosophical Institution, a bandstand for concerts. One great advantage of the place was the large number of women out walking on their own or in pairs. Most of them were middle-aged and I assumed that they were invalids there to take the waters or comfortably-off widows living in the terraces and hotels. Their presence meant I wasn't conspicuous on my own.

At this time of day at least, it wasn't a town for young men. I saw nobody resembling the gentlemen jockeys I'd seen up on Cleeve Hill, or anybody at all who looked like a racing man. In one way this was a relief, because I was in no hurry to encounter Henry Littlecombe. In other ways, it was disappointing because I was hoping to pick up some gossip about the missing Peter Paley. That was one of my reasons for coming to town; the other a need to find somebody who knew about Jack Picton's radical and probably revolutionary activities. I hadn't been specific about either of them to Mr Godwit, because I knew he'd disapprove of both. After a while I went back to the hotel, ate a good lunch at a table of my own in the dining room, and asked a rather surprised porter for directions to the Mechanics' Institute. In Albion Street, he said, not far from the hotel. I walked there in the afternoon sunshine and found the doors closed, hardly surprising because the mechanics of the town were likely to be at work. A noticeboard beside the doors gave an idea of the serious-mindedness and politics of the place: a lecture by a Chartist who'd been in prison for his views, an appeal for everybody to sign the petition demanding reprieves for the Newport rioters and, more surprisingly, a meeting of the women's branch of the local working men's association. I pushed one of the doors and it opened. A woman was sweeping the hall floor inside. I apologized for troubling her and said I was hoping to find Mr Barty Jones. She looked me in the eye, sizing me up.

'Who wants him?'

'My name is Liberty Lane, but that won't mean anything to him. I'm a friend of a man he knows in London, a printer named Tom Huckerby.'

It was hard to tell from her expression if the name meant anything to her. Tom had friends and allies in most parts of the country.

'Mr Jones isn't here.'

'Do you know when he might be? I could call back later.'

'You could try this evening, if you like. There's a meeting on at seven.'

I thanked her and walked back to the Promenade, wondering how best to burrow into local gossip. It would probably come my way naturally if I stayed in town a week, but I couldn't wait that long. Still wondering, I came back to the Literary and Philosophical Institution. Quite a different atmosphere here from the Mechanics' Institute, more leisurely and less political. The notices outside advertised concerts and lectures, including one happening this afternoon on the habits and habitats of British butterflies. Ladies and gentlemen strolled in and out. I went inside and found the reading room. Elderly men were taking an after-lunch doze in leather armchairs; a clergyman and a grey-haired woman sitting side by side at a table were reading newspapers. With nothing much in mind, I settled myself at a small table with a pile of local newspapers. For a small town, Cheltenham seemed to generate quite a few. At the top of the pile were copies of the *Cheltenham Looker-On*. It turned out to be a cheerful and gossipy publication, mostly chronicling recent arrivals in the town. A name in an edition of a few weeks ago caught my eye: *Mr D'Israeli, the veteran author of* Curiosities of Literature *and other well-known works, is at present sojourning amongst us.* My laugh woke up one of the sleepers and brought a look of reproach. This veteran author was the father of my now ex-friend, Benjamin Disraeli MP. It seemed I couldn't get away from the family. I read through the next edition, wondering whether the senior Mr D'Israeli was still in town. Then, quite unexpectedly, I came across another name I knew. The paragraph was curt and not at all sociable.

> Mr Colum Paley wishes it to be known by all concerned that from the present date onward he will not be responsible for any debts or obligations incurred by his son, Peter Paley, however and whenever they were entered into.

Somebody had taken the trouble to circle the paragraph in thick black pencil. I checked the date. It was the week before Mary Marsh was killed and Peter Paley had disappeared. Mr Godwit had mentioned that Paley senior had grown impatient with his son's debts, and here was the proof of it.

Wondering who might have been interested enough to circle the announcement, I looked up and found the clergyman had stopped reading his paper and was looking at me. He was holding a pencil. It looked very much like the sort of pencil that would make thick black marks. I met his eye and gave a questioning look towards my paper. Sure enough, it brought him over to stand beside me.

'Allow me to introduce myself. Reverend Francis Close, vicar of this parish. Do I take it that you're a visitor here?'

His voice was low but sonorous, as if he created the acoustics of the pulpit round himself wherever he went. He was a good-looking man and, I guessed, conscious of it. The woman he'd been sitting beside was watching him with devotion. I gave him my name and admitted to being a visitor.

'I see you're observing our depravities,' he said, nodding towards the paper. 'I'm afraid we have many of them.'

'More than other places?'

He frowned, aware I wasn't taking him quite seriously. 'I believe so. Card playing, dancing, racing and gambling among the wealthy and idle; ingratitude, Chartism and socialism among the working men. Now we are being told we must submit to the arrival and departure of railway trains on the Lord's Day. We shan't allow it.'

'Cheltenham didn't strike me as particularly sinful,' I said.

'That's because you don't know it yet.'

'Did you know this young man in the paper?'

'Only by reputation, as a typical young gambler, wasting his substance and his life.'

'That seems to be his father's opinion, certainly.'

He frowned. 'Like father, like son. I wouldn't want you to take away the impression that because Colum Paley is at last acknowledging his son's sins – for the preservation of his own purse – he has none of his own. If anything, the father is worse than the son.'

'In what way?'

'In ways that I shall not even sully your ears by mentioning. I refer to his reputation only because some misguided people in our community have chosen to treat him as an honourable man. I should not wish an innocent visitor to fall into that error.'

Judging from his expression, he was only just giving me the benefit of the doubt on the question of innocence. I thanked him for his concern, disappointed at not getting more specific information, and walked out of the reading room.

The butterfly talk had just finished. Some of the audience were coming out of the lecture room, others lingering inside to look at collections of butterflies and pictures of them on the walls. I went in, trying to weigh up who would be most likely to join a stranger like me in a cup of tea and a gossip. Most were women, with a few gentlemen. I've no taste for looking at dead butterflies under glass, so I pretended to concentrate on the pictures. It was a temporary exhibition, mounted on cards rather than framed, mostly amateur and of varying quality. The colour more than anything else drew my attention to a small painting of the common blue butterfly. It was carefully done in watercolour from three different aspects: on a birdsfoot-trefoil flower with wings folded to show the underside, wings spread and then in flight. The artist had worked with precision, showing every vein in the wings. Equally carefully, he or she had added the date bottom left: April 1840. The signature was on the right-hand side. I glanced at it from idle curiosity and then must have made some sound or movement because people were staring at me. The artist's name was Mary Marsh. A tall woman with curly grey hair was standing next to me. She smiled.

'Yes, it's very well done, isn't it?'

'The artist . . .' I said.

'She's dead now, poor girl. We had a series of classes on painting butterflies earlier this year. She brought her pupil to them, but the girl wasn't very interested. Mary had much more talent.'

'Barbara Kemble,' I said. 'Mary Marsh was her governess.'

I was trying to catch up, staggered at coming close to Mary Marsh so unexpectedly.

'You knew Mary?' said the woman. She was kind, taking my surprise for distress.

'No, not really. That's to say . . .'

A male arm in a black sleeve reached out between the woman and me. While I'd been looking at the picture, I'd been aware of steps coming up behind me and somebody standing there, but I had been too absorbed to take much notice. I half turned, surprised at the rudeness. A hand came past my cheek, scrabbled at the edge of the picture and, before the woman or I could do anything, tore it off the wall and let it drop to the floor. Reverend Close stood there with the self-satisfied look of an Old Testament prophet watching a sinful town destroyed.

'It should not be there,' he said, in a voice that carried all around the room.

'Why not?' I said.

He spoke to the room, not to me. 'To the pure, all things are pure. From the impure, everything is impure.'

'Only half of that is in the Bible,' said the woman beside me, with some spirit.

He disregarded her, turned on his heel and walked out, leaving first a silence, then a surge of the over-bright conversation that comes from general unease. Although some of the people had put on church-going expressions that suggested they agreed with the vicar, I sensed that others were embarrassed by him. I bent down and picked up the picture. The butterfly with wings spread was torn right across.

'I'm so very sorry,' the kind woman said. 'It can be mended, I think.'

'But why did he do it?'

'Because he's exactly the kind of man who would cast the first stone. He thinks he has a monopoly on the scriptures, but there are other people who can read the Bible as well.'

She was indignant, cheeks flushed. 'I'm so sorry this should have happened to you.'

I accepted her suggestion that we should go for a tea and we went to the refreshment room next door. Her name was Felicity Dell, a doctor's widow. I told her that I was staying with Mr Godwit, without introducing the distant relation fiction. She'd met him several times and liked him. When tea had been brought, I turned the conversation back to Mary Marsh.

'Why is Reverend Close so insulting about her?'

'Because he listens to rumours.'

'What rumours?'

'I feel as if I'm being disloyal to the poor girl's memory, even passing them on. People are so ready to believe the worst.'

'Believe me, Mrs Dell, I've no interest at all in harming her reputation. But I have reasons for wanting to know why she was killed. I'm afraid I can't tell you what the reasons are, but if the rumours had anything to do with her death, I'd like to know about them.'

'They have, yes. Some people say she was . . . let's say, she was too friendly with the man who's accused of killing her – with Picton.'

'Did those rumours start before or after she was murdered?'

She looked around, making sure nobody was listening. 'Most of them afterwards, but . . . I haven't told anybody else this, because I didn't want to blacken her reputation any further. But the fact is, I did see her and the Picton man together.'

'Recently?'

'No, in early May, at the time of the butterfly classes. It was a series of five, over five weeks. We worked in pairs, two to a specimen case, and as it happened she and I were usually together. Her pupil, Barbara, was put with one of the other girls. I liked Miss Marsh. She seemed very quiet in her manner at first, but when you got to know her, she had some incisive opinions and a sense of humour. She seemed to enjoy the classes, so I was surprised when she didn't attend the last one. Barbara wasn't there either, so I assumed the girl was ill and Mary had had to stay with her. When the class was over, I went to see a friend of mine in St James Square. The parish workhouse is just behind the square. I know it well because my husband used to be a visiting doctor there. I walked past the workhouse and there was Mary, talking to a man just outside it. I'm sure that man was Picton.'

'You'd have recognized him?'

'Oh yes. Jack Picton is pretty well known in town – the demon king as far as some people are concerned.'

'You were surprised to see them together?'

'Yes. I couldn't think how they'd have met.'

'Did you say anything?'

'No. I was on the other side of the road. They were deep in conversation. I'm sure she didn't see me. To be honest, I didn't think of it again until those rumours started.' She stared at the tablecloth and then added, quite fiercely: 'Some people, they assume that if a woman gets murdered she must somehow have brought it on herself. I hate that.'

There was nothing else she could tell me. We exchanged cards and she invited me to call next time I was in town. Before we parted, she offered to take the blue butterfly painting and have it mended for me, but I decided to keep it for the time being. It was the closest I'd come yet to Mary Marsh.

EIGHT

A t half past six I was back at the Mechanics' Institute inquiring for Mr Barty Jones. A young man with a fierce scar on his face that looked as if it had been made by hot metal told me his meeting had already started, so I was too late. He had no notion when it might finish. His manner wasn't especially obstructive, but not welcoming either. I strolled around in the warm evening. Most of the invalids had gone back to their hotels for early dinners and the sociable part of the evening hadn't properly begun. The assembly rooms and the Literary and Philosophical Institution were closed. The main signs of life were a phaeton clopping along the Promenade, taking a party for an airing, and voices from the open doorway of a public house. A small breeze from the west stirred the dust. I wondered what kind of welcome Amos had found when he came home to his people and whether he'd sold the nervous charger. I missed him. All the time my mind was running on what Mrs Dell had said. Because of that, I followed her route to St James Square, looking for the workhouse.

Even though I expected it, the place still came as a shock. After the elegant buildings of the rest of the town, it looked like some grim factory. The central building was a hexagonal three-storey block of red brick, with two lower wings radiating out from it at angles. One of them was longer than the other, with an iron cross at the apex of its roof. I guessed that one wing was for men and the other for women, the normal system, with a chapel where, for an hour or so every week, a man and wife kept in the separate wings might have sight of each other. I walked round it. At the back, great wooden gates, ten feet high, were firmly barred. Round the side, a smaller entrance with one word – Workhouse – carved in the stone lintel. The board of guardians who ran the establishment might have saved the money they'd paid to have it chiselled. The place couldn't be anything other than a workhouse, except perhaps a prison. It really wasn't very different, except the men and women inside were guilty of poverty and homelessness, not wrongdoing. If Jack Picton and Mary Marsh really were meeting secretly, why should they have chosen this ill-omened spot of all the places in town and country? Wondering that, I hadn't noticed somebody walking up behind me until he spoke.

'So, you're admiring our Bastille.'

For the second time that day, I was being addressed in a voice used to making itself heard in public. But this was different from the self-satisfied tones of Reverend Close. This was a working man, speaking with the local accent. I turned and saw a man of perhaps forty-five or fifty. He was medium height or less and looked as tough as a brick, rectangular in build with broad shoulders, jaw and forehead, his body braced on rather bandy legs. His dark hair was short, flecked with grey.

'Bastille?'

'A hell on earth.'

'The Bastille fell.'

'So will this, one day. Not soon enough, though.' He gave me a long look, as if waiting for disagreement, and then added: 'You were looking for me?'

'You're Mr Barty Jones?'

A nod. 'They said a young lady was looking for me.'

The slight emphasis on 'lady' didn't sound like a compliment. I gave him my name and asked how he knew where to find me.

'I know a lot of things.'

It sounded like a warning. He could have known where to find me only if somebody at the Mechanics' Institute had pointed me out as soon as I'd left the building and he'd followed me. That might mean that he'd heard about my earlier visit and had been waiting when I came back, not in a meeting at all.

'You say you know Tom Huckerby. What's he doing now?' he said.

Definitely a challenge, not just a polite inquiry. I kept my temper and told him the truth, that Tom was still producing his radical pamphlets from his print shop off Fleet Street.

'So how does a lady like you come to know the likes of Tom Huckerby?'

'He was a friend of my father.'

It was the truth, but Barty Jones looked sceptical.

'So, what do you want from me?'

'I want to keep Jack Picton from getting hanged,' I said. 'If he's innocent, that is.'

'What's Jack Picton to you?'

'Nothing at all, until two weeks ago. I work as an investigator. I was approached by a person who wishes him well.'

Not entirely Mr Godwit's standpoint, but I couldn't say more without revealing his part in the case.

'Who?'

'I can't tell you. But if you're a friend of Picton, isn't it your business to help me?'

The sun had shifted. The edge of the shadow of the great hexagonal tower was falling on us. I felt cold – and impatient when he didn't answer immediately.

'Well, isn't it?'

'How do you know who my friends are?'

'Well, at least you share his politics?'

'What do you know about my politics?'

'Very well. For all I know, you might be a Conservative.' He spat, past me rather than at me. 'Well, then,' I said.

'So how do you reckon I can help Picton?'

It was far from a surrender, but a decision had been taken.

'The question is: what he was doing on the night Mary Marsh was killed? He's refusing to tell anybody. As far as I can tell, there might be three reasons for that. One, he's trying to protect somebody. Two, he was doing something illegal. Three, he's guilty.'

'He's not guilty.'

'You know that for certain?'

A nod.

'So which is it – protecting somebody or doing something illegal? Or both?'

'Both?'

'For instance, if he'd been out with the Raddlebush Brotherhood.'

That surprised him and for a second he let it show.

'So he's in that, is he?' he said.

'People seem to think so.'

'People think a lot of things that aren't true.'

'Is it true?'

'How would I know?'

He knew; I was sure of that from his eyes.

'If you know anybody who is in the brotherhood, could you ask him to speak to me?' I said. 'If he wanted, I wouldn't even ask his name or tell anybody I'd met him.'

'What use would that be? I thought you were looking for some-body who'd stand up in court for him.'

'That would be the best thing, yes. But I can see that a man might not want to incriminate himself. If he could at least give me a hint to begin with, I might find out some other way.'

He stood with one hand propping his chin, the other cupping his elbow, as if thinking were a weight that needed support.

'I'll do what I can,' he said at last. 'I can't say more than that.'

'Thank you.'

'Where would I get word to you, if I did happen to know of anyone?'

'You could leave a message for me at the post office. I'll send somebody to inquire every evening.'

He nodded and I expected him to walk away, but he stood there.

'So, where are you going now, my lady?'

If I'd said back to the hotel, he might make inquiries and find out that a local magistrate was paying my bill there. After his stratagem of following me so that he could meet me on his own terms, I knew I shouldn't underestimate Mr Jones.

'I think I'll stroll round the town for a while,' I said.

'We can't have a lady walking round all on her own. There are some socialist ruffians at large, as you know. Will you permit me to escort you?'

Back to sarcasm. He expected that I wouldn't want to be seen with a working man who was quite probably one of the local rabble-rousers. I looked him in the eye.

'I should be very grateful, Mr Jones, if you have the time.'

When we started walking side by side, I realized that his wide-legged stance must come from some weakness or injury because he walked with a limp, swaying from side to side. We probably looked a strange couple and when – as if in a deliberate challenge – he made for the Promenade, we received curious looks. People who'd eaten early dinners were now soothing their digestions with an evening stroll and the pavement was quite crowded. Some of the looks were hostile as well as curious, confirming my impression that Barty Jones was a known political agitator. He rolled along as slowly as any of the respectable invalids, demonstrating that he had as much right to the evening air as any of them, but when a clock struck the half-hour he started walking faster, his swaying limp suddenly purposeful.

I thought we might be on our way back to the Mechanics' Institute, but instead he took us towards the assembly rooms. Lamps were already lit outside its wrought-iron entrance canopy and two gentlemen in evening dress were getting out of a carriage. Clearly, some function was about to start. I wondered if Barty Jones intended to invade it and steeled myself for more hostile looks, or worse. Instead, he came to a halt a few dozen yards away and looked round. A man in a workman's cap and jacket came unobtrusively up beside us. Barty Jones spoke without turning to look at him.

'Where is he?'

'On his way,' the man said, and then went away and leaned against a wall. When I looked round, there were a surprising number of working men who seemed to have nothing better to do than watch prosperous citizens arriving for a dinner, or whatever the function was. There were at least a dozen, as far as I could see, mostly gathered in twos and threes, apparently casual but with their eyes fixed on the entrance to the assembly rooms. A gentleman in evening dress and top hat turned the corner and came walking towards us. The man who was leaning against a wall came suddenly upright. The others, still unobtrusively, started moving towards the entrance. Barty Jones's hand slid into his jacket pocket. For a heart-stopping moment, I thought I was about to see an assassination, but he had no pistol, only something small enough to be clasped in his palm. Seeming unaware of what was happening, the gentleman walked on. He was only a few steps from the entrance canopy when Barty Jones raised his right hand and the air was suddenly full of missiles.

Small and regularly shaped missiles, they were, just dots against the pale evening sky. Some hit the gentleman's top hat, knocking it sideways; others clanged against the canopy or fell with metallic clicks on to the paving stones. At first there was no sound apart from that. Then people started shouting. Most were shouts of alarm and anger from men running from the assembly rooms, but the loudest came from Barty Jones.

'Eighteen of them, Mr Paley. That should see your lad all right for a week.'

The man he was shouting at gave one glance in his direction. He was an imposing-looking man, in his fifties, with an angular face, as if a sculptor had chiselled the planes but not had time for smoothing touches. Then he turned away, removed his hat calmly just before it fell off of its own accord and walked into the assembly rooms. He must have said something to quieten the gentlemen who had rushed out to see what was happening because they all disappeared inside. The men who'd thrown the missiles were disappearing too, quietly but without wasting time. No sign at present of a constable or anybody else in authority, but there'd been enough noise to attract attention. Barty Jones turned to me, smiling.

'If you'll excuse me, I'll leave you here, Miss Lane. I'm sure you'll find some gentleman to take you wherever you're going.'

He started rolling away. I walked after him.

'Was that Colum Paley?'

'That's right.' He said it over his shoulder.

'But what was it all about?'

'I'm sure you'll find out, you being an investigator.'

That was clearly all I was going to get from him, so I let him go and went back to the entrance of the assembly rooms. Still no constable, but a gang of small boys had arrived and were scrabbling on the pavement and in the gutter for the things that had been thrown. Something glinted in the lamplight, caught in a crack between paving stones. I got to it just before one of the boys and straightened up with the thing in my hand, the boy pulling at my skirts and wailing in disappointment. It lay there in my glove, only adding to the bewilderment.

'Miss, it's not fair, miss. Please, it's mine. I saw it first.'

So I gave it to the boy. After all, it was only a penny. One of eighteen of them according to Barty Jones; totalling one shilling and sixpence. About what an unskilled working man might earn in a day, thrown at a rich man to see his son all right for a week. Far from helping me solve a puzzle, Mr Jones had handed me another one.

NINE

Mr Godwit arrived an hour late to meet me next day at the hotel, red-faced, flurried and apologetic.

'I only just managed to get away. I've spent most of the morning with Penbrake. There's been another of these raddle bush atrocities.'

'A rick burning?'

'Just the bush, so far, tied to the farm gate. Penbrake thinks they'll come back tonight. He's all for calling out the militia.'

He told me the rest as we hurried to where he'd left the gig, a boy coming behind with my bag. The red thorn bush with black rags for ribbons had been found on the gate of a prosperous farmer who lived a little way out of the village, on the far side of the Kembles' estate. The farmer had galloped straight to the chairman of magistrates, Mr Penbrake, and Penbrake had convened an emergency meeting of the bench at Mr Godwit's house, since it was closer to the scene of the crime than his own. In fact, as far as I could make out, no crime had yet been committed, but Mr Godwit was being carried along on Penbrake's urgency. I asked what the farmer had done to annoy the brotherhood.

'Nothing especial. He turned away one of his men last week for insolence, and now this has happened. He doesn't want trouble. He asked if we thought he should take the man back, but Penbrake told him it was his duty to stand out against them.'

By his standards, Mr Godwit drove fast on the way back, the cob hammering along the roads. It needed all his attention, so I couldn't have reported on what I'd been doing in Cheltenham, even if I'd wanted to. I didn't want to, because I could make no sense of any of it. Months earlier, Mary Marsh had neglected a painting class to meet Jack Picton outside the workhouse. The vicar considered her to be a woman so impure that her butterflies were an offence to a respectable wall. Colum Paley might have been richer by one shilling and sixpence if he'd stooped to pick up pennies.

While we were waiting for a farm wagon to get out of the way, I tried Mr Godwit on one thing.

'I met Reverend Close.'

He turned, looking alarmed. 'Oh. What did you make of him?'

'The most uncharitable clergyman I've ever encountered.'

He looked so solemn at first that I thought he admired the man. If so, I'd probably have given up his case there and then, but he smiled suddenly. 'Do you know, I quite agree with you . . . only one mustn't say so.'

'Why not?'

'Quite a lot of people think he's the salvation of the town. Penbrake's all for him.'

The cart got itself out of the way and we went on at a fast trot.

Mr Penbrake was waiting on the drive as the gig drew up. He was one of those men who seem to take up a lot of space – no more than averagely tall, but solidly built, standing chest out as if breasting an invisible sea. He'd obviously shaved that morning, but dark stubble was already appearing on his cheeks, as impatient as the rest of him to get on with things. His face was handsome enough, with a broad forehead and well-shaped lips, but his chin was too small and rounded, adding a petulant air.

He started talking at Mr Godwit before he could get down from the driving seat, a cannonade of names of people he'd been in contact with through the morning. Mr Godwit insisted on helping me down and introducing him to me. He gave me a barely civil touch of the hand and a few words, and then he was off again. To his annoyance, the authorities hadn't given in to his demand to call out the militia, but he was doing his best with the county constabulary and as many farmers and landowners who could be recruited from the estates round. The Duke of Wellington before Waterloo couldn't have been busier. He tried to resist Mr Godwit's suggestion that we should eat a late luncheon: beef between slices of bread was enough for a campaigning man. But when it came to regular meals, Mr Godwit was determined, so the three of us sat down to a luncheon of cold cuts and salad, brought in by Mrs Wood herself. It was usually Suzie who served at table. I hoped she and Tabby weren't up to some devilment together.

As soon as I could escape, I went to find Tabby. She was up a tree in the orchard, looking down at Rancie and the cob.

'Where's Suzie?' I said.

'Mrs Wood sent her on an errand somewhere. Who's the man making all the confloption?'

'Chairman of the bench. Did you manage to find out any of the things I wanted?'

'The Kemble girl's maid's coming to see her mother in the village tomorrow morning, if she can get away. Suzie thinks she might talk to us then.'

'Good. What about Sal Picton?'

Until then Tabby had been talking down to me from her perch in the tree. Now she came sliding lightly down the trunk, getting leaves in her hair and bits of lichen on her dress.

'I went to see her this morning. She was feeling low-spirited because her mother kept her awake all night. The mother's stomach had got upset from all the food. Sal had to wash the sheet and I helped her peg it out. That was when we got talking and she told me about her sister.'

'I thought there was a sister somewhere. What about her?'

'She got transported.'

'What!'

'Earlier this year, it was – to Van Diemen's Land. They were going to hang her, but a lot of people signed one of those things to the Queen . . .'

'Petition.'

'Whatever it was. Anyway, the Queen said they shouldn't hang her, so she was transported for life instead.'

'What had she done?'

Tabby scuffed her toe in the grass. 'She killed her baby.'

'Why? How did it happen?'

'Dunno. Sal said she wasn't supposed to talk about it and that was what had made her mother like she is. She wouldn't say any more. I think she was sorry she'd said that much.'

The thought in my mind was that Mr Godwit must have known, so why hadn't he told me? If it hadn't been for the presence of Mr Penbrake, I'd have gone to have it out with him there and then. The same applied to William Smithies, though it was more defensible in his case because he wouldn't have wanted to gossip about his friend's family affairs to a stranger. At least I understood now the message he'd asked me to pass on to Jack Picton. They were campaigning to have the girl brought back from Australia, although it seemed the faintest of hopes. She was lucky to be alive – always assuming she'd survived the voyage out in a convict ship. I wasted most of the afternoon waiting for a chance to confront Mr Godwit, but the two magistrates stayed closeted in the study. Now and again farm boys arrived with messages and lingered by the back door drinking beer before leaving with replies, sometimes at a run. Later an official-looking man who turned out to be an officer in the county constabulary rode up to join the planning session. By then I had given up hope of getting any sense from anybody and gone back to the paddock. The two horses belonging to the visitors had been turned out there and Rancie wasn't pleased with competition for the grazing. Tabby joined me.

'I tried to listen at the door, like I knew you'd want, only Mrs Wood caught me. She's in a bad mood, with Suzie away and that one staying for dinner. She said to tell you it will be half an hour early and not to change because it's campaigning order and not formal.'

'Campaigning order! Heaven help us! What did you hear?'

'Not much. They were away from the door, standing round something on a table. A map, I think it was, but I could only see a bit through the keyhole. The stubble-faced man was saying something about cutting them off if they came down from the top road and not shooting till he gave the order.'

Worse and worse. Penbrake might have been denied use of the militia, but angry farmers with shotguns might do nearly as much damage. After a while the gardener arrived to catch the constabulary cob. The old man looked harassed and, without much persuasion, revealed that he'd spent most of the afternoon searching stables and outhouses for pitchforks, shovels and anything else that might be used as weapons and loading them into the gig. More time had been spent finding and cleaning Mr Godwit's old shotgun.

'Doesn't know one end of it from the other,' he grumbled. 'Be more danger to himself than the rebels.'

So protesting farm labourers had been elevated to rebels now, the way that birds are promoted to game when men go out to take their lives. I was growing more and more worried. When the man from the constabulary had mounted his cob, the two magistrates came out to see him off and Mr Penbrake couldn't resist giving him more instructions. At least I guessed that was the case because the man on the cob was looking grave and nodding. I dodged into the house and made for the study.

Tabby had been right about the map. It was a large one that looked as if it had been professionally surveyed, showing the town

and the countryside for several miles around. It was easy to pick
out the farm that was the subject of the Raddlebush Brotherhood's
latest threat because somebody, Mr Penbrake probably, had ringed
it in red ink. Red ink arrows converged on it from the north, with
names and numbers beside them, with green ink ones coming from
the south. I tried to make as much sense of it as I could in the few
minutes that were probably all I had. The farm was about half a
mile past the Kembles' land and uphill of it. It was isolated, with
only two buildings near it – probably farm cottages. To the south,
the main road went close, with a lane off it leading up to the farm.
Green arrows clustered either side of the lane. Above the farm was
a dead-end track, leading only to a quarry. Woodland ran along
some of the hillside between the quarry track and the farm and
could conceal a group of men. It would be a good place to start a
surprise attack, with nothing but a field or two between saboteurs
and farmyard. Penbrake clearly thought so too because two sets of
red arrows pointed towards a copse of trees and an area carefully
marked 'dead ground' between the quarry road and the farm. If the
brotherhood came from that direction, there'd be men in hiding
waiting to ambush them.

I'd been too intent on the map. Before I was aware of steps in
the passage outside, the study door was opening and Mr Godwit
and Mr Penbrake were back.

I turned, not trying to hide my embarrassment and confusion.

'Oh, I'm sorry. I know I shouldn't be here, but I'm so scared
and worried.'

I spoke to Mr Godwit, but it was Mr Penbrake who answered.

'My dear young lady, you mustn't disturb yourself. We promise
that we'll keep you and everybody else safe, won't we, Stephen?'

He spoke like a kindly uncle to a child of seven, noticing me
now because I was playing my proper part in their drama. Mr Godwit
was making small soothing noises. I edged away from the map.

'I'm sure you will, but it's you and Mr Godwit I'm scared for.
The guns . . .'

Two of them, propped up against a bookcase. Mr Godwit's might
have been used in King George's time, but the other looked modern
and businesslike.

'My dear, I promise you we'll bring him back safely. Sleep tight
tonight and don't worry, and we'll be back with you by breakfast
time, safe and sound,' Mr Penbrake said.

Somehow he'd got hold of my hand and was patting it. I'd always hated that, even when I was a child, so I pulled it away, pretending a need to get my handkerchief out of my pocket. Naturally, he assumed I was trying to hide a nervous tear. After a few more soothing sounds, we went in to our campaigning dinner, where Mr Godwit only toyed with his food but Mr Penbrake ate steak and kidney pudding like a hero. I left the table as soon as I decently could, but not before suffering a toast from Mr Penbrake: 'To hearth, home and the ladies. May they always find defenders.'

Tabby, sensing action, was waiting in my room upstairs with my plainest dark wool dress laid out on the bed and my good stout walking shoes under it. She was wearing her urchin boots, visible because she'd already hitched her dress up to shin level.

'Are we off now?'

'We'll let them go first. They probably won't be long.'

The gig, loaded with rustic weaponry, was already on the drive under our window, with the cob in the shafts, the gardener standing beside it, holding the reins of Mr Penbrake's horse.

'Do you want me to get Rancie ready?' Tabby asked.

'I think we'll go on foot.'

There'd be fields to cross and I had no intention of putting Rancie at unknown hedges in the dark. The battle party went off soon afterwards. Watching from the window, we saw a group of what looked like local farmhands, who had been waiting by the church, fall in behind Mr Godwit and the gig. I guessed that they'd been ordered by their employers to come to another farmer's defence, whether they liked it or not. They probably liked it. A rural worker's life can be pretty monotonous.

'Whose side are we on?' Tabby inquired. It sounded as if she didn't mind one way or the other.

'We're not on anybody's side. We're just trying to prevent bloodshed.'

I'd no great sympathy for people who burned ricks, but my father had brought his children up to be on the side of the working man. Also, Mr Godwit was too old and too gentle to be dragged into battles in the dark.

Tabby and I waited half an hour. Then we put on our cloaks and walked uphill, in the opposite direction to the way the battle party had gone. It was around half past seven, still broad daylight. Penbrake's tactics were probably to put one party by the main entrance to the threatened farm and a larger one in the fields at the back, between the farm and the quarry road. He'd want to get both groups in place before dark. The Raddlebush Brotherhood couldn't risk arriving by daylight. Their attack would come late, possibly even in the early hours of the morning. We could all be in for a long wait.

'We could have done with a lantern,' Tabby said.

'Probably. There'll be a half-full moon, but it doesn't rise till much later.'

I'd consulted Mr Godwit's almanack before we left and put a few inches of candle in my pocket, along with a flint lighter. Tabby fell behind and then caught up, holding two stout hazel sticks that she'd taken from a hedge. She offered me one of them.

'Better'n nothing,' she said. 'If you hold it by the thin end and bring it down like this.'

Her swing made it whistle through the air like a hornet.

'For goodness' sake, Tabby, we're supposed to be stopping them, not joining in.'

Still, I accepted the stick. It had a comforting feel. As we walked, I explained my plan to Tabby. Mr Penbrake was probably right in thinking the attack would come from the quarry track because the brotherhood would expect the front gate of the farm to be defended. We'd wait on the track or in the quarry with the aim of intercepting the attackers and warning them that the farm was defended with guns and a much larger party than they'd been expecting. If there was a brain among them, they'd surely call off the attempt. If not, then at least we'd done what we could.

As we turned on to the quarry track, the sun was going down over the western hills, a great copper hemisphere in a pale sky, with home-going rooks silhouetted across it. Smoke was rising from chimneys down in Cheltenham. I imagined the Raddlebush Brotherhood gathering on street corners or in public houses and then setting out for their long walk. Barty Jones would be with them, I was sure. He hadn't even expected me to believe his pretence of knowing nothing. The road was deeply rutted by quarry carts, so we were glad of the hazel sticks for balance. It was high and exposed, apart from a few old and twisted oaks on our left. Rabbits hopped across and a fox came out of the woods, then turned quick as flame and went back under the trees when he saw us. The roof of the Kembles' house came into view above the trees. I supposed

Rodney Kemble and his father would be out with the defenders. Further on, we saw a prosperous-looking farmhouse with several barns and a whole row of haystacks, giving plenty of targets for the brotherhood. Two large copses, one close to the farm and another nearer our road, would be good hiding places for the magistrates' forces. There'd be men in there already, sitting on tree trunks, checking their weapons. When I thought of that, a flaw in my simple plan occurred to me. Even though they wouldn't be expecting the attack till much later, they'd be keeping an eye on the quarry road and Tabby and I would be all too visible as we walked along it. We decided we'd better take to the woods and helped each other clamber over a keeper's stile into the shelter of a copse. We walked, sometimes in clear patches over dead oak leaves, sometimes shoulder-deep in bracken and foxgloves. It was slow going, but then we were in no hurry.

By the time the belt of woodland ran out, we were past the farm and almost at the quarry. The light was going by then, so we felt safe enough scrambling through a hedge into the quarry itself. The cliffs of cut stone on either side of the entrance looked like huge doors that might close on us, but everything was peaceful inside and still warm from a day of sunshine on pale limestone. We settled on a block of cut stone, our backs against the rock face, and prepared for a long wait. Once or twice voices came up from the fields between us and the farm. It was a reminder of how sound travels on still evenings, so when Tabby and I talked we kept our voices low.

'Do you think Sal Picton would talk to me about her sister?' I said.

'Nah. I told you, she wished she hadn't talked to me.'

'Everybody must know about it, though. Something like that would be the talk of the village for months.'

But then it wouldn't be something they'd talk about easily to strangers. It explained, perhaps, why the other villagers had shown so little charity to Sal and her mother. A rioting and fire-raising brother was bad enough; a woman who'd killed her baby far worse. But none of that excused Mr Godwit for not telling me. Since there was no progress we could make in that direction, I told Tabby about my discoveries in town. She thought the explanation for Mary Marsh's meeting with Jack Picton was the obvious one.

'They were sweethearts; then he got tired of her and killed her. Like I said.'

'That simple? Then we can pack up and go home tomorrow.'

'Wouldn't mind.'

'There's more to it than that. How would they have met in the first place?'

'Don't know, but they must have.'

'We must try to speak to Barbara Kemble's maid tomorrow. She'll have some idea if there was any gossip about the governess. Then I think I'd better call on young Barbara herself.'

'Will she see you?'

'Probably, yes.'

If I called and left my card, social convention would almost demand that she invited her neighbour's visitor to tea.

We waited. Bats criss-crossed each other in the air, catching insects in the upward draughts from the warm stone. Owls hooted from down in the copse. Some of them sounded strange and I wondered if they might be signals among the various groups of the farm's defenders. Usually, Tabby was good at waiting, but country-side made her fidgety.

'If I was to go back the way we came, I could whistle to you if I heard anyone coming.'

'Better not whistle. Wait along the track if you like. Only don't try to tackle them or speak to them. Run back here.'

She went. The air was chilling now and the bats had gone. Soon it was almost completely dark, an overcast night with not even stars showing. I wrapped my cloak tightly round me and strained my ears for any movement in the fields or back along the track. It was a long time before anything happened. Then somebody was running towards the quarry, only one person and light steps. Tabby appeared, a darker shape against the darkness, gasping for breath.

'In the fields already. Four or five of them, I think.'

She'd heard them and seen shapes pushing through a hedge into a field soon after the turning on to the quarry track. I'd thought they'd keep longer to the track before they went cross-country, but they'd wrong-footed us. Their route across the fields to the farmhouse would take them close to one of the copses where Penbrake's men were waiting. Tabby and I ran back along the track, stumbling on ruts, and pushed our way through a dark mass of hedge, hoods up to protect our faces from thorns. On the other side, we fell into a group of sheep. They'd been sleeping till then and scrambled to their feet, setting up an outcry of baaing that would have been audible a mile away. Somehow we got clear of them and started downhill, heading for the copse. The men from the brotherhood would have to make a diagonal course across the fields to reach the farm, and at some point our straight downhill line would intercept it. Simple in geometry; not so in dark fields with shoe soles sliding on dry grass and sheep droppings.

We came to a stone water trough in the hedge and scrambled over it into the next field. A sheepdog was barking down in the farm. I put out a hand to stop Tabby. Between the barks there were noises much closer to us. Footsteps and a muffled curse from a hedge at right angles to the one we'd just crossed. They sounded near enough to hear if I called to them, but we might be quite close to the defenders in the copse by now. I fumbled in my pocket and found the few inches of candle and the lighter. The rasp of the flint sounded terribly loud. As soon as a bud of light formed round the candle wick, I kept my hand round it, so that it wouldn't be seen from the copse but might be visible to the men who'd just come through the hedge. It worked. The footsteps stopped. We could see nothing outside our cave of candlelight.

'Who's there?'

A whisper, but still too loud. I thought I recognized the voice, and when the speaker took a few steps towards us, I knew from the rolling walk that I was right.

'Who's there?' he said, more urgently.

No point in keeping quiet now. The men in the copse might already be alerted.

'There are men waiting with shotguns,' I said. 'A lot of men, this side of the farm.'

Barty Jones stopped a few yards away from us.

'I know that voice. It's the Lane woman.'

'No names, for goodness' sake. Just get away or you'll be dead or arrested.'

I don't know whether he believed me, but luckily one of the men in the copse must have broken discipline. Penbrake, or whoever was in charge of the group, had probably heard voices in the field and told his men to get ready to fire. Through nervousness or over-eagerness, somebody discharged his shotgun without waiting for the next command. The sound of it blew the night apart and echoes rolled back from the quarry, out over the fields. By the time they died away, Barty Jones and his men had melted away into the dark.

I blew out the candle and dropped it. Drips of hot wax had already soaked through my glove and scorched my hand. Shouts were coming from below us. The men from the copse, with no hope now of surprising the invaders, were spreading out in the fields, searching for them. Tabby sized up the situation as soon as I did and we were running together uphill, back to the quarry track. I caught a toe in my dress hem and fell full-length, just managing not to cry out. She turned back and dragged me up and on, so fiercely that my feet didn't make contact with the ground again for yards. We found the stone trough and scrambled back over it, hugger-mugger so that our clothes trailed in the water. By the time we reached the hedge between the last field and the track, we were both gasping and the pain under my ribs was as sharp as glass. Somehow we bundled ourselves through the hedge and on to the track. The sheep were bleating again, but that didn't matter because of the noise coming from below us. Men were shouting to each other across the fields and down in the farmyard. More distant shotgun blasts suggested that those posted at the main gate of the farm were shooting at random.

We turned along the quarry track, back the way we'd come. No need for caution now in the dark, with everybody's attention elsewhere. Below us some of the men had lanterns and their lights were criss-crossing the fields. The farmyard had so many lanterns lit that the barns and haystacks showed clearly as unscathed silhouettes. They were safe for tonight at any rate. I hoped Barty and his men were safe as well. So far there'd been no sounds of triumph or excitement to suggest that anybody had been shot or captured. Once we'd turned off the quarry track, on to the road leading back to the village, we stopped and reorganized ourselves as best we could, wringing out the wet skirts of our dresses, using our fingers to comb the worst of the leaves and thorns out of our hair. After that, we went on at a more normal pace. I was sure we'd get back before Mr Godwit and Mr Penbrake. It sounded as if the confusion would take a long time to die down and there'd probably be endless arguments about what had gone wrong. Mrs Wood was another matter.

'She sleeps heavy,' Tabby said, picking up my thoughts. 'If we take our boots off, we might get up the back stairs. Suzie won't tell on us.'

'How do you know she sleeps heavily?'

'Suzie says. And she snores, so we can listen and make sure.'

As so often, Tabby was right. We crept up the back stairs to my room and arranged our outer garments across chairs and washstand to dry. Then Tabby went to her own bed – presumably still on the floor of the maids' room – and I went to sleep. My last waking thought was that Barty Jones owed me now.

TEN

It was daylight before the gig came rolling home and I heard Mr Godwit treading wearily upstairs. But he was there at the breakfast table, neatly dressed as ever, although hollow-eyed.

'They didn't come,' he said. 'Penbrake thinks they must have known we'd be waiting for them.'

He looked as if he needed to spend the morning dozing in his summer house but, as all too often, I had to add to his troubles.

'I'd like to talk to you after breakfast,' I said. 'About Jack Picton's other sister.'

He flinched. 'Oh.'

Mrs Wood came to clear the table, still looking annoyed about the disturbances of the day before. Mr Godwit led the way into the garden and stood staring at the bumblebees rummaging his hollyhocks.

'You must have known about her,' I said. 'Why didn't you tell me?'

'It's a painful and distressing subject to talk about to a young lady.'

'You hired me as an investigator. You must see that it might be relevant to the charge against Jack Picton.'

'I don't see that there's any connection between them.'

'He's keeping something from us; we know that. His friend got me to take a message to him in prison about bringing her back.'

'I'm afraid that won't happen.'

'But that must mean he's concerned about her,' I said.

'He wasn't very concerned when the poor girl was in the workhouse.'

The words came from him suddenly and harshly.

'Workhouse?'

'That was how it happened. She absconded from the workhouse with the baby.' He was still staring at the flowers but, I was sure, not seeing them.

'You're on the workhouse board of guardians,' I said.

'We didn't know she'd gone, not until too late.'

'She'd have appeared before you, as a magistrate.'

'Initially, yes. But of course we had to commit her to the assizes. We had no choice.' He sounded utterly miserable.

'Tell me about it, whatever you know,' I said.

'The girl's name is Joanna. The baby was born over a year ago, in the spring of last year. She wouldn't name the father. At first her mother took her in. But it has to be said that Joanna was a wilful girl and of course there was no money to maintain a baby. By the autumn they'd quarrelled so badly that her mother threw Joanna and the baby out. With no other resource, she walked into Cheltenham, carrying the child. I don't know what she expected to find there. Charity perhaps, or she might have had friends who she hoped might take her in. If so, she was disappointed. It was a lot to ask, after all. The result was that Joanna was found with the baby, sleeping in a church porch. The curate took her to the workhouse. When she was admitted, she was asked again to name the father of the child, and again she refused.'

I guessed that she'd have come under some pressure. Men who fathered illegitimate children could be made to support them in the workhouse. The neat, kindly man standing beside me would have been one of the people who questioned Joanna.

'How old was she?' I said.

'Eighteen then. Seventeen when the child was born.'

'So she was taken into the workhouse?'

'Yes. And I'm sorry to say that from the start she proved difficult. The supervisor several times reported her to the board of guardians for laziness and disobedience. She was quarrelsome too and had to be disciplined for fighting with one of the other women in the laundry room. On the credit side, everybody agrees that she cared for the baby. In fact, some of her problems came from trying to get better treatment for him over the other children. Of course, other mothers resented that.'

He went quiet for so long that I had to prompt him.

'You said she absconded from the workhouse.'

'Yes. It seems she just walked out one evening with the baby, before the doors were locked for the night. Somebody should have noticed she was gone, but nobody did. There'd been another quarrel that day and Joanna had been sulky, but that was nothing out of the way. In the morning she and the baby were missed. The other women said they hadn't noticed anything. Good riddance was their attitude.

In fact, it might have been the general attitude, except for what happened next.'

'The baby died.'

'Yes. The thing to understand was that by then it was November and the weather particularly harsh – rain most days, puddles in the road, water in the ditches, temperatures down to freezing at night. When the guardians heard she'd left, we were sure she wouldn't stay more than one night outside. She'd be found in some doorway, begging to be taken in again. Only that didn't happen. For some reason she decided to leave the town entirely and make for Gloucester.'

A matter of ten miles away.

'Why there?'

'Simply because it's the next big town. She hoped to find work there. At least, that's what she told the woman at an inn where she stopped.'

'She had money to stay at an inn?'

'No. It was the morning after she left the workhouse. She'd probably spent the night in a barn somewhere. She came to this inn not far out of Cheltenham and knocked on the door, begging for a cup of milk for the baby. The landlord's wife says she was shivering, blue with cold. She was a kind-hearted woman – asked her in to get warm by the kitchen fire and gave her some milk for the baby, bread and tea for herself. Joanna wanted to know if they needed a maid, but they didn't, so after getting warm she moved on with the baby. It must have been slow going, because it was just after daylight the next morning when a carter found her sitting on a bank on the outskirts of Gloucester. Without the baby.'

'What had happened to it?'

'She told the carter she'd lost it. She wanted him to take her back along the road to look for it. She was pretty well paralyzed with cold and exhaustion, couldn't walk any further. Of course, the carter couldn't go back because he had his rounds to do, but he gave her a ride into Gloucester and put her in the care of a constable. They took her back to look for the baby. She identified more or less the place where she'd last seen it. She said it was dark, that she'd had to stop and step off the road into some bushes to . . . er . . . adjust her dress . . .'

A call of nature, I guessed, but he was too delicate to say so.

'So she put the child down on the bank, but she must have come out of the bushes in a different place and couldn't find him again. She went up and down in the dark looking for him and, by her account, shouting for help. But it was on a lonely stretch with no houses and nobody coming by. Then it occurred to her that she needed somebody with a lantern, so she started running and fell and twisted her ankle, didn't even know which direction she was heading. In the end, all she could do was sit down and wait to be found.'

As he told the story, he'd been talking more and more quickly and had to pause for breath.

'And they found the baby dead?' I said.

He nodded. 'In a ditch, in about a foot of icy water. She said it was where she'd left him on the bank. She hadn't known there was a ditch.'

'So he'd rolled down and drowned?'

'That was the defence case. She had a good young barrister, acting *pro bono publico*. He did what he could.'

'But the jury didn't believe him? Or her?'

'No. There was her record and character, you see. The prosecution made the point that if she'd really cared for the child, she'd have stayed where he was safe, in the workhouse. Their case was that she'd wilfully absconded, felt burdened by the child and deliberately drowned him.'

He hadn't looked at me while he was telling the story. He didn't look at me now, bending to pull a groundsel seedling from the border of mignonette. When he had the small weed in his hand, he stood staring down at it, as if puzzled how it had come to be there.

'But you believed her?' I said. 'You think it was accidental?'

'It was out of my hands. It wasn't for me to decide. She was sentenced to death at the Lent assizes.'

His nervous determination to see fair play for Jack Picton was easier to understand now. He'd failed Joanna and dreaded repeating it with her brother.

'Did you sign the petition to the Queen against hanging her?'

'Yes. Some people thought I shouldn't, as a magistrate.'

'Where was Jack Picton in all this? Surely he should have kept his sister out of the workhouse, at least,' I said.

'Where indeed? This happened just after that dreadful business at Newport and he was hiding himself away somewhere.'

'So, what was the first he knew about what was happening to his sister?'

'I don't know for certain. He only reappeared in public after she'd been sentenced.'

'What did he do then?'

'To be fair to him, moved heaven and earth – letters, the petition. His Chartist friends marched through Cheltenham. The Smithies father and son had a lot to do with that. There was even talk that young Smithies had a tendresse for Joanna, until she turned into such a wilful girl. The wilder sort were even talking about a raid to snatch her away from the gallows if they tried to hang her.'

'Did the wilder sort include one Barty Jones by any chance?'

He nodded.

'And in all this nobody ever knew who the father of the baby was?'

'No.'

'Why in the world didn't she say? She was going to be hanged – what worse could anyone do to her?'

'The child died and it was her fault. What difference did it make who the father was?'

Quite a lot of difference, I thought. In spite of the sunshine and scent of flowers, the cold and dark of that November road had got into my body, and I guessed it wouldn't easily go away. Mr Godwit looked longingly towards his study window. Perhaps the cold had got to him as well and he wanted to take refuge among his books and papers. I wasn't quite ready to let him go.

'You said her mother took her in at first, after the child was born. So she'd been living away from home until then?'

'Yes. To be precise, the mother took her in before the birth, once her condition became so obvious that she had to leave her employment.'

'What employment?'

'As a maid.'

'Where?'

'In a local household.'

It was like trying to drag out a tooth. His shoulders were hunched, his words directed at the mignonette.

'Which local household?'

At first I thought the wriggle he gave was a physical sign of reluctance to answer. Then I realized that he'd nodded his head down to his right shoulder.

'Oh dear, not the vicarage,' I said, trying to follow the direction. At least the misunderstanding made him say it in words.

'No, not the vicarage. The Kembles.'

I stared. 'Joanna Picton was working for the Kembles?'

A nod.

'Have I understood this right? She was working as a maid for the Kembles, she became pregnant, she was dismissed when her pregnancy became obvious and everything else followed from that?'

'Well, yes.'

'And the obvious connection never occurred to anybody?'

'What do you mean?'

'Mr Godwit, did you hire a fool?'

'Fool?'

'Because you seem to think I am one. May we please put delicacy aside? When a female servant becomes pregnant in a household where there's a son, there's a question that everybody asks himself.'

'I'm quite certain that Rodney Kemble is an entirely moral young man.'

'His father, then?'

'Quite out of the question.'

'What did Jack Picton think? Did he suppose it was quite out of the question?'

'I don't know or care what Jack Picton thought.'

'Perhaps you should care. He comes home from somewhere and finds out, if he doesn't know already, that his sister's in prison and sentenced to death. He already hates the Kembles because of his father's accident. What conclusion do you think he'd draw?'

Somehow I must have jolted him into using his brain, or admitting that he possessed one. He looked at me for the first time in the conversation.

'In that case, why kill the governess? Why not kill Rodney Kemble?'

It was a good question and, since I had no answer to it, I let him go.

When the mind is unquiet – and mine was very unquiet – there's no better treatment than watching horses graze. I went to the paddock and leaned on the gate. Rancie was disappointed that I wasn't bringing a carrot as usual but graciously accepted a few handfuls of the longer grass that grew on my side of the gate. The cob stayed in the shade of a tree, recovering from his exertions of the day before. After a while Rancie went to join him. I watched them, lulled by the gentle rasping of their teeth against grass blades.

'That mare's getting a grass belly on her as big as a pumpkin.'

I'd been thinking that and was mildly surprised that the observation had expressed itself in Amos Legge's voice. Then I turned and there he was, standing beside me. He was dressed for the country, in breeches, leggings and yellow waistcoat, but as spry as in Hyde Park and smiling broadly.

'Where did you spring from,' I said. 'I thought you'd be in Herefordshire by now.'

'I was, but I came back. Business with a horse.'

That was nothing new, but I was surprised that he'd spent no more than a couple of days at home.

'Heard there'd been a bit of bother here last night,' he said. 'Something to do with you, was it?'

'I didn't start it, but I was there, yes.'

He nodded, unsurprised and asking no questions.

'Your business going well?'

'No.'

We both stood, watching Rancie.

'So, aren't you going to ask me about my business?' he said.

'You told me. A horse.'

'Bay gelding I picked up in Ledbury.'

A market town, about halfway between here and his home. It seemed a lot of journeying for one sale.

'A bargain, was he?'

'I reckon the man who sold him was glad to get rid of him. He was kicking the front of the cart into next week's firewood.'

'A bad-tempered carthorse? That doesn't sound up to your usual standards.'

'He had a fair bit to be bad-tempered about. For a start, he wasn't a carthorse.'

He waited, the grin broader than ever. I gave in.

'So what was he?'

'A racehorse, I'd say. Not the best but not the worst either.'

The world is full of racehorses, most of them bay, but his expression and tone of voice suddenly brought a picture to mind – an early morning in July and two farm workers watching a bay and his rider galloping in the distance.

'You don't mean young Paley's horse?'

'Could be.'

'But what was he doing in Ledbury? As far as I can gather, Paley was going in the opposite direction.'

'That's the point. I reckon whoever got his hands on the horse took him well away from where he found him.'

'Stolen?'

'I reckon.'

'But how do you know? Young Paley might have sold him. We know he had no money.'

'If he'd sold him, he'd have made sure he got something like a proper price for him and he wouldn't have turned up kicking the daylights out of a market cart. I asked the man I bought him off where he got him, and he was a bit shifty, like. I reckon he bought him at a knock-down price and guessed he wasn't the other man's to sell.'

'So it doesn't mean that young Paley went to Herefordshire?'

It would have been surprising. London or even a Channel port would be a more likely destination for a fast-living young man down on his luck.

'Just the opposite, I'd say. Suppose some tramp or tinker finds a good horse wandering on its own. He steals it, but has just about enough sense to take it a fair distance before he sells it. The man I bought him off had only had him a week. The horse was thin as a slice of toast, kibbled with botfly bites and missing one shoe. That says to me he was on the road for a week or two with a wandering man who didn't know much about horses.'

'But why would young Paley abandon a perfectly good horse?'

'Perhaps he had no choice.'

I looked at him.

'You mean . . .'

'Don't jump to conclusions. He might have been robbed, or taken a fall and stunned himself. Doesn't mean he's dead. Still, his family's got to be told.'

I thought of Colum Paley in a hail of pennies. Father and son seemed fated to trouble.

'Are you going to tell him?'

'And take him the horse. If he wants to pay me what I paid for him, and a bit over for my trouble, I won't refuse. If not, he can have him any road.'

'Where is the horse now?'

He nodded towards the road. 'Outside. Want to come and look at him?'

A boy was holding the horse while it grazed on the verge. One look at the animal confirmed everything Amos had said. He was a thoroughbred, fallen on hard times quite recently. Amos had got him a new set of shoes, but his ribs jutted and parts of his coat were worn bald from rubbing at fly bites.

'Is that his own tack?'

'No. I reckon whoever took him sold that off separately. I had to make do with what I could get.'

They'd spent the night in Gloucester. Amos intended to let the horse graze for a while longer and then ride him down to Cheltenham. I offered to fetch some refreshment for Amos but he preferred his pipe. While he puffed away at it, I gave him a summary of what I'd done so far. For once he didn't have much to add. I asked how he intended to get back to Hereford if he left the horse with Colum Paley.

'I'll stay down in Cheltenham the night, see if I can pick up something to ride back. If not, I know the driver of the Mazeppa coach that goes through tomorrow night. He'll let me ride up beside him.'

'I'd like to know if it really is Paley's horse,' I said. 'I'll ride down tomorrow and find out what happened.'

'Come with me today if you like. Your mare could do with the exercise.'

I was tempted, but today might be my one chance of talking to the Kembles' maid and that had become more urgent since I heard Joanna's story. We settled that I'd ride down the following morning and inquire for Amos at the stables of the Star Hotel, where he knew the head ostler.

'I'll come as early as I can,' I said. 'If you've found another horse, you'll be wanting to get home.'

'No hurry, as long as I'm home by Sunday.'

I laughed. 'I didn't know you were a church-going man, Amos.'

'Not as a matter of course, only they're reading the banns so I ought to be there.'

'Wedding banns? Whose banns?'

He took a pull on his pipe. 'Mine.'

I staggered. My gasp took in a mouthful of his pipe smoke and made me splutter.

'You're getting married? That's sudden. You've only just got home.'

'Not so sudden.' Through my surprise, it struck me that he didn't look very happy for a man soon to be married. 'The fact is, there was this girl I was more or less engaged to before I went away. Her father owns land next to my father, so it seemed a good enough arrangement. What with being away so long, and not being much of a hand at writing letters, I thought she'd have forgotten all about it. I always thought she liked my cousin better, any road. But when I get home, it seems I've been properly engaged all this time without quite knowing it, so naturally everybody's thinking I've come back to get married. She's a decent sort of girl and I don't want to disoblige her after all this time.'

I managed to smile and congratulate him, horrified to find myself so near tears. I'd known that Amos would return home at some point, and it was only to be expected that such a fine-looking – and now prosperous – man would marry. Only for three very tumultuous years he'd been so central to my life that I couldn't imagine things without him. Hyde Park itself wouldn't be the same without Amos in his hat with the gold lace cockade, riding out as the most popular groom in London. As for the morning rides on Rancie that had kept my heart up in some of the worst times, I couldn't see how they'd happen at all. From when I'd lost my father, Amos had been the man I'd brought my troubles to, and time after time he'd either solved them or made them bearable. Now a great blow had fallen and all I could do was stand there watching a horse crop grass. I think Amos felt something too, because he said no more until it was time to mount and go. When he was in the saddle, he spoke at last, though there seemed something forced about his cheerfulness.

'See you tomorrow, then.'

'Yes, tomorrow.'

I watched until they were out of sight along the road, not trying to hold back the tears any more.

ELEVEN

Tabby arrived soon afterwards with a welcome distraction.

'She's at her mother's now, only she can't stay long because she's got to be back to serve lunch.'

The Kembles' maid – Maggie by name – was allowed a few hours' leave now and then to visit her mother in the village. According to Tabby, the timing of that leave was unpredictable and it might be weeks before we had another chance to speak to the girl away from her employers. I collected bonnet and sketch pad from upstairs and we hurried to a line of rickety-looking cottages not far from the church. A stream ran past them with a stone slab across it by way of a bridge. On our side of it, a big black and white sow rootled with her snout in the grass. The church clock showed half past eleven. I hoped we hadn't missed Maggie, but Tabby glimpsed a white bonnet through the cottage window and said she was still inside.

'I was keeping a lookout and saw her when she came. I said there was a lady who wanted a word with her on the way back, not mentioning your name.'

'Was she surprised?'

'Didn't seem to be. Perhaps she thinks you're looking for a maid.'

I took off my glove and scratched the sow's neck. Ten minutes later the cottage door opened and a girl in a maid's black dress and white apron came across the bridge, carrying an empty basket. She was about fifteen years old, small and plump, neat as a beetle. Tabby did the introductions, after a fashion.

'This is the lady I told you about. We'll walk back with you.'

Maggie didn't seem put-out that she had no choice in the matter. I walked beside her on a footpath that ran past the church to the road. Tabby fell in behind us, but near enough to listen.

'I understand you work for Mr Kemble,' I said.

'For Miss Barbara, mostly. I was the parlourmaid, but now she's grown-up I'm her lady's maid.' Justifiable pride in her voice for having taken a step up the servants' ladder. Then she added, less happily: 'I still have to do cleaning, though.'

A hint there, perhaps, that she was open to offers. I didn't want to take advantage of her.

'I'm not looking for a maid,' I said. 'What I'm looking for is some information.'

That puzzled her. She went on walking, biting her lip.

'What about?' she said at last.

'Mary Marsh.'

'Oh.'

We turned off the footpath and on to the road. She glanced up at the church clock and started walking faster.

'I'm supposed to be back by half past twelve.'

'And about Joanna Picton,' I said.

'Oh, her.'

When I'd mentioned Mary Marsh, she'd sounded wary. In the case of Joanna, her voice was openly contemptuous.

'You didn't like her?' I said.

'I didn't have much to do with her. She was taken on as scullery-maid and she wasn't even any good at that.'

'A living-in scullery-maid?'

'Of course.'

'So you lived under the same roof. You must have seen something of her.'

'No more than I could help. They should have hanged her, not just sent her away – drowning the poor little mite like that.'

'I gather the Kembles dismissed her when they found she was pregnant.'

'Not before time. We all knew.'

'That she was pregnant?'

'Yes.'

'Did anybody know who the father was?'

'Could have been anybody, the way she went on.'

Her voice and the expression on her face made her seem twice her age.

'Was there any gossip about her and anybody in the household?'

She stopped and glared at me.

'Her! None of the men would have touched her with a dish clout.'

She started walking again, faster. It was clear from her voice that she was talking about the male household servants. If it had entered her head that gossip might have involved a member of the family, she was disguising it very well.

'So she had men friends?' I said.

'Must have had, to get the way she was.'

'But nobody in particular?'

'She wasn't particular.'

'How can you be so sure about that? You say there was nobody inside the household, and I don't suppose she had much chance to get out.'

For a scullery-maid, perhaps one Saturday a month if she was lucky.

'She got out when it suited her,' Maggie said. 'She was lucky she wasn't sacked before, 'specially when she sneaked off to the races that time.'

'Races?'

'There's a fair on when the races are. She'd made up her mind she was going to the fair, so off she went and came back drunk and her clothes all over the place.'

Jack Picton had told me to ask people about what happened at the race fair. But he'd said that in relation to Mary Marsh's death, not anything to do with his sister.

'When was this?'

'July, two years ago. She should have been sacked then, but it was when Mrs Kemble was ill, so everything was upside down.'

The roofs of the Kemble's house were in sight now. It was clear that if anybody from the household had been responsible for Joanna's condition, I shouldn't find it out from Maggie. In the little time left, I tried a different approach.

'Do you like working with the Kembles?'

'It's the only place I've ever had. I wouldn't mind going some-where livelier. I'm hoping when Miss Barbara gets married and moves away, she'll take me with her.'

'Is she going to be married soon?'

'I expect so. She's eighteen and she's been engaged once already, only that was broken off.'

'She was angry about that, wasn't she?'

Angry enough to throw things at her maid, but Maggie didn't mention that.

'Terrible arguments they had about it, Mr Rodney and her. Colonel Kemble threatened to send her away if they didn't stop it,' she said.

'So it was her brother she blamed for breaking off the engagement?'

'Her father sided with her brother, but yes, it was him mostly.'

'And now Peter Paley's disappeared.'

'Yes. I think he went off to kill himself because of being heartbroken.'

Cheery little soul, she was. I felt like saying that from what I'd heard of young Paley, he was more purse-broken than heartbroken.

'Miss Barbara's having a sad time,' I said. 'Her mother's dead, her engagement's ended, the man who was her fiancé disappears and her governess is murdered.'

Maggie gave a merely conventional nod to that.

'Did you see much of Mary Marsh?' I said.

'Not much. She didn't take her meals with the servants. Most of the time when Miss Barbara didn't need her, she'd be up in her room reading and writing or going out for walks. That's what she pretended, anyway.'

'Didn't you like her?'

'She was a sly one. Pretending to be so quiet and ladylike, when all the time she was—' She stopped suddenly.

'She was what?' I said.

Maggie's cheeks had flushed, her lips set in a pout like a sparrow's beak. A struggle was going on between love of gossip and discretion.

'You mean seeing Jack Picton?' I prompted.

She nodded.

'Were you the one who saw them together in the woods?' I said.

'No. That was Abby, the downstairs maid.'

'When did she see them?'

'A few weeks before he killed her. May, it would have been.'

'You're sure he killed her?'

'Of course he did. It was bound to happen, wasn't it, her going on like that?'

Maggie set her lips again and walked faster. Before I could ask any more questions, we came to a lane that turned out to be the servants' way in to the Kemble house. She turned down it without a goodbye, saying she'd better hurry.

Tabby glanced at me.

'Do we go after her?'

'I don't think so. I doubt if there's anything else she can tell us.'

'What was all that about the race fair?'

Until then I hadn't told Tabby about Joanna because the story was almost too dismal to bear repeating. I told it now as we walked along the road. She listened, head bent and without reaction.

'The dates fit,' I said. 'Joanna Picton's baby was born in the spring of last year. April, say. That would be nine months after the race fair.'

'Doesn't get you any nearer knowing who the father was,' Tabby said. 'Maggie thought it could be anyone.'

'Maggie's a malicious little baggage. Of course she'd think the worst of poor Joanna.'

'Poor Joanna?'

'Yes. Whatever she'd done, she didn't deserve what happened.'

Tabby didn't comment, but then she'd only heard Maggie's hostile account. Joanna was a bad servant, a girl without morals, wilful and wild. It went with her reported conduct in the workhouse: lazy, sullen and quarrelsome. The rest of the story from Mr Godwit hadn't been so very different, but there'd been touches there of a girl who wasn't entirely bad. She'd been protective of her baby, misguidedly loyal to the man who'd fathered him in refusing to name him, as misguidedly brave in walking to look for work with a baby in her arms on a winter's night.

'In any case, she can't have had many opportunities,' I said. 'A scullery-maid works morning till night, and if she'd run off without permission as often as Maggie implied, she'd have been dismissed very smartly. All we know is that she went to the race fair two years ago and came back drunk.'

Joanna, longing for an escape from kitchen drudgery, thinking why shouldn't she have her day at the fair like anybody else? Sneaking out of the house in the early morning in whatever poor bit of finery she possessed – a bonnet or a ribbon, say – and walking miles and miles to the racecourse. Joanna, excited at the fair but with no money, happy to accept drinks from young men who saw a servant-girl in her best bonnet as fair game. Joanna returning, drunk and distressed, her clothes all over the place.

'I'm certain it was at the fair,' I said.

Tabby said nothing. There wasn't much to say, because it got us no further. Half the men in the county would have been at the races and the fair: farmhands and sporting gentlemen, hucksters and gamblers, aristocrats and jockeys. If I was right, any one of them could have fathered the child that died in a ditch.

'You realize that Maggie's done away with one of our theories,'
I said. 'It was in our minds that Rodney Kemble might be the father.
If there'd been any gossip in that direction, Maggie would have
known it.'

'But she might not have passed it on,' Tabby said, reluctant to
let go. 'Especially if it had been made worth her while not to.'

Thinking about Joanna and also Amos, I was preoccupied as we
walked along. Tabby sensed that and didn't ask her question until
we were about half a mile beyond the lane where Maggie had left
us.

'So, where are we going now?'

'To ask the Kembles' butler for permission to sketch on their
property.'

We were in sight of the stone pillars at the main entrance. The
tall iron gates were shut, but a smaller gate at the side let us in to
the drive. As an object for sketching, Colonel Kemble's property
was not inspiring. The house was comfortable rather than grand,
three storeys high and built no more than a generation ago from
local limestone. The drive was shorter than the grand gateway might
have suggested, with six young oak trees staked on either side of
it like recruits for military inspection, sheep grazing round them.
Behind the house, trim meadows dipped into a wooded valley and
up again. One of the meadows had a line of birch-brush fences, for
training horses. A stable block to the right was large in proportion
to the main house. Nobody was visible at the windows as we walked
up the drive. It was lunchtime, with family and servants occupied.
I asked Tabby to wait on the gravel sweep at the bottom of the front
steps, holding my sketching things prominently, while I went up
and knocked on the front door. It was some time before the butler
appeared, looking harassed. Callers at mealtimes were a nuisance.
I apologized, introduced myself and said I was staying with Mr
Godwit.

'I'm interested in drawing some of the best local views to take
home with me. I'd be very grateful if Colonel Kemble would give
me permission to sketch in his parkland.'

'Parkland' was overstating it, but there was no harm in flattery.
The butler's eyes had gone at once to the gravel sweep and registered
that there was no carriage there, not so much as a gig – only Tabby
clasping the sketchpad like a weapon. The best I could hope for
was a verdict of genteel eccentricity. He replied, without enthusiasm,

that permission would almost certainly be given, if I would kindly leave my card. I handed him two.

'I wonder if you would give the other card to Miss Kemble. I really should have called on her by now, and I believe that she has an interest in sketching as well.'

All I knew was that she'd attended, with no notable enthusiasm, a class on painting butterflies, but any well-brought-up girl sketches.

'I'll come back this afternoon, if I may,' I said.

The butler nodded and closed the door.

'So it's the daughter we want?' said Tabby as we walked up the drive. 'Why?'

'Because we still know next to nothing about Mary Marsh.'

I had no notion how Barbara Kemble had felt about her governess, but she must have spent more time with her than anybody else. I'd wandered a long way from the question of who killed Mary Marsh and it was time to come back to her.

Mr Godwit still looked worn and tired at lunch. We kept to his rule of not discussing the case at mealtimes, or at least he thought we did, because I turned the conversation to the race fairs again, particularly to the troubles of two years ago.

'It's not so much the races themselves; it's all the things they attract – gambling booths of all kinds, hazard, whist, dice, roly-poly wheels. Then there are the beer and gin tents and other things I shouldn't mention to you. It all gets the races a bad name. You heard a group of townspeople burned down the grandstand some years ago?' he said.

'Yes. It seems rather an extreme reaction.'

'Reverend Close had been preaching some very powerful sermons against the races.'

That man again. I tried to keep my tone light.

'What was so much worse than usual about the race fair two years ago?'

'As you know, I wasn't there so I can't say for certain. I'm not sure it was so very much worse in itself, but Reverend Close had been on the subject again. He persuaded Penbrake that the magistrates should attend along with the police, to see for themselves.'

'What happened?'

'Quite a large number of arrests were made. In fact, I gather there was something like a riot.'

Something like a riot? A drunken mob with the constables trying to make arrests, under the eyes of the magistrates. Caught up in it, head fuddled with gin, a scullery-maid on a truant day out. Joanna Picton might have counted herself lucky to escape without being arrested that day, but she'd been the unluckiest of them all.

I told Tabby about it as we were walking back to the Kembles' house. She said it didn't tell us anything we hadn't guessed already, which I had to admit was true.

This time we were carrying full sketching paraphernalia – an easel and folding chair borrowed from Mr Godwit's study and my parasol. When I knocked on the door, the butler conveyed to me the colonel's kind permission to sketch wherever I wanted, with the addition that the view of the house was considered more imposing from the other side. I took the hint, not because the house looked very much better but because the other side had a summer house with a tea table outside, overlooked by a terrace and large windows of what was probably a sitting room. We set up my sketching things in the shade of a big cedar much older than the house and I began work with my pencil while Tabby kept an eye on the windows. Although Barbara was our target, I wondered what to do if her brother Rodney appeared instead. He'd recognize me from our strange meeting in the woods, but might have his own reasons for not wanting to talk about it. If he did, I could pretend to have been reconnoitering places to sketch. Unconvincing, in a nettle-choked glade at dusk, but he could hardly call me a liar. I was hoping that the problem wouldn't arise. The menfolk – father and son – should surely be out supervising things on the estate or in the stables.

I had the outline of the house sketched in when Tabby reported a sighting.

'Somebody in the right-hand big window.'

'Man or woman?'

'Woman. I think it's her. Light brown hair.'

'What's she doing?'

'Just sitting there, looking out. Now she's gone.'

To get her parasol, I hoped. I was relying on the fact that life in the country can be uneventful, especially for a fashionable young lady of eighteen with a quick temper. The arrival of a sketching woman on the lawn would be far from exciting, but probably better than nothing. A few minutes later the door to the terrace opened and out came a pink parasol, followed by a girl in a pink and white print dress. She took her time, lingering on the terrace and pretending not to see us, drifting down the steps and halfway across the lawn before letting her eyes move in our direction. An amateur actress making an entrance would have moved like that. She was young, pretty and practising on anybody. When she came closer, I stood up, introduced myself and asked her to thank her father for permission to sketch.

'I'm sorry not to have called on you,' I said. 'I sent my card in this morning.'

She showed she'd received it by a gracious inclination of the head, spoiling the effect by biting one side of her lip in her pearly teeth. She wanted to look grown-up, but her mother's death had left her as the lady of the household before she was ready for it. The seven years between her age and mine would be a great gulf to her.

'I love your dress,' I said. 'I saw a print quite like that in Bond Street, only not so pretty.'

It was hardly proper manners, adopting such an intimate tone so early in our acquaintanceship, but the smile she gave me was real and impulsive.

'You shop in Bond Street? Oh, you're so fortunate. Everyone's positively months out of date here and we have to take our fashions from magazines.'

Several minutes of fashion gossip followed. I did my best, shamelessly dropping in references to receptions and operas I'd attended. She thought Covent Garden must be heaven, sheer heaven. She'd love so much to live in London. The years between us were vanishing and I was fast becoming a dear friend. I was puzzled, though, when she suddenly adopted one of her stagey attitudes, moving a few steps out of the shade and into the sunshine, hand resting on her furled parasol. Then I saw that sunlight made her light brown hair golden and took the hint.

'I'd like to include you in the sketch, if you don't mind. I might work it up later in watercolour.'

'Like this?'

'If you'd just turn your head sideways a little . . . yes, just so. And bend your neck as if you're looking at a daisy on the lawn.'

The fact is I've no great skill at drawing faces but can usually manage profiles. It turned, surprisingly, into one of my better efforts and she was delighted when I let her look at it. I promised to work it up and send it to her.

'You positively must stay to tea,' she said. 'Wait in the summer house. I'll go and tell them to bring it out.'

Tabby had been listening all the time, unobtrusive near the trunk of the cedar. The look she gave me asked why we'd been wasting time on sleeves and sashes.

'Getting the measure of her,' I said. 'What did you think?'

'Silly.'

'Yes, but I like her, I think.'

'She threw a scent bottle at Maggie.'

'Wrong, I agree.'

And yet there'd been a self-satisfied malice about Maggie that might make me want to throw things. I told Tabby she'd better rest in the shade of the cedar while Barbara and I had tea. I knew very well that she'd be listening at a crack in the summer house before we'd taken our first sips, but didn't want to encourage her. Barbara came back, followed soon afterwards by the tea tray, brought by a maid who looked even younger than Maggie. The maid arranged the tea things on a rustic table and left. Barbara poured with careful concentration, still unpractised in the role of hostess. I guessed that her father and brother didn't do much entertaining.

After answering more questions about the glories of London life, I turned the conversation back to sketching. Barbara said she used to sketch quite a lot, but not recently.

'Since your governess died, I suppose.'

She sighed. 'Before that. My father said I should learn how to run a household. It's achingly tedious.'

'I saw a painting of butterflies by Mary Marsh when I was in Cheltenham on Tuesday,' I said. 'It was very good.'

I didn't add that it was now in my trunk, torn nearly in half. Barbara gave a shrug and a twist of the mouth, indicating boredom.

'Oh, that class . . . all those old women. Mary insisted. She told my father it would be good for me.'

'So it was your governess's idea?'

'Yes. The last one, I flatly refused to go, but she went anyway. Father would have been angry if he knew she'd taken the pony cart in to Cheltenham just for herself, but I didn't tell him; otherwise, he'd have wanted to know why I wasn't with her. If she wanted the butterflies so badly, let her have them.'

Only she hadn't gone for the butterflies, I thought. She'd gone to meet Jack Picton.

'Did you get on well with your governess?' I asked.

She poured us more tea and considered. 'Most of the time, yes. She was kind about my engagement and when my mother died. She was so serious, though, making me learn a lot of history and geography I'll never need. What does it matter where coalmines are or what Oliver Cromwell said? I ask you: were you ever at a ball and had a gentleman talk to you about coalmines?'

Oddly enough, the answer would have been yes, and very interesting he was, too. But it wasn't the one Barbara wanted.

'You must have spent a lot of time together,' I said.

'Not as much as we did. Once I was sixteen, my father agreed I shouldn't have to do lessons any more, but Mary was to stay as companion and chaperone.'

'Were you glad about that?'

'Quite glad; otherwise, it would have been my mad old aunt.'

So, in the last year of her life, Mary Marsh would have had time on her hands. According to Maggie, she read and went for walks. I wondered what else.

'It pleased Rodney at any rate,' Barbara said. She spoke almost under her breath, looking down at the tablecloth. Her cheeks had gone as pink as rose petals.

'Your brother was pleased that Miss Marsh was staying?'

She gave a nod, still looking down. It was clear what was happening. Barbara, with a rare chance to talk to somebody who seemed to her a woman of the world, was practising adult gossip. I suppose I should have changed the subject, but this was too good to miss.

'There was a *tendresse* between them?'

'*Tendresse.*' She liked the word and lingered on it. 'Yes, from him at any rate. Perhaps from her, but then they quarrelled. Just as well. Father would never have allowed it.'

'What did they quarrel over?'

'She wanted him to do something and he wouldn't. I don't know what it was.'

'When was this?'

'Oh, months ago. Last year.'

'Was Miss Marsh very beautiful?' I asked.

She made a face. 'Some people thought her so. She was tall, though, and quite brown-complexioned, with a lot of dark hair that wouldn't stay up. Quite old, too. I was teasing her once and she admitted to being nearer thirty than twenty.'

She smoothed a lock of bright brown hair over her cheek. The pink was fading, now that her experiment in gossip was achieved. We'd finished our second cup of tea. I said I must go and promised to get up the sketch and send it to her. She was reluctant to let me leave.

'You said you were in Cheltenham on Tuesday. Did you see a lot of people?'

Of course, she assumed assemblies, tea parties and the like. She thirsted for social news, even from a few miles away. No point in telling her about Barty Jones and the Mechanics' Institute. Then I thought I could give her something, so I told her about the strange attack on Colum Paley at the entrance to the assembly rooms. Since I owed her some gossip, I told the story as vividly as I could and saw that I had her full attention. She listened, biting her lip. When I described the pennies raining down on him, she gasped.

'Eighteen pennies,' I said. 'At least, that was what somebody said.'

'Oh no.'

Her hands flew to her face and almost covered it; only a pair of startled grey eyes peered over them.

'I'm sorry, I didn't mean to distress you,' I said.

She drew her hands down, but the eyes were still startled.

'Did . . . did he say anything to you . . . if he'd heard from Peter.'

I remembered that I wasn't supposed to know the details of the broken engagement.

'I didn't actually speak to Mr Paley,' I said. 'It was hardly the moment to be introduced to him. Was . . . is Peter Paley a friend of yours?'

I spoke as gently as I could. She looked annoyed as well as distressed.

'You really didn't know? Nobody told you?'

'Told me what?'

Her eyes brimmed over with tears. 'That we were engaged, Peter and I. We still are in secret, only you mustn't tell my brother. He hates him. He said I must break the engagement, only we didn't, not really. And now I don't know where he is.'

The last words were a wail. I went over to her and put my arms round her and she sobbed against my shoulder.

'Everything's gone wrong . . . gone so terribly wrong. I don't know what to do.'

It would have been inhuman, and probably useless, to put more questions to her. It was a relief to see the maid advancing from the house, to clear up our tea things. When I mentioned that, Barbara sat up and dabbed at her eyes with a table napkin. She managed to answer the maid's 'Will that be all, ma'am?' with 'Yes, thank you, Annie,' but kept her face turned away from the girl. It was obvious that what Barbara really wanted to do was run up to her room and have a proper cry, so I thanked her and went.

TWELVE

Tabby joined me as I walked up the drive.

'What was that thing between them?'

I had to think about it for a moment. '*Tendresse*. Meaning Rodney Kemble liked the governess. Probably more than liked.'

I watched her face. She was the one who'd been suspicious of Rodney Kemble from the start.

'And she liked him, too. Then they quarrelled. What about?' she said.

'I'd like to know.'

'He still wants her, but she won't have him, so he knocks her on the head?'

'Is that how it happened, do you think?' I said.

We were through the gates and back on the road before she answered. 'Nah.'

'No, I don't think so either. But why not?'

'She said him and the governess had their row months ago. If he was going to kill her, he'd have done it then.'

The answer might be simmering resentment and hurt, coming to a head over long months. I remembered Rodney Kemble's face when we met in the place where Mary Marsh had died. A murderer returning or a man grieving? It could be both, of course. In spite of my instincts, I couldn't rule out Rodney Kemble.

'The puzzle is, why she wouldn't have him,' I said.

Over the past few days, Mary Marsh had become real to me: a tall, good-looking woman, in her late twenties, well educated, dutiful and serious-minded. Not dull, though. Her painting class friend had credited her with humour and incisive opinions. She was kind, too; at least kind to Barbara when she'd needed it. Rodney Kemble probably lived a secluded life, with the estate to run. It wasn't surprising, or unprecedented, that the son of the house should fall in love with the governess. If his intentions were honourable – and it sounded as if Rodney Kemble's had been – what a piece of luck for the governess. From being a servant of the house, she becomes its mistress. For a woman in Mary Marsh's position, the luck would be even greater. With Barbara almost launched on the world, she wouldn't be needed any more. With no more than a quarter's wages in her pocket, she'd soon have to pack up her trunk and move to a new position – perhaps one less pleasant than the Kembles' home. All she'd have to look forward to for the rest of her life would be a succession of other people's children, solitary meals and lonely walks. Rodney Kemble was a presentable man, probably reasonably handsome when he wasn't miserable. His father's objections might have been overcome in time. After all, the Kembles were simply wealthy landowners, not aristocrats. So why not jump at his offer?

'I wonder what it was that she wanted him to do and he wouldn't,' I said.

'Run off with her and never mind his father,' Tabby suggested.

'Somehow I can't see her wanting that.'

Tabby gave me a look, as if to ask how I knew. Simply, it wasn't how the Mary Marsh in my mind would have behaved. We got no further on the walk back. I found Mr Godwit in the garden and broke to him the news that I was going to Cheltenham again next day. There seemed no harm in telling him why.

'My friend Amos Legge thinks he might have found Peter Paley's horse. I'm curious to know whether it is or not.'

'The animal he had with him when he called on you this morning? Poor Paley. It can't be good news, can it, a horse without his rider?'

He offered to take me in the gig as he had to be in town the next day for a magistrates' sitting, but I said Rancie needed the exercise. I agreed to meet him for tea at the Queen's when we'd finished our day's work.

'Are you anywhere near forming a conclusion about Picton?' he said.

It was a fair question. The assizes were only ten days away and so far I'd delivered to him nothing but anxiety. I hesitated before answering.

'I don't know. Sometimes I feel yes, I am nearer a conclusion, the way you sense some animal or bird's near you before you see it. But I haven't seen it yet.'

'If I were to ask you now, is Picton guilty, what would you say?'

'I should say no,' I said.

The answer surprised me, and yet I shouldn't have wanted to go back on it, even if I could. He nodded, rather sadly it seemed to me.

'But I'm nowhere near proving it,' I said. 'I'm following a lot of threads, but they're so tangled I can't even see if they're connected. One thing I'm sure of is that Mary Marsh's death had something to do with Joanna Picton.'

A little frown at that. He wouldn't disagree with me outright, but Joanna worried him.

After dinner, the boy from the vicarage came over with mail from town. I'd had a word with him the day before and given him a shilling to ask at the post office for any messages for me. There was one, a folded sheet of good-quality white paper with my name written on the outside in clerk's copperplate. Inside, it had no address or salutation at the top, only the day's date.

If Miss Lane would inquire for the undersigned at the Mechanics' Institute at her earliest convenience, he would be obliged. B. Jones. I laughed at the contrast between Barty Jones's appearance and manner and his formality on paper.

'A friend?' Mr Godwit inquired, busy with his own mail.

'After a fashion.'

It was a pleasant ride to town next morning, with some good long canters on grass verges. When we got there, I made straight to the stable yard of the Star, and there was Amos, smoking his pipe and rubbing neats foot oil into a stirrup leather. As always, I felt warm and reassured when I saw him. Problems always seemed simple in the presence of Amos. Then I remembered that there wouldn't be many chances to see him in future and the warmth ebbed away. He seemed the same as always. He corked up the oil bottle, wiped his hands and arranged with his ostler friend to have Rancie stabled for the day, taking his time and making me wait for his news as usual.

'Well, was it the horse?' I said.

He nodded. 'Head groom recognized him as soon as we got into their yard, called Mr Paley down and no doubt about it.'

'How did Mr Paley take it?'

'He tried not to show it, but I think he was a touch shaken.'

'Not surprising. As far as I can gather, he's not been very concerned until now, or has pretended not to be. Now he knows something's badly wrong.'

'Any road, he thanked me, gave me what I'd paid for the horse and a bit over beside. I did wonder if, up to the time I'd brought

the horse in, he thought he knew what the boy was doing and now
he doesn't.'

That chimed with my impression that young Paley's disappearance hadn't been as impulsive as it looked.

'Had Mr Paley any explanation for the horse being found where
it was?'

'No. He agreed with me: someone had stolen him or found him
and taken him as far off as he could to sell him. He says the son
would never leave a valuable horse wandering around on its own
like that, not in his right mind.'

'So is he suggesting Peter wasn't in his right mind?'

'He's not suggesting anything. But he's a worried man. That's
why he made me the offer he did.'

'Offer?'

'He started by asking me what I knew about the man who was
using the horse to pull his cart, or trying to. Not much, I said. So
he says, Go back to him, find out all you can about the man he
bought it off, then find that man and so on until we get back to
where young Paley and the horse parted company.'

'A reasonable idea, if you could do it.'

'Very reasonable. The man's not a fool. Far from it.'

'So are you going to do what he wants?'

'I thought I might as well have a try at it. After all, I'll be going
back in that direction anyway. I told him I'd do what I could and
come back and give him a report sometime next week, one way or
the other.'

'And you'd tell me as well?'

'Course I would.'

He looked at me as if I must be crazy to think otherwise. From
Amos's point of view, nothing between us had changed. Not yet,
at any rate.

I said goodbye to him and walked to the Mechanics' Institute.
A man in the hallway said yes, Mr Jones was expecting me, and
showed me into what looked like a lecture room, with rows of chairs
and a low platform with a blackboard. Barty Jones was sitting with
his legs stretched out. He stood up when I came in, but his greeting
had the same note of sarcasm as at our first meeting.

'Good morning, Miss Lane. You got my note, then. Kind of you
to call.'

I said I hoped he and his friends got home safely on Wednesday night, returning the sarcasm in kind. I wanted to remind him of the debt he owed me. I might as well have saved my breath.

'We did. Are you comfortable, lodging out there with the magistrate?'

Goodness knows how he'd found out where I was staying. Perhaps somebody had spotted me with Mr Godwit in town.

'Is that what they do with government spies, then? Billet them with the magistracy to save public money?' he said.

I was suddenly blazingly angry. After all, it had been my refusal to be a government spy that had tipped me into this tangled affair.

'If you think I'm a spy, why did we take so much trouble to warn you?' I said. 'If it hadn't been for Tabby and me, you'd have led your men straight into an ambush of shotguns.'

I was glaring at him. He glared back.

'So how did they know we were coming in the back way?' he said.

'Because a boy of ten with a box of toy soldiers would have done the same. Leave a warning on the front gate and come in at the back. If that's your idea of tactics, I'm surprised you've stayed out of prison so long.'

He stared at me for what seemed like a long time and then began laughing, a deep laugh from his bootsoles.

'Are you trying to teach me tactics, miss?'

'Somebody should. If you must know, the chairman of the magistrates left a map on the table showing where he was going to put his men. I saw it and came to warn you. I'm not a government spy and I expect you to take that back or I'm leaving.'

He stopped laughing. 'What makes you think I have stayed out of prison, in any case? I've picked oakum in my time.' He spread out his square, calloused hands. 'All right, for the present we'll assume you're not a government spy.'

It wasn't the retraction I'd demanded, but it would have to do. I sat down at the end of the front row of chairs. 'So, what have you got to tell me about Joanna Picton?' I said.

It took him a moment to register that I'd said her name, not Jack's. He blinked.

'Joanna?'

'You helped Jack with the campaign to stop her being hanged – the petition, the march. You know a lot about Joanna.'

He sat, four chairs away from mine. His eyes were wary.

'Jack came home to find her in prison on a capital murder charge,' I said. 'He might not have been a very good brother until then, but he did what he could.'

'It was criminal what they did to her,' Barty Jones said, a sincerity in his voice I hadn't heard before. 'She'd have no more intended to kill that baby than the kindest mother in the land. They drove her to it – the magistrates and the board of guardians and the rest of them. What will she do in Australia? She'd hardly been out of the parish before all this happened to her. It's just killing her another way.'

'She never named the father,' I said. 'Not to the magistrates, the assize judge or anyone. Did she tell her brother?'

He shook his head, staring down at his big hands.

'Did he ask her?'

'They never let him see her. Jack's no favourite of the law, not the kind they let go prison visiting.'

'But he wanted to know?'

'Oh yes, he wanted to know.'

'And was he trying to find out?'

'Of course he was. He said whoever had fathered the baby should be standing in the dock alongside Joanna, no matter if he were the highest in the land.'

'So he suspected it was somebody of high position? Did he know more than that?'

'I don't know what he knew. Jack was always a close one, but he was even closer after he found out what had happened to his sister.'

'I think there was somebody trying to help him,' I said.

'We were all trying.'

'Somebody else. Mary Marsh.'

He looked at me, saying nothing.

'There was something between him and Mary Marsh,' I said.

He scowled. 'That's what they say when they're trying to make out Jack killed her.'

'I don't believe it was a love affair, but I know for certain that they met secretly at least once,' I said. 'Joanna worked in the house where Mary Marsh was governess. She was still working there at the time the child was fathered. Mary might have offered some information to Jack when Joanna was sentenced to death.'

'Why would she do that?'

'Humanity? A sense of justice?'

He considered and then nodded. 'You're right. Jack did meet Mary Marsh, and more than once. They met at my house a couple of times, when Mary had to bring the girl in for a ball or a party or somesuch.'

'When?'

'After Joanna was sentenced, when the appeal was going on.'

'But he didn't tell you what it was about?'

'I guessed it was something to do with the sister.'

'I think she told him a name,' I said. 'I think he's determined to bring that name out at the assizes, whatever happens to him.'

'He thinks he's a dead man in any case. He's always said the judges and the politicians won't rest until they've hanged him on some trumped-up charge or other. He'll go down fighting.'

'By naming the man?'

'Probably.'

'And do you know the name?'

'I'll leave that to Jack. If he wants to name him at the assizes, I'm not stealing his thunder. But if you're as sharp as you think you are, you'll have worked it out by now.'

I didn't rise to the bait because something that had been at the back of my mind had grown to a near certainty.

'I'm surprised you're going to let him be hanged without even telling a lie for him,' I said.

I'd caught him by surprise, but he tried not to let it show. 'What lie?'

'It would have been the easiest thing in the world to say he was with you all that evening and night. With the reputation you and he have, people might even have believed that you were out together looking for ricks to burn down.'

'You think a judge would take my word for anything?'

'Probably not, but it might have been worth trying. A man might risk perjuring himself for a friend.' He said nothing, but I could see his pride was hurt. 'But it wouldn't have been any use, would it?' I said. 'Because you're pretty sure you know where he was that evening.'

'Do I?'

'At the Kembles' house. He was seen not far away from it.'

'His mother lives near there.'

'A good mile away, and he wasn't very dutiful about visiting his mother. He was hoping to see Miss Marsh.'

It was a toss of a coin whether he said anything or not. While he was making his mind up, he stared at me like a craftsman judging the grain in a piece of wood. Then he gave one quick nod of the head, decision made.

'It was the other way about. She'd sent him a note asking him to meet her.'

'That evening?'

'Yes.'

'You saw the note?'

'Jack showed me. Two lines, asking him to meet her at ten o'clock, in the usual place.'

'What was the usual place?'

'Somewhere in the woods behind the house.'

'And he intended to go?'

'Yes. I warned him it might be a trap, but he said he'd have to take the chance.'

'Why a trap? She'd been helping him.'

'She *had* been, until they got at her.'

'What do you mean?'

'I only know what Jack told me. Right up to the time the poor girl was transported, the Marsh woman was helping Jack find out who was responsible for what happened to her. As soon as she's gone, Miss Marsh changes her tune, doesn't want to meet Jack any more. She tells him she's been wrong all along, that the father wasn't who they thought it was. She's been told another name, so she says, but she won't let him know this time till she's certain.'

'How did Jack Picton take that?'

'How do you reckon? He thought she'd been bribed or threatened into turning against him. I agreed. I was surprised all along that she'd done as much as she did, and now she'd gone back to her own side.'

He meant what he was saying, I could see that.

'But why a trap?' I said. 'And what sort of trap?'

'Can't you guess? He goes to meet her in the woods in the dark, she screams out as if he's laying hands on her and Master Kemble and half a dozen keepers rush out of the bushes and accuse him of rape. Ten years in prison and who's going to believe a word he says about anything?'

I looked at him, wondering if he realized that he had just produced a convincing motive for his friend to kill Mary Marsh. He must have seen that in my face.

'He didn't kill her,' he said. 'He'd never have killed her, even if she had turned against him.'

'Then why did he run away and hide?'

'He'll have his reasons. Maybe they'll come out in court, if they'll let him speak.'

I said nothing to that, convinced that the more Picton said, the more he'd turn judge and jury against him.

I thanked Barty Jones and walked with him to the door. I'd liked to have asked him if he still believed I might be a government spy but guessed he didn't give up anything easily, suspicions included. I was lucky to have got as much as I had from him. He'd confirmed my guess that Jack Picton and Mary Marsh were working together and then added the twist that she'd turned against him. I found that hard to accept. As for the idea that she'd let herself be the bait in a cruel trap, it was close to unthinkable. The likes of Jack Picton and Barty Jones saw traps and plots everywhere. Stick to what seemed likely: Mary had been helping Picton in trying to find the father of Joanna's child. Soon after Joanna was deported, Mary decided that they'd suspected the wrong man. Did that mean that she'd found out for certain who had fathered the boy who'd drowned in a ditch?

I strolled along the Promenade, sorry that I'd agreed to meet Mr Godwit for tea, still two hours away. If it hadn't been for that, I could have collected Rancie and ridden back. As it was, I was in riding habit on a hot August afternoon with no very clear idea what to do next. Worse, I was getting looks. Riding habit and top hat were not normal wear for afternoons in a place where other women were in muslins or cotton prints and ribboned bonnets. As it happened, my riding habit was a smart one with tight waist, tapering sleeves and an overskirt caught up with a button on the left side. It looked well on horseback in Hyde Park, but the glances I was getting from some of the women showed all too clearly that it was considered racy for Cheltenham. That, along with the heat and the confusion in my head, put the devil in me. I started to feel angry with the perfectly inoffensive invalids in their bath chairs, the ladies with their little crystal bottles for collecting spa water, the leisurely citizens sitting in the shade of trees, listening to the band. Where had they been the night Joanna Picton walked between freezing puddles carrying her baby? If she'd knocked on any of their doors, would they have let her in? Unfair, of course. Most of us aren't heroes of generosity, or any other kind of hero. Mary Marsh, it seemed, had been a hero. I was convinced now that she'd gone a long way outside social boundaries and risked her own reputation in trying to help Joanna, even associating with her outlaw brother. In the end, it had cost her not only reputation but life. Until then I'd been doing my duty by trying to help Jack Picton, whether he deserved it or not. It was more than duty in the case of Mary Marsh. She deserved justice.

I was walking along, not looking right or left, when I heard somebody calling my name.

'Miss Lane, I say, Miss Lane.'

The voice rang out like a huntsman calling hounds to order. I turned, and there was my acquaintance from the racecourse, Henry Littlecombe, lounging against the trunk of a tree near the bandstand. Like me, he was dressed for the saddle, in his case breeches, soft-topped boots and a checked waistcoat. It had been a mistake to turn. He took it for encouragement, straightened up and came striding towards me.

'I say, what a piece of luck to meet you again. I've been looking out for you every morning, but you never came.'

His high-pitched voice would have been audible across several fields, let alone the Promenade. People weren't just glancing now; they were openly staring at me. I should have given him a cold nod and walked on, but the devilish part of me decided that if I was being judged as a fast woman, or worse, I might as well live up to it. So I wished him good afternoon and raised no objection when he came up and walked beside me.

'Are you in town on your own, Miss Lane? Beastly hot, isn't it? May I offer you a lemonade or an ice or some such?'

A lemonade would be very welcome, I said. A tea garden was in sight, with tables under trees around a small fountain. We headed towards it. Since the fates had thrown Henry Littlecombe in my path, I thought I might use the occasion to confirm some things I thought I knew.

We took our seats under a tree. The lemonade arrived. Mr Littlecombe uncorked his hip flask under the table and poured from it into his lemonade so deftly that I almost missed the action. When he saw I hadn't, he gave the grin of a naughty schoolboy and waggled the hip flask at me with an inquiring lift of the eyebrow.

'No, thank you.'

He chattered on, about a horse he intended to buy, an atrocious bill for which his saddle-maker was threatening to dun him. Then, at last, something nearer the purpose.

'Did you hear Paley's horse was brought home yesterday? Some horse dealer just walked into his old man's yard with it, cool as you please. Wouldn't say where he got it.'

I decided not to say that I knew the last part of the story was untrue.

'And no news of Mr Paley himself?' I asked.

He shook his head. 'Dead, everyone thinks. Perhaps somebody shot him and took the horse off him. Dashed shame. A thorough sportsman, Paley was. Everybody liked him.'

'Except Rodney Kemble,' I said.

For a moment he looked ill at ease. 'Bit of a misunderstanding between them. I'm sure they'd have made it up if—'

'Hey, there you are, Littlecombe. Thought you'd gone to ground. What are you doing, inflicting your clod-hopping presence on this lovely lady?'

Just when my companion might have been on the point of saying something useful, he was interrupted by another loud-voiced young man in riding clothes. I recognized him as one of the group I'd seen up on the racecourse. Two more young men of the same stamp were standing behind him, grinning. Their red faces suggested they too had been at their hip flasks, probably without benefit of lemonade.

'Well, if it isn't our belle amazon,' the newcomer said, lifting his hat to me. 'Are you arranging a return match with her, Littlecombe? If so, my money's on the lady.'

The three of them ordered Henry to introduce us properly and then asked my permission to sit down with us at the table. I gave it. As far as the Promenade was concerned, my respectability was already past saving and I was determined to salvage some scrap of information from the situation. Their four heads combined might be more useful than Henry's alone, though there probably wasn't much sense in any of them. The new arrival, referred to by his friends as Postboy (because, they explained, he'd once raced a Royal Mail coach for a bet and won), seemed determined to lead the conversation. He asked me why they hadn't seen me at last month's races.

'Because I wasn't there,' I said. 'Did I miss a lot?'

They shook their heads sadly. 'Dashed tame,' Postboy said.

'Dullest they've been for years. If the killjoys have their way, it will be all temperance banners and Sunday school picnics.'

'I gather it was livelier two years ago,' I said.

'I should say so. We had to hide young Henry here under a circus wagon because a leg he owed was out for his blood. Then there was a fist-fight between two Gypsies over the lurcher racing and . . .'

And so on, all of them contributing to the catalogue, voices growing louder, sidelong glances to see who was impressing me most.

'Then the police and magistrates arrived,' I said.

Sudden silence. They looked at each other. In the end, the one who'd been slightly less noisy than the rest answered.

'Truth to tell, things did get a little bit out of hand that year.'

Henry Littlecombe made a sound midway between gulping and chortling.

'It was Holy Fanny's fault.'

The others shushed him and looked at me.

'He means the Reverend Francis Close,' the less noisy one explained. 'He took it on himself to lead a crusade against the infidels.'

'Beadles, magistrates, the lot of them,' Littlecombe said, only slightly subdued. 'Knocked over the booths, arrested people right, left and centre.'

'While the races were going on?'

'Afterwards. There was a certain amount of drinking and gambling and so on, but no harm done.'

'Were any of you arrested?'

'No. It was mostly the commoner sort, the legs from out of town, the gambling booth keepers and so on.' Another gulping chortle. 'I'll tell you who did . . . I mean, very nearly got arrested, and that was Paley and Kemble.'

'What for?' I asked.

'Public brawling.'

'Brawling?' It seemed a long way from the Kemble I'd met.

'They had their jackets off and were squaring up to each other; then Penbrake comes running up, wanting the constables to arrest both of them. Paley senior appears and gives the constables a piece of his mind, so Penbrake went off to find some easier game.'

'Luckily for Kemble,' Postboy said. 'Peter would have floored him.'

'If he could see him,' Littlecombe said. 'Paley was pretty drunk and Kemble was as sober as a judge. Angry, though.'

I'd known the two disliked each other, but had no idea it had gone this far.

'What was he angry about?' I said.

Littlecombe and Postboy looked at each other. Male secrets.

'We don't know,' Postboy said. 'Whatever it was, they've been on bad terms since.'

'I heard it was over a girl,' the less noisy one said.

They didn't actually shush him, but he was given a couple of warning looks.

'Was that before the engagement between his sister and Peter Paley had been broken off, or after?' I said.

'Just before.' Littlecombe said it quietly.

He seemed more subdued now. I stood up, thanked Littlecombe for the lemonade and said I had another appointment. Postboy and his friends pressed me to stay, or come back at least. Their clamour attracted attention and I felt eyes turning to me again as I walked away. But one pair of eyes, at least, wasn't curious or hostile. The eyes belonged to a tall man in yellow waistcoat and gaiters, standing in the shade of one of the trees. It looked as if he'd been there for some time. Goodness knows how Amos Legge had found out where I was, but he'd been watching in case one of the sportsmen overstepped the mark. He took off his hat to me.

'Good afternoon, Miss Lane.'

'Good afternoon, Amos.'

In a public place, it should have been 'Mr Legge', but the sense of what a good friend he was came over me, and how much better he was than the sportsmen I'd been sitting with, even though the world would regard them as his betters. As I walked the short distance to the Queen's Hotel, I knew he was watching me and the devilment drained out of me, leaving only sadness.

Mr Godwit was waiting at the hotel, with tea things laid out and an older man sitting beside him. They stood up, the older man rather unsteadily, and Mr Godwit introduced him as his fellow magistrate, Septimus Crow. He made the introduction with that slight 'don't blame me' air of a man burdened with an unwanted companion. Since Mr Godwit had described the third magistrate on the bench as old, deaf and entirely under the thumb of the chairman Penbrake, I'd envisaged somebody small and quiet. Mr Crow was certainly elderly and deaf – an ear trumpet on the table among the tea things confirmed that – but he was plump, cheerful and loud. Since he had trouble hearing other people, he assumed that they had equal trouble hearing him and spoke in a voice that could be heard on the other side of the tea room. At first we discussed the usual things – the heat, the number of visitors, the difficulty of finding anywhere to park carriages. I could see that Mr Godwit was anxious that I might let slip my true reason for visiting, and tried to calm him by playing the obscure female relative as well as I could. I was only too grateful that he hadn't seen me with the sportsmen.

Mr Crow remarked it had been hot in court. Mr Godwit tried to change the subject, worried that any mention of the court might set me asking inconvenient questions. Mr Crow wouldn't be deflected.

'And the smells, eh? I hope you won't think I'm being indelicate, Miss Lane, but there was a fellow we sent up the hill for poaching – you'd have thought he'd brought his ferrets into the dock with him.'

Teacups rattled all around the room. A plump woman fanned the air in front of her nose as if the smell had been carried in by the mention of it.

'Up the hill?' I asked.

'House of correction in Northleach. He'll be taking his exercise on the treadmill for the next three months. We sent them a brace of poachers and a pickpocket today. Fifteen on the clerk's list and most of them wasted our time pleading not guilty when we knew their faces as well as our own.'

Mr Godwit murmured something about not discussing the affairs of the bench in public. He was disregarded.

'Total of twenty-two pounds, fifteen shillings and sixpence in fines,' Mr Crow bellowed cheerfully. 'And what about the young Prewett fellow, eh? Five pounds, eighteen shillings and sixpence, all on his own. If he'd been able to pay up, it would have made it a record for the day.'

The last part was said in what was intended to be a confidential aside to Mr Godwit, which meant that only the neighbouring three tables would have heard it.

'He couldn't pay up?' I said.

'Not a chance of it. So it was up the hill for him too, young dog. At least he won't be making himself liable for any more up there.'

By now Mr Godwit was acutely uncomfortable, signalling to the waiter to bring his bill.

'Nearly six pounds is a pretty stiff fine,' I said.

'Ah, but he'd been building it up every week over eighteen months, hadn't he? Eighteen months and one week exactly. He'd never have got away with it so long if the board of guardians had been—'

Abruptly, Mr Godwit stood up.

'Miss Lane and I really have to go. I hope you'll excuse us. See you next week, Crow.'

He plonked half a crown down on the table and practically marched me outside.

'I do apologize for Crow. He's a good enough man in many ways, but does tend to forget himself.'

I said I'd liked him. Mr Godwit insisted on walking with me to the Star to collect Rancie. The gardener was waiting for him with the gig at another hotel not far away. There was no sign of Amos in the yard. An ostler brought out Rancie and helped me mount, and I rode out of town towards the hills in the cool of the evening.

On the way, my mind kept going back to the indiscreet chatter of Mr Crow. I wondered how the young dog Prewett had come to build up such a fine. Eighteen months' uninterrupted poaching would have been a tall order. Drunkenness, perhaps. I'd have liked to ask Mr Godwit over dinner, but took pity on him. In my room, the small question still nagged at my mind, perhaps as an escape from all the large ones. Idly, I picked up a pencil and did sums on the blotter. Five pounds, eighteen shillings and sixpence, divided by eighteen months and one week – seventy-nine weeks that would be – to give the weekly total of the young dog's fine. When I'd worked it out, I stopped being sorry for Mr Godwit and was angry with him again.

THIRTEEN

'One shilling and sixpence a week,' I said. 'That's eighteen pennies.'

It was just after breakfast on Saturday morning. Mr Godwit had disappeared into his study with unusual promptness. I'd invaded it and found him in the urgent task of labelling a collection of dried fern leaves. He looked up at me, face pained and apprehensive.

'Mr Crow was about to say that the fine wouldn't have mounted up for so long if the board of guardians had been paying attention,' I said. 'You're on the board. He was talking about something to do with the workhouse, wasn't he?'

'Properly speaking, it's not precisely a fine,' Mr Godwit said. 'Crow could never be made to understand the difference.' He was playing for time. I didn't give it to him.

'What is it, then?'

'It's a matter of paying for upkeep.'

'Upkeep for somebody in the workhouse?'

A nod. Remembering Crow's tone of voice and a certain look on his face, I was certain that the young dog's debt had not been incurred for maintaining his mother.

'Or rather, I should say, for two people in the workhouse,' I said. 'A mother and her baby.'

A law had been brought in quite recently, vulgarly known as the Bastardy Act. The flush on Mr Godwit's face showed I'd hit the target.

'Crow shouldn't have talked about it in front of you. I'm afraid Prewett is quite a deplorable case.'

I wasn't interested in Prewett. 'If a man fathers a child out of wedlock and won't marry the mother, he can be made to pay towards her keep and the baby's in the workhouse. That's the case, isn't it?' I said.

'It's not fair that all the charge should fall on the parish,' he said, not looking at me.

'And the amount he has to pay is eighteen pence a week. Which is precisely the amount the men threw at Colum Paley. One of the men shouted that it should see his lad all right for the week. I told you about it. You must have seen the connection, but you didn't tell me.'

'It wouldn't have been right to tell you about it.'

'Because you didn't think it was respectable to talk about it? How can I work if you won't tell me things in case they shock me? I assure you, I'm not so easily shocked.'

'I don't doubt it.' He looked at me now, prepared to be mildly combative. 'I meant that it wouldn't be fair to Colum Paley and his son.'

'You don't even like the man very much. But I suppose it's a case of gentlemen holding together. The likes of Prewett go to the house of correction and the likes of the Paleys laugh over their brandy about the number of bastards they've fathered.'

He gasped. 'That's a very irresponsible allegation.'

I sat down on a chair opposite his desk.

'Very well. If I'm irresponsible, then you won't want to go on employing me. But before I leave you're entitled to a report on what I've found out so far. Is this a convenient time to give it to you?'

I glanced at the pressed ferns spread over his desk, not bothering to keep the sarcasm out of my voice. He looked at me and then sat on the chair behind his desk, on his dignity and as businesslike as he could manage.

'Then give your report.'

'We'll go back two years – the day of the races the year before last. Joanna Picton goes to the fair without her employer's consent and falls into the hands of some men, or gentlemen, who give her too much to drink. One of them, possibly more than one, takes advantage of her.'

When I thought of that quick, probably brutal, coupling behind a tent or under a wagon, it was as much as I could do to keep my voice level, but I didn't want Mr Godwit to see how it affected me.

'The poor girl's already in a state of panic when something else happens. Reverend Close and your magistrate friend Penbrake choose that day to make a stand against gambling and drunkenness at the races. A lot of people are arrested and Joanna probably thinks herself lucky not to be one of them. She runs back to her workplace and again is lucky not to lose her job. Months later she finds that she isn't lucky at all. You know the next part of the story. It's public knowledge. Only there's one aspect of it that almost nobody knew.'

I had his attention now. I took a deep breath and embarked on what was still speculation.

'Joanna seemed as alone as a girl could be. The child's father would be no use to her, even if she knew who he was. She was on bad terms with her mother, and her brother was away somewhere stirring up riots, more or less an outlaw. But as it turned out, she did have one friend in a most unlikely place.'

I waited to see if he'd say anything. He didn't.

'The governess,' I said. 'Mary Marsh. Normally, a governess wouldn't condescend to notice a kitchen-maid. But Mary Marsh was different. It's odd about governesses, isn't it? They have to be so conventional and respectable and yet they're educated women, with opinions of their own. Mostly, they can't show them. But Mary had courage and a warm heart. She knew from the servants' gossip that Joanna was expecting a child and wanted to help if she could. She talked to her, and the whole story came out, including the likely identity of the father.'

I imagined the girl crying on the back staircase, the governess stopping to comfort her. Joanna had probably not experienced many kind words in her life. Naturally, she'd have told Mary Marsh everything.

Something like alarm showed in Mr Godwit's eyes now, but he said nothing.

'It's quite possible that Joanna herself didn't know a name,' I said. 'But she told Mary Marsh enough to put her on the right track. As it happened, Mary had another source of information. Rodney Kemble had fallen in love with her.'

It looked as if Mr Godwit was going to protest.

'Why not?' I said. 'She deserved to be loved. She went to him to ask him to help the girl, perhaps to persuade his father to have her back when the baby was born. Perhaps she'd already guessed who the father of the child might be. If not, she could have found out from Rodney.'

'I simply won't believe it of him. I've known Rodney since boyhood. He's an entirely moral and admirable young man.'

It wasn't the time to talk about sins committed by moral and admirable young men, so I reassured him.

'I'm not saying it was Rodney himself, only that he had a very shrewd idea of who the likely father was. In fact, he'd almost come to blows with him at the fair where it happened.'

I guessed that Rodney Kemble had probably wanted to avoid his sportsmen acquaintances at the fair. When he'd seen one of them trying to calm a distressed girl, or perhaps even mocking her, he might even have passed by, except that he recognized that girl as his father's kitchen-maid. Was it concern for her or a sense of ownership that had made him stand up to the other man? No way of telling, so give him the benefit of the doubt.

'You knew Rodney Kemble and Peter Paley had quarrelled,' I said. 'Didn't you wonder what it was about?'

'We all assumed it was to do with the breaking-off of the sister's engagement.'

'I think you'll find the breaking of the engagement followed what happened at the fair. Rodney told his father, so of course letting Barbara marry young Paley was out of the question. Only they wouldn't tell her why. All this male delicacy again. It's possible that Mary knew all this before she went to Rodney Kemble to ask for help, and didn't get it.'

I imagined that she'd have to choose a time when Rodney was on his own, probably out walking the estate. The young man would have seen that as a god-sent chance to confess his warm feelings for her. Even if he weren't especially vain, he might have expected that she'd welcome his confession with a blush, bright eyes and beating heart. Perhaps she'd done exactly that. Why not? But then . . .

'As I said, she asked him to help Joanna. I guessed it was help to keep her job, but perhaps it was more than that. Perhaps she wanted him to stand up in public and say that Peter Paley was the father of Joanna's child.'

The look of shock on Mr Godwit's face showed what an unthinkable demand that would have been. A man in love might swim oceans and fight monsters at his beloved's request. To outrage his social circle with accusations about the parentage of a kitchen-maid's brat was asking too much.

'Whichever it was, he wouldn't do it,' I said. 'So there wasn't much she could do for Joanna. I don't suppose Mary had more than a few pounds she could call her own and she was in no position to offer Joanna a roof over her head. So Joanna and the baby went into the workhouse. Even then, I don't think Mary gave up trying.

If you made inquiries among the workhouse staff, you might even find that she'd managed to visit her.'

I suspected more than visit, but I didn't want to go into any more detail to Mr Godwit. Mary might have planned some way of getting mother and baby out of the workhouse. If so, something must have gone wrong with the plan and Joanna was left wandering alone with her baby. Then what a burden of guilt Mary would be carrying, with Joanna in prison and condemned to death.

'So, Joanna's in prison and that's when Jack Picton comes on the scene,' I said. 'How he and Mary Marsh found each other, I don't know. His Chartist friend, William Smithies, might have met her, or possibly an agitator named Barty Jones was involved.' Mr Godwit shuddered at the name. 'In any case, they met and agreed to do what they could to help Joanna. The first thing was the petition. They succeeded in getting the death sentence commuted to transportation, but it didn't end there. Jack Picton was determined to do something about the injustice of the whole thing, and Mary helped him, doing great harm to her reputation when people found out that she was meeting him.'

More than meeting, I wondered? Certainly, that was not a road I intended to go down with Mr Godwit, but I couldn't help being curious. On the one hand, the handsome, self-assured outlaw; on the other, the warm-hearted governess with radical opinions that she'd had to suppress for most of her working life. Would it be so surprising if their alliance led to something more? But Mary had suffered enough from speculation and gossip in her life, and if I could help it, I didn't want to add to it after her death.

'Then Mary Marsh was killed,' I said. 'And – the day after – Peter Paley disappeared.'

I expected some protest from Mr Godwit, but it didn't come. He looked older, weary. I thought that until then he'd somehow managed to convince himself that the whole business would blow over like a summer cloud. He'd hired me to quiet his conscience so that he could go back to his ducks and bees thinking he'd done his best. In that way, I'd failed him.

'It must have occurred to you,' I said, more gently.

'You think young Paley killed her?'

'Yes.'

'And that's why he went?'

'That sudden departure of his was nowhere near as impulsive as it looked. He practically forced that bet he lost on the other man. When it seemed as if he might win it, he made his horse stumble. His father might even have helped him plan it when he put that advertisement in the paper repudiating Peter's debts. The rumours that young Paley was the father of Joanna's baby were already circulating and Paley senior might have told his son to vanish for some time until the scandal died down. But they had to concoct a reason that had nothing to do with Joanna.'

'But why kill the governess?'

'Because she'd talked to Joanna. She was the one who knew who the father was. I think that, almost until the last, young Paley was reluctant to do his disappearing act. If he could persuade or frighten Mary Marsh into saying somebody else was the father, there'd be no need for it. But it went wrong, so disappearing was even more necessary.'

Mr Godwit leaned back and closed his eyes.

'You can't prove any of this?'

'Not yet.'

'There does seem to be a flaw.' He spoke slowly. You could almost sense the reluctant movement of his brain. 'Your whole case turns on the parentage of the child, and the belief that Peter Paley was the father?'

'Yes.'

'Then – forgive me – I must say something that might offend you, but things have already been said that I should not have dreamed of discussing with you in normal circumstances. So I'll ask you this question: was fathering the bastard child of a kitchen-maid something so serious that the Paleys would go to such lengths to hide it?'

He opened his eyes before I could hide the surprise on my face. I waited.

'As you've gathered, I'm no great friend of Colum Paley,' he said. 'I consider him arrogant, purse-proud and something of a bully. I know little about the son, and what I do know is not to his credit. But there's one thing I will say for Colum Paley – and anyone will tell you the same: the man's honest, sometimes brutally so.'

'Even an honest man may be tempted when his family's threatened,' I said.

'But how was it threatened? I have to tell you this. To my certain knowledge, Colum Paley has fathered at least two bastards and provided for them liberally. It's said there are others, but I don't know about that. If the son had come to him and admitted that he'd got a servant-girl pregnant, Paley might have been annoyed but he'd have paid her off and that would be an end of it. Twenty pounds in hand would be a fortune to a girl like that. End of the matter.'

'Suppose Colum Paley didn't know until Joanna was in prison and there was already a scandal.'

'It was her scandal by then, not young Paley's. She was the one responsible for the child's death.'

I wanted to argue about that, but now that he'd decided to talk candidly at last, there was no stopping him.

'Another thing – you say it's the gossip in the streets that Peter Paley was the baby's father. It's true there's gossip. Those pennies you saw thrown weren't the first, at father or son. But that gossip only started after Jack Picton came back and began stirring up trouble. As far as I know, until the day she was transported, Joanna herself never named the father. When she came into the workhouse, the guardians questioned her repeatedly on that point and she wouldn't say. Why not? She had no reason to protect Peter Paley. Even if she didn't know his name, she could have described him and his friends at the races. Not a word out of her.'

He looked at me with the nearest thing to a glare I'd seen on his face. It wasn't his expression that worried me as much as the fact that what he said was sense. If Colum Paley was shameless on his own behalf and his son's, my theory had lost one of its supporting columns. I was inclined to believe Mr Godwit, mainly because it had cost him such an effort to say what he did.

'So if Jack Picton intends to stand up in the dock and say that Peter Paley was the father of Joanna's child . . .' I said, trying to adjust my mind to this new state of affairs.

'Then he'll be wasting his breath,' Mr Godwit said promptly. 'It will be stale news to most people and simply set judge and jury against him.'

'I don't believe he killed Mary Marsh.'

'But you haven't a shred of evidence to prove it.'

There was no arguing with that.

'Very well,' I said. 'Tabby and I will move out tomorrow morning. I'm sorry to have let you down and thank you for your hospitality. In the circumstances, I shan't be sending in an account.'

He blinked and was all mildness and apology again.

'My dear, that wasn't what I meant. And tomorrow's Sunday. You can't start such a long journey at the weekend.'

'We shall only be going as far as Cheltenham.'

'And onward on Monday? In that case, you really might as well stay . . .'

'Just Cheltenham. We'll stay until next week when the case comes up at Gloucester assizes.'

I thought we'd have to find a cheaper hotel than the Queen's. This case would turn out to be an expensive one for me.

'So you still think you can help Jack Picton?'

I was tempted to tell him the truth: that Jack Picton was not the main reason. Yes, I thought there was at least a reasonable chance that he was innocent. Yes, it was anybody's duty to save an innocent man from being hanged. But something stronger than keeping Jack Picton alive was tying me to the case, and that was a duty to two women, one of whom had been transported to the other side of the world and one of whom was dead. To a rebellious kitchen-maid who'd wanted one day at the fair. To a brave governess who'd cared about her when nobody else did. I didn't think Mr Godwit would understand if I tried to explain, so I didn't try.

'I don't know,' I said.

He urged me again to stay and I said I would, until the assizes. Before we parted, I borrowed his box of watercolours and spent the morning working up my sketch of Barbara Kemble. Better, perhaps, than doing nothing while recovering from the damage to my precious theory, but not so very much better.

FOURTEEN

I took the picture with me to church on Sunday, hoping that nobody would think it irreverent. The service was much the same as the one the week before, with the Kembles in the front pew and Rodney looking no better, but the sermon was shorter. By chance, the banns were read for a local couple. I thought of Amos in his home village away to the west, sitting in a pew in his Sunday best, with the woman he was going to marry alongside him, listening to those same words. Afterwards, while the father and son were talking to the vicar, I found Barbara under a big yew tree in the churchyard, alone and bored. She cheered up when presented with the watercolour and declared it a perfect likeness, only too, too flattering, of course. I was a genius like Reynolds and Gainsborough, simply divinely talented. She ran out of compliments at last and asked if she might request a favour. She said it so solemnly that I thought it must be something dark and secret. My hopes of some new development in the case rose, but sank again when it turned out that all she wanted was a chaperone for a shopping trip to Cheltenham.

'Mary used to come with me, but now I have nobody. I simply have nothing to wear for autumn, and with you knowing all about the London fashions, it would be so divine if you could come.'

'When were you planning to go?'

'As soon as we can, or all the latest things will be sold. What about tomorrow?'

'Well . . .'

'Oh, you are such a darling. I'm sure Father will let us have the carriage. I'll go and ask him now.'

She practically dragged me back to the church porch and prized her father away from the vicar. Colonel Kemble seemed only mildly surprised to be told that she positively must have the carriage for the whole of the next day, because the perfectly angelic Miss Lane was taking her to Cheltenham on an essential shopping mission. He put up little resistance, beyond telling me that I mustn't let his daughter make a nuisance of herself. It was arranged that the carriage would call for me around ten o'clock next morning.

'Am I coming, too?' Tabby asked, when we got home. Naturally, she'd been listening.

'You'll be bored, in and out of shops.'

'I'm bored here.'

I took pity on her. It was likely that Barbara would be bringing her maid, Maggie, so there seemed no harm in having Tabby along.

But when the carriage arrived on Monday morning, half an hour late, it turned out to be a brougham with only two seats inside, so no Maggie and no room for Tabby.

'I'll ride on the back,' she said.

'It's raining,' I said.

The weather had broken, the sky grey and drizzle falling.

'Doesn't matter.'

So I borrowed a waterproof for her and we set off with the Kembles' coachman on the box and Tabby on the back, firm as a barnacle.

'Do maids always ride on the back in London?' Barbara said.

I resisted the temptation to say it was the latest fashion. 'Tabby usually does.'

The rain was heavy by the time we reached town, but it didn't quench Barbara's enthusiasm. She was like a colt let out to pasture, explosive with energy, wanting to gallop in all directions at once. It reminded me how gloomy life must have been for her over the past couple of years, cooped up in the big house with a mourning father and love-sick brother. I resolved not to press her, even tactfully, for details to support my case and simply try to give her a day's pleasure. We spent the first hour in the finest draper's in town, poring over fabrics and fashion plates. The shopkeeper and his assistants unrolled bolt after bolt of material for her, cut off samples for her to try against her cheek in the mirror. All the time she was appealing for my opinion. If I said something suited her, she'd be firmly decided on that for all of two minutes, but then something else would catch her eye. Wouldn't this do better? Did they have it with a red stripe instead of a brown? What did I think? Altogether, it was weary work and I could see Tabby fidgeting by the door. We finally managed to order three dress lengths of fine woollen fabrics and various trims, to be delivered to her dressmaker and charged to her father's account. Then it was on to the milliner with a swathe of samples and a folder of fashion plates. While Barbara was in serious consultation about feathers, I caught Tabby wearing a flowered bonnet and making faces at herself in the mirror. I told her she'd better go off and amuse herself and meet us at four by the church, and I gave her a handful of small change for a pie. She was out of the door like a squirrel up a tree.

After the milliner, Barbara agreed that it was time for refreshment. I suggested cups of tea at the assembly rooms, confident that there'd be no chance there of an embarrassing meeting with my sporting acquaintances. But, as luck would have it, we were on our way there when I caught sight of the gentleman they called Postboy on the other side of the street. Barbara gasped and clutched my arm.

'That man – don't acknowledge him.' He'd raised a hand and looked like crossing over to us. 'Don't look at him,' Barbara hissed. 'Just keep walking.'

That was exactly what I'd intended, though not at Barbara's panicky speed. She waited until we'd turned a corner and then walked more slowly, hand to her ribs.

'He's not coming after us, is he?'

Of course he wasn't. Even a sporting gentleman can't run after ladies intent on ignoring him.

'You know him?' I said.

'He used to be one of Peter's friends. I don't want to meet him.'

Perhaps she'd managed to convince herself that the rumours about her fiancé and Joanna weren't true by pushing any blame there might be on to his friends. I wondered if she'd had any communication with Peter Paley since their engagement was broken, but I decided to keep to my resolution for the day and not ask questions.

We drank our tea without incident, but her mood seemed to have changed. She spread the fashion-plate pictures out on the table and made some attempt at discussing them, but her heart didn't seem to be in it any more. She kept glancing at the clock.

'So, it's your dressmaker next?' I said.

It was how she'd planned the day. With the fabrics chosen, the next step was a session with her dressmaker and a final decision on styles. From the morning's evidence, it was likely to take a long time. She nodded and stood up heavily. She looked pale and tired.

'Have you a headache?' I said. 'We could leave the dressmaker for another day.'

She shook her head impatiently. The dressmaker lived at the

Montpellier end of the Promenade. We walked there mostly in silence. She seemed to have something on her mind. On the dressmaker's doorstep, it came out.

'The chestnut velvet reverse isn't right with the brown stripe. It should be the moss green.'

Since that point had been discussed at length in the draper's, I had to fight to keep the impatience out of my voice.

'The chestnut will look very well.'

'No, it will be terribly drab. It must be the green. They won't have delivered it yet. Will you be an absolute angel and go and tell them to send the green instead?'

I felt some irritation at being converted into a messenger, even an angelic one, but at least it would spare me from more clothes discussion. I left Barbara on the dressmaker's doorstep and walked back towards the centre of town. The rain had stopped and I took my time, enjoying being in the open air. Somewhere along the way I realized that Tabby was walking beside me.

'We going back yet?'

'Soon, I hope.'

We delivered the message at the draper's and stopped on the way back to watch the convalescents drinking spa water.

'Tastes horrible,' Tabby said.

'I think that's the point. You bought a glass?'

'Nah. Somebody had left half theirs so I tried it.'

I rang the dressmaker's bell and told Tabby to wait outside. It was nearly four o'clock by then and at half past we were due to meet the driver with the brougham. I'd been away nearly an hour and hoped Barbara would be ready to go. When the maid came down, I asked her to let Miss Kemble know that I was waiting. She stared.

'Miss Kemble?'

'Yes, she came for an appointment. I suppose she's still with you.'

The maid closed the door and bolted back upstairs.

'What's biting her?' Tabby said.

After a while the door opened again. The woman standing there was clearly the dressmaker herself, a tape measure round her neck and a pin cushion strapped to her wrist. I explained that I'd come to call for Miss Kemble.

'Miss Barbara Kemble?' She seemed slow of understanding.

'That's right. She arrived for an appointment with you about an hour ago.'

'There must be a mistake. I've made clothes for Miss Kemble, but I haven't seen her since spring. She had no appointment with me today.'

At first I was simply irritated. I thought Barbara had mixed up the day of the appointment. She must have remembered her mistake even before she rang the doorbell and either rushed off to look for me or gone to the place where we were supposed to meet the carriage, outside the Queen's Hotel. If so, I only hoped she hadn't driven straight home and stranded us. I sent Tabby to the hotel to check and hurried back to the draper's. No sign of her there. They hadn't seen her since our visit that morning. The same story at the milliner's. I tried a few other shops without result and then went back to the assembly rooms, hoping to find her sitting down with a cup of tea. Nobody there but a couple of elderly women. A maid clearing tables had seen nobody of Barbara's description in the past hour. I still wasn't really worried, expecting to find her waiting at the carriage, but a doubt was forming in my mind. When I got to the Queen's and found Tabby and the driver sitting up on the box, but no Barbara, the doubt flared into something like panic. Even then, I couldn't believe that she'd simply vanished, so Tabby and I wasted another hour scouring the town in likely and unlikely places, even looking inside the church and the public rooms of the main hotels. No Barbara. We went back to the coach.

'You'd better wait here in case she arrives,' I said to Tabby. 'I'll come back when we've told her father.'

The entire journey, I was looking out of the window in the unlikely hope that she'd decided to walk home, though I guessed that she would have no enthusiasm for long walks. The journey seemed all too short, considering the task waiting at the end of it. As we came down the drive, Colonel Kemble was standing on the steps outside his front door. He looked annoyed. It was past seven by then and his daughter's lateness was keeping him from his dinner. He was alongside the brougham before the wheels stopped turning. Then he opened the door and saw only me inside. I got out.

'Barbara's gone,' I said. Then, realizing the ambiguity of it: 'She's disappeared.' I told the story as coherently as I could, not that there was much to tell. The staff inside must have sensed that something had happened – perhaps someone was watching from the window

– because the butler, housekeeper and several others came out. The colonel had aged ten years in a few minutes, but he gave orders like the military man he was. The butler was sent to find Rodney, the housekeeper to fetch the maid, Maggie.

'Miss Lane, you'd better take the brougham and report to Godwit,' he said to me. 'It's a matter for the constabulary. Send the brougham back as soon as you get there.'

He was holding in his anger. I couldn't have resented it if he'd raged at me for being such a spectacular failure as a chaperone.

Mr Godwit took longer than the colonel to size up the situation. At first he seemed so bewildered that I had to fetch the gardener from his cottage and help harness the cob to the gig. For the sake of speed, I drove us back to town. When we got to the Queen's, the Kembles' brougham was already standing outside, with Tabby beside it. As soon as she saw me, she shook her head. Barbara wasn't back. Inside the hotel, a kind of council of war had convened in one of the downstairs rooms. Mr Penbrake was in conference with a man who turned out to be the head of the county constabulary. The parish beadle was there and several other official-looking men. Mr Crow was on the outskirts of the group with his ear trumpet, trying to follow what was going on. Mr Godwit drew him aside and asked where the colonel and Rodney Kemble were.

'Gone to have it out with Colum Paley,' Mr Crow yelled happily. 'Accusing him and the son of kidnapping his daughter.'

The other conversation stopped and everybody turned towards us. Mr Penbrake recognized me and I had to repeat the story of Barbara's disappearance again. He stared at me all the while as if I was an unreliable witness.

'Did Miss Kemble say anything to you to indicate where she was going?'

'Nothing.'

'Did she speak to anybody while you were in her company or did anybody speak to her?'

'The draper, the milliner – only what you'd expect. But a more important question is who she didn't speak to.'

I'd been thinking about it on the way there and was almost sure of my ground. At any rate, it had to be said. Penbrake looked annoyed, as if I was deliberately speaking in riddles.

'There's a sporting gentleman called Postboy by his friends,' I said. 'I don't know his proper name, but I'm sure any of the racing fraternity could tell you. He looked as if he intended to come over and speak to us. Barbara was quite disturbed and determined to avoid him. She said he used to be a friend of her former fiancé, Peter Paley.'

'That was perfectly proper of the young lady,' Mr Godwit said. 'It was wrong of the man to even think of forcing his company on you both.'

I could have left it there, with Barbara's reputation intact, except some things mattered more than reputation.

'I'm not convinced that was the reason,' I said. 'I wonder if she had an arrangement to meet the man Postboy, only later when she'd managed to get away from me. Her confusion might have been that she'd almost run into him by accident and was afraid I'd suspect something.'

Now they were all staring at me.

'Why should Miss Kemble have an arrangement to meet him?' Mr Penbrake said.

I took a deep breath. 'Isn't it possible that she'd decided to elope with Peter Paley, and Postboy was to take her to wherever he is?'

Everything went very quiet.

'Have you any reason for such an accusation?' Penbrake said.

That was difficult. My main reasons were feelings, Barbara's hectic excitement in the morning, then her growing nervousness as the time to take her decisive step came close.

'Consider the alternative,' I said. 'Miss Kemble's disappeared – there's no doubt about that. Either she went away of her own free will or she was abducted against her will. I left her in the middle of the afternoon, in broad daylight, in a place where she only had to scream to attract the attention of several dozen people. Shouldn't we at least consider the possibility that wherever she went, she went willingly?'

I could sense them wrestling with the notion that it would be ungentlemanly to consider any such thing. When the head of the constabulary made the suggestion that hired ruffians might have thrown a cloak over her head and carried her into a waiting carriage, it was greeted with a relief. When I asked sarcastically if that kind of thing often happened in Cheltenham, he said it could happen anywhere and they all nodded. Then the Kembles came back. Rodney Kemble's face gave nothing away, but the colonel was tight-lipped and furious. Penbrake asked him what Colum Paley had said.

'Nothing to the purpose. Still claims he doesn't know where his son is or what he's doing.'

'He offered us his servants and horses to help look for her,' Rodney said, more quietly. 'He said if there'd been an elopement, it was without his knowledge and consent.'

I noticed that he'd used the word 'elopement', not 'kidnapping', and his father hadn't contradicted him. The two men who knew Barbara best weren't denying that she might have gone voluntarily.

Well into the night, men were coming and going with reports. The management and the ostlers at all the inns and hotels had been questioned, but none of them had seen Miss Kemble. Nobody had rented carriages that day to customers apart from their usual ones, for routine journeys. Two stagecoaches had departed since Barbara was last seen, but she hadn't been on either of them. At some point I went out to Tabby and suggested she might use her skills in talking to some of the street urchins and the sharp-eyed boys who hold horses. When she returned with nothing much to add, I arranged for her to eat and drink in the servants' room. Quite late in the proceedings, somebody remembered the new railway line to Birmingham and a constable was sent running to find the ticket clerk. Again, he drew a blank. By then the constables and volunteers were spreading their net more widely, riding to inns and toll houses on all the roads from town, asking if anybody had seen a young lady and one, or possibly two, gentlemen in a cart or carriage. My suggestion that they should look for two or more riders on horseback was dismissed by both Rodney and the colonel. Barbara was a reluctant horsewoman and would never have consented to ride any distance, especially at night. At least Mr Penbrake took my information about Postboy seriously enough to send somebody to inquire at his lodgings, which I gathered were a room over one of the town's less respectable inns. He was away, but his landlord seemed to think that wasn't an unusual state of affairs. Sometimes he was away for days without leaving a forwarding address.

By midnight the room was cluttered with empty cups and the remains of sandwiches. Most of the men were drinking brandy and some were smoking cigars. None of them asked my permission because all but one of them had forgotten I was there, which suited me. I lay back in one of the big armchairs, tired but too strung-up to sleep. The one who hadn't forgotten was Colonel Kemble. He stood by a window, not eating or drinking, still wearing his greatcoat to be ready to dash outside the moment there was news. Now and again he'd glance towards me, then quickly away as if he couldn't trust himself to control his anger. Rodney Kemble wasn't there. He'd gone out with the riders along the country roads.

It was a relief when Mr Godwit came up and suggested we should go home. We were doing no good there and his housekeeper would be worried. I sent a waiter to the servants' room to collect Tabby and the three of us squashed together in the gig, with Mr Godwit insisting on doing the driving. This meant we crept along at a snail's pace in the dark and it wasn't far off dawn by the time we got back and unharnessed the cob. We said our goodnights and went upstairs. Tabby should have continued up another flight to the room she shared with Suzie, but we needed to talk. At a nod from me, she followed me into my room. I lit the candle, threw my cloak and bonnet off and settled into a chair. Tabby perched on the bed.

'You see what I did wrong?' I said.

'Sent me away.'

'Oh, if you'd been with me, you'd have seen what she was doing, would you?'

'You'd have sent me back with the message, so she couldn't have got away from you like she did.'

It wasn't the answer I'd expected, but she was right. Barbara had not brought her own maid into town with her and might have been disconcerted when Tabby was added to the party. Then, unknowingly, I'd solved the problem for her myself.

'Barbara's been lucky as well as clever,' I said.

'Her, clever!'

Still sitting on the bed, Tabby performed a lightning mime of a girl fluffing out her hair and adjusting her ribbons, all simper and flutter.

'Yes, that's what I did wrong: I underestimated her. Almost as soon as she met me, she saw a way to use me.'

'So she wasn't run off with?'

'No. I'm almost certain she's gone to join Paley, wherever he is. Though how they communicated, I don't understand.'

Gone to join a man who was a rapist and, quite possibly, a murderer, through my fault.

'Do you think it's possible that she knew all along he'd killed Mary Marsh?' I said.

'She might have helped him do it,' Tabby said.

'Can you see her doing that?'

'You've just said you couldn't see her running off like that, until she did it.'

True. If I stopped seeing Barbara as a silly girl, a lot of things fitted together. She seems, obediently, to accept the breaking of her engagement when rumours about young Paley and Joanna circulate. But somehow they still communicate. Paley convinces her of his innocence. She is furious when she finds out from him that her own governess is the source of some of the rumours. Even if she didn't help him kill Mary Marsh directly – and I still could not imagine that – she might have contrived things so that the governess was waiting in the woods when Paley came for her.

'The important question at the moment is how we find her,' I said.

Arrogant, perhaps, to assume that it was work for us. Even now, one of the scores of men who were out looking for her might have discovered her, along with Peter Paley, in some country inn. Or perhaps a clergyman in a quiet parish would be interrupted at his breakfast by a gentleman with a special licence and an urgent need for a wedding ceremony.

'Pity Mr Legge's not here,' Tabby said.

I agreed with her but wished she hadn't said it. Amos was hunting for Peter Paley too, but from a different direction, following the trail of Paley's horse. He wouldn't know yet about Barbara's flight.

'You remember what he says: if a person goes somewhere, it must be on four feet or two,' I said. 'The magistrates and all those other gentlemen are looking for horses and carriages, just what Mr Legge would do. That leaves the two feet.'

'I don't see that one walking far,' Tabby said.

I thought back to the shoes Barbara had been wearing the day before – fine brown leather with small heels and buckram rosettes on the toes. Definitely not what a girl would choose for serious walking.

'No, she didn't walk far. And a well-dressed young woman walking anywhere out of town would stand out, whether she was with a man or not. And none of the boys you spoke to had seen anybody of her description?'

Tabby shook her head. I put more trust in her informal efforts than all the questioning by police officers.

'I suppose whoever met her might have brought overshoes and a cloak to put over her clothes,' I said. Yet somehow the image of a cloaked and shuffle-footed Barbara wouldn't stay in my mind. 'But she'd hate not looking her best, wouldn't she, especially if she was going to meet her fiancé? Tabby, I think we're missing something, or somebody.'

She should have been as mazed as I was by a long day and lack of sleep, but it didn't take her long to work it out.

'Maggie.'

'Yes, her maid. Wherever she's gone, Barbara will want clothes. She'd have been unhappy about leaving all her nice things and not having fresh linen. She might have made arrangements to have her clothes sent on to her.'

'Her father would be looking out for that, wouldn't he?'

'Yes, so whoever did it would have to be secret and clever. She'll have paid Maggie well. Perhaps the idea is that Maggie will go and join her wherever she is, taking a trunk of Barbara's best clothes along.'

I remembered that when we'd talked to Maggie, she'd been discontented with country life, sharing her employer's longing for the city. Ambition and a hefty tip would recruit her to whatever Barbara was plotting.

'So we watch Maggie,' Tabby said. 'If she's not gone off already.'

That was possible. If Barbara had been really clever, she'd have told Maggie to go ahead of her, while she was shopping in Cheltenham and before the hue and cry started. But surely Colonel Kemble or his son would have mentioned the maid's absence at the hotel last night. It would have made it almost certain that Barbara had planned her own disappearance. Since it hadn't been mentioned, Maggie had still been under the Kembles' roof when they'd left yesterday evening. Tabby was on her feet, making for the door.

'Where are you off to?' I said.

'To keep a lookout for her.'

We were nearer daylight than dark by now, but only just.

'She won't go at this hour. Too conspicuous,' I said. 'Either she's gone already, in the turmoil last night, or Barbara has worked out a way for her to go later without being followed. She'll have a trunk with her, remember. That means a cart of some kind.'

Reluctantly, Tabby agreed to catch a few hours' sleep, curled like a puppy in a nest made from my coverlet and pillows on the floor.

Both of us woke up a couple of hours later to the sound of Suzie's footsteps going down the back stairs. Tabby laced up her boots.

'Eat something at least,' I said.

'Suzie does herself tea and toast before she rakes out the ashes. A bit smoky, but all right.'

She went. I knew better than to give her advice on how and where to keep watch on the Kembles' house. Nobody knew more about watching back doors, grand or humble, than Tabby did. My task was to find out what I could through the front door, and after the way Colonel Kemble had regarded me last night I wasn't looking forward to it.

FIFTEEN

Mr Godwit was up early too, face pale and dark rings round his eyes.

'Do you suppose they've found the poor girl? We shall go and inquire straight after breakfast.'

The question was whether we went to the heart of the search down in Cheltenham or the half-mile to the Kembles' house. It was resolved when we visited the paddock and Mr Godwit decided that the cob was too worn out from his exertions the day before to be harnessed. I doubted that. Some horses have an instinct for avoiding work and the cob was one of them. Still, that suited me. I turned down a tentative suggestion from Mr Godwit that we should try Rancie in the gig by saying she'd assuredly bolt. In fact, she was too polite to do any such thing, but I wouldn't hurt her dignity by putting her between shafts. So Mr Godwit and I walked in the fine summer morning, between fields refreshed with the rain of the day before, along the road and down the drive to the house. Even the look on the butler's face as he opened the front door to us showed that there was no good news of the young lady. He told us that the colonel was at home, and if we'd kindly wait in the small sitting room off the hall, he'd have our names sent up.

The colonel came down almost at once. He'd shaved and put on clean linen since the night before but obviously hadn't slept. He glanced at Mr Godwit's face, found no good news there and then shifted his eyes to me. No hostility in them today, only puzzlement. I guessed that he'd done a lot of thinking through the night and shared my belief that his daughter had deceived both of us. He offered coffee. We accepted, more for something to do than any need for it.

'Rodney's still down in the town,' he said. 'He promised to send a message up at any hour if there was news. I came back here in case of . . . developments.'

He meant, I suppose, the faint hope that Barbara would return home. He said he was about to ride back down to Cheltenham and hoped we'd excuse him. We should wait and finish our coffee. I took the plunge.

'I wonder if you'd allow me to speak to Miss Kemble's maid.'

He frowned. 'The girl's no help, I'm afraid. Maggie's as puzzled as any of us.'

'All the same, she may have noticed some small detail that would be significant to a woman rather than a man.'

An expression of embarrassment and alarm came over his face at the idea of female mysteries. 'By all means, talk to Maggie if you think it would help. Talk to any of them. She's tidying up my daughter's room, I think. I'll get the housekeeper to send her down.'

'Would you allow me to go up and find her?'

By now all he wanted was to be on his way. He nodded, opened the door for me and said Barbara's room was the second door on the left, from the first landing. I told Mr Godwit not to wait for me and went upstairs.

The second door on the left was ajar. I gave a single knock and walked straight in. Maggie might have been sitting on the pink brocade chair by the window because when I walked in she was standing beside it, looking startled.

'Have they found her?' Then she added quickly: 'Ma'am.'

Hard to tell from her voice and expression if the thought that Barbara might have been found alarmed her. Certainly, there was no particular sign on her face of grief or even a sleepless night. Clothes were strewn round the room – a couple of cotton and muslin dresses and an embroidered nightdress on the bed, a bonnet and a straw sunhat on the stool in front of the dressing table, a velvet cloak over a chair. Maggie's own white frilled cap was sitting on the dressing table among scent bottles and various pots. Had she taken it off to try on her employer's hats? Hardly appropriate in the circumstances. When she saw my eyes on it, she blushed, grabbed it and pinned it deftly back in place.

'So, you've been asked to see if any of Miss Kemble's clothes are missing,' I said.

'Yes, ma'am.'

She grabbed the excuse promptly, but I doubted it was true. Even if the colonel was facing the possibility of elopement in his own mind, he wouldn't risk having it discussed among the servants.

'Colonel Kemble has asked me to help you,' I said.

Only a slight stretching of the truth, I thought. Maggie looked far from overjoyed at the idea, but couldn't object.

'Have you found anything missing so far?'

'No, ma'am, apart from what she was wearing when she went.'

The door of a big wardrobe was standing open. I walked over and looked at the dozen or more costumes hanging neatly from hooks, the shelves piled with silk and linen undergarments, the tidy row of shoes and pumps.

'It must be hard to tell what's gone and what hasn't, Miss Kemble having so many clothes.'

'Nearly impossible, ma'am.'

Another hasty snatch at an excuse, and a mistake by Maggie. A lady may lose count of her own clothes, but a lady's maid doesn't. It's her pride and skill to know every stitch, hook and seam. Nobody had suggested that Maggie was a bad maid in that respect; she wouldn't have lasted long with Barbara if she had been. All the time I was looking for evidence of a small trunk or large bag that Maggie might be packing. I picked up a green satin pump and dropped it, as an excuse to bend and look under the bed. Nothing. Maggie was making a great business of folding up one of the dresses.

I went over to the chest of drawers and pulled out one drawer after another. Stockings and garters, spare lengths of lace and ribbons, linen handkerchiefs worked with Barbara's initials. All the drawers seemed pretty full. The dressing table had two small drawers at the sides. One of them was empty; the other held a small pot of lip rouge, half used. Her father wouldn't have approved, which was probably why it wasn't with the other pots and bottles on top of the dressing table. They were pretty thickly clustered, but where Maggie's cap had rested was a white circle, about the diameter of a coffee cup, standing out against the dark varnish of the dressing-table surface.

'What a pity,' I said. Maggie came over to see what I was talking about. 'It can easily happen if you're not careful,' I said. 'You have a favourite flask for your toilet water; then, when you're refilling it, some of the toilet water runs down the outside and makes a mark.'

She stared as if seeing for the first time. She must know very well that none of the bottles on the dressing table was the right size and shape to have made that mark. Therefore, Barbara's favourite flask of toilet water was somewhere else, along with the manicure set and chamois buffing pad that she would surely have kept in the now empty dressing-table drawer. Either mistress or maid had packed carefully, but the trunk or bag had already gone. Any hope of knowing where would rely on Tabby's efforts.

I suppose I could have bullied Maggie into saying something, perhaps with a threat of telling the colonel. But he'd have gone by now and it might be best to leave Maggie unsettled and see what she did next. I was about to go and give Tabby fresh instructions when I realized I was missing an opportunity. Here I was, on the bedroom floor of the house where Mary Marsh had lived, with freedom to go pretty well where I pleased.

'Was Mary Marsh's room on this floor?' I said.

Maggie was so relieved to face a question on something else that she didn't hesitate.

'Yes. At the end, facing the other way on.'

I told her I might be back later, to keep her anxious, and walked to the end of a corridor and a door at a right angle to the others. It opened on to a small but comfortable room, looking towards the stable block. The rug, desk and two armchairs were rather worn, as if they'd migrated there from more important rooms, but, by the standards of many governesses, Mary Marsh had been comfortably housed. The bed had been stripped of its linen and pillows, with just a coverlet over it, but apart from that it looked as if nothing much would have changed since Mary last walked out of the room. It only needed a second glance to see that the books in the bookcase were her own. This wasn't the usual tidy and unread assembly that you find in the guest rooms of country houses, but rather the mixed, sometimes tattered collection of a woman who loved reading. Some were novels, both in French and English, others poetry, history, geography, geology, natural history, showing a lively and wide-ranging mind, well beyond the demands of her work. The fact that they were still there, a month after Mary's death, showed how alone she'd been, with no family or friends to come and claim her possessions.

If her books were still there, perhaps her other things were as well. I looked into the corridor to make sure that nobody was near, closed the door and started searching. The chest of drawers was empty, but a small leather-covered trunk beside it, marked M.M. in faint white paint, was unlocked and full of her clothes, neatly folded. The housekeeper had probably done that after her death. I sorted through it layer by layer, looking for anything that might link her to Joanna Picton or her brother. Nothing – no old newspapers, not a scrap of writing. I replaced the clothes and went across to her desk, still unlocked. When I opened the flap, the reality of her was so intense that I half expected her to walk into the room and ask what I was doing. It had a cheerful untidiness, showing it had been much used, but with an underlying sense of order. The large central compartment held her watercolour box, with most of the paints worn down, several pencils and charcoal sticks and a small sketch pad of good-quality paper. I sat at the desk and looked through it – more butterflies; various flowers, carefully labelled with English and Latin names; a few attempts at birds, spirited but less successful. No people at all, with just one exception and that was only a back view of a man on a horse.

That was one of the last sketches, near the few blank pages at the end of the book. It was done in quick charcoal strokes, less neat and careful than most of the sketches, but with force and feeling. He looked like a young man, tall and firm in the saddle, but there was somehow a loneliness about the way he and his horse were standing there against a background of trees, his shoulders down, head slumped forward. The horseman was sad and the artist was sorry for him. I got up and took the sketch over to the window. As I'd thought, there were those very same trees to the left of the arch into the stable yard. She'd caught the twists of the oak trunk in a few clever strokes, sketching the scene from her window. I was sure the man on the horse was Rodney Kemble. He'd loved her and the sketch proved that she, once at least, had had feelings for him. Whatever had driven them apart must have mattered very much to her.

I went back to the desk and replaced the sketchbook. The left-hand compartment contained her professional work, plans of lessons for Barbara going back several years. Mary had been conscientious, marking up calendars with each day divided into periods of study: French, divinity, drawing, use of globes, Shakespeare, fractions and long division, piano practice. I only hoped Barbara had benefited from it all. There was no work calendar for the present year, Barbara having graduated from the schoolroom. The right-hand compartment, the most disorderly, contained her correspondence. Like many people who enjoyed writing, Mary had kept letter books, with letters she'd received pasted inside and copies of her replies so that she could look back on a complete correspondence. There were three of them, in plump exercise books with varnished cloth covers. I riffled through them. Many of the letters were exchanges with a woman who was also a governess. She seemed to be younger than Mary, or newly entered on her profession, because Mary was giving her sound practical advice, with good humour and occasional gentle mockery of their charges. Not a word to the purpose, though. Not a hint about the young man of the house being in love with her, or a handsome outlaw, or a scullery-maid who might hang.

Only one letter had something that might touch on it. Her correspondent had complained about how spoiled her pupils were, not charitable or grateful for their luck in being rich. Mary had replied:

> Oh, how well I understand you. Thank goodness I do not have your trials, my girl being kind enough at heart, but there are times when I sit by the fire, playing whist with the colonel, and think of the poor wretches on the road outside who could be called from death back to life by even five minutes of the comforts I take for granted, and it's all I can do not to overturn the table and run out and look for them. Or so I flatter myself, as I suppose we all do, being creatures so very tenacious of our comforts.

I checked the date, the December of the previous year, soon after the arrest of Joanna Picton. It was surely the baby's death that Mary had been picturing, and wondering how much of her own precarious comfort she might risk to help Joanna.

Apart from the letter books, what remained were mostly small, sociable things – an invitation to tea from her friend Mrs Dell, politely declined because of the difficulty of getting home afterwards, a thank you for a book she'd sent somebody. One note, ornamented by cut-out pictures of hearts and roses, wished her happy birthday from Barbara, but had no date.

A few scraps of paper carried memoranda to herself, mostly facts to be checked when she next visited the library in town. Only one was of interest. It looked like a copy, in her handwriting, of a page from a road book giving times of stagecoaches between Cheltenham and Gloucester. Then just two words: St Luke's. She'd written it thriftily on the back of a receipt from a bookshop, with a date in early May of the present year. So, sometime after that date, Mary had either made or contemplated a visit to Gloucester to go to a church. If she'd needed a church, there were many closer than Gloucester and there'd been nothing in her letters to suggest particular piety. Could the distance even be the point of it, wanting to talk about her dilemma to somebody outside the circle of Cheltenham gossip? If so, why that particular church? I read the note again, memorized it and then put it back, closed the desk and made sure everything in her room was as I had found it. On my way back along the corridor, I looked into Barbara's room, but Maggie had gone and the clothes were tidied away. I went downstairs, found the butler and asked him to give my compliments to the colonel when he returned. Nobody was watching me from the windows, so after I'd gone a little way up the drive, I turned off it and walked round a shrubbery towards the side of the house.

A whistle too shrill to be a blackbird's sounded from a big cedar. Tabby was sitting comfortably on a wide branch, legs stretched along it and back against the trunk. When I signalled to her, she slid down, landed neatly on her feet and reported.

'Nothing's come out except the pig bins earlier on, and you wouldn't hide anything in those because of the stink.'

'We missed it,' I said. 'I'm nearly certain Barbara arranged for Maggie to send it somewhere while we were away yesterday in Cheltenham, only I don't know how.'

Tabby and I walked in silence. She was frowning, clearly thinking hard, and when we were nearly back at Mr Godwit's, she announced the result.

'I think I know.'

'How she sent it?'

'With you.' I supposed my jaw dropped, because she laughed. 'You know when you sent me away – well, I walked around for a bit, looking at things. Then I saw the carriage we came into town on, the same driver. He was on a road going out of the town. There was nobody inside, just him.'

'Odd, yes.'

'So I thought I'd follow him for a bit,' Tabby said. 'He didn't go far. Just outside the town, there's a public house with three stars on the board. He drove into the yard. I thought that was just a place he liked to drink at, so I came back and didn't think any more of it till now.'

'You didn't see him unloading anything?'

'We weren't looking for anything then, were we? If it was only a little trunk, he might have kept it up at the front, under his driving box, and we wouldn't have known it was there.'

The more I thought of it, the more convincing it sounded. The driver wouldn't even have to be conscious of Barbara's plot. It would be quite a normal thing to deliver something to a staging post to be picked up by somebody else, although the usual place would be one of the big coaching inns, not some out-of-town establishment.

'You could take us there?' I said.

'Course I could.'

We were both ravenous so we stayed for lunch, I with Mr Godwit, Tabby with Suzie in the kitchen. Afterwards we groomed and tacked up Rancie. When I'd told Mr Godwit that we might be away for the night, he'd hardly raised any objection, dazed by all that was happening. Once I was in the saddle and we'd buckled on the saddlebag, Tabby hopped on to the mounting block and up behind me. Having your maid riding pillion was country manners and would raise a few eyebrows in the streets of Cheltenham, but I was used to that. I shouldn't have inflicted it on Rancie with anybody else, but Tabby was so light and well balanced that a horse would hardly feel the extra weight. We enjoyed a few long canters and were in town by mid-afternoon.

'Straight on, past the statue thing,' said Tabby, directing from the back.

As it happened, it was the main road towards Gloucester, so quite busy. After less than a mile, we came to the public house, three faded gold stars on a flaking blue background, a couple of out-of-work farm labourers drinking slow pints on a bench outside. A girl like Barbara shouldn't even have known such a place existed, but a sporting gentleman might pause there for a quick glass on horseback to break a long hack home. Paley's suggestion to her, probably. How long had they been planning this?

We slipped off and I left Tabby holding Rancie while I went to the door and waited. One of the labourers stood up and called 'Lady to see you' into the dim, beer-smelling depths of the room. A tall, very thin man in a green apron came out.

'I'm sorry to bother you,' I said. 'My friend's coachman left a trunk here yesterday. I wonder if it's been collected yet.'

'Yes, ma'am. First thing this morning. He was here before I got the doors unlocked.'

'Did he give a name?'

'Why should he? He'd come to collect a trunk, he collected it and off he went in a hurry. Didn't even stop to wet his whistle.'

'A young man?'

'Pretty young.'

'What sort of vehicle was he driving?'

'Two-horse curricle, nice one.'

A sporting man's vehicle. That fitted.

'Was he a tall red-faced gentleman with dark hair and side whiskers?'

I was describing Postboy, sure that he was in the plot somewhere. The landlord shook his head.

'Tall, very tall. Not dark or red-faced, though, and no side whiskers. Light-coloured hair and blue eyes, I noticed. Didn't come from round here, judging by his voice.'

'Where from, did you think?'

He jerked his thumb westwards. 'Somewhere that way, I'd say.'

'Which way did he go?'

'Towards Gloucester. Handled the horses like he knew what he was doing.'

It was unbelievable, and yet it fitted too well. I tried another question.

'What was he wearing?'

'Jacket, boots and gaiters, ordinary wear but neat.'

'And his waistcoat?'

'Yellow as a canary bird. So you know the gentleman?'

He looked relieved when I nodded. I suppose he'd feared trouble about the trunk. I thanked him and went back to Tabby and Rancie.

'It was collected first thing this morning,' I said. Then added, still not quite believing it: 'By Amos Legge.'

SIXTEEN

We walked westwards along the road, leading Rancie and trying to make sense of it. The idea that Amos had simply been recruited as a bag-carrier in an elopement was ridiculous. Why and wherever he'd taken the trunk must have been to do with his search for Paley. How he'd got to it before we did was a puzzle. When I'd parted from him, he'd been on his way home to Herefordshire, pausing at Ledbury to follow the trail of Paley's horse. On Sunday morning he'd have been sitting in church next to his fiancée, hearing their banns read. In two days he'd somehow picked up the trail and ridden back here. Given Amos's ability to lay his hands on a fast horse or a pair of them at need, it was possible but still surprising.

'Why in the world didn't he tell us what he was doing?' I said.

'Because we weren't there,' Tabby said, defending him.

A fair point, I supposed. Amos might have been looking for us while we were looking for Barbara.

'The trunk must have had a delivery address on it, or what would be the point in taking it?' I said, trying to think it through. 'Or perhaps he hoped there'd be something inside it that would tell us where Barbara's gone.'

'How would he have known she's gone?'

'You know Amos. He only has to spend five minutes in any stable yard to catch the latest gossip. The whole county's been buzzing with people looking for her.'

We walked on another half-mile.

'Where are we going?' Tabby said.

'Gloucester. It's only another nine miles or so.'

The decision seemed to have made itself. Perhaps it had been made as soon as I looked at that scrap of paper in Mary Marsh's desk.

'Because that's where he's going?'

'I've no notion where he's going,' I said. 'He might have turned off anywhere between here and Gloucester. We'll probably have to wait for him to find us.'

'So, why are we going there?'

'To find a church.'

'Another one?'

She sounded far from impressed, but I was working on a guess so wild that I didn't want to talk about it until I'd tested it, not even to Tabby. She saw that and walked on without resentment. In theory, we were on foot for a while to give Rancie's back a rest, but she was still as fresh as paint and could have carried us both cheerfully. The real reason was another notion too eccentric for me to explain. We were following Joanna Picton. Soon after we'd left the Three Stars, I'd realized that this must have been the road she'd walked, with the baby in her arms, on that icy November night nine months ago. The Three Stars might even be the public house where a kind landlady had let her warm herself at the fire, or another one like it along the way.

It was true that the circumstances could hardly be more different. Joanna was walking in the dark, scared and hungry, with nothing but sodden ploughland and flooded ditches round her. We were going between golden stubble fields with fat pheasants clacking, pastures full of grazing sheep, pink mallow and creamy meadow-sweet growing along the roadside verges. She had the weight of the baby in her arms, probably crying by now, and walked on workhouse shoes that would let in water. It would have been surprising if she'd possessed gloves, so her hands would be blue with cold, probably chapped and chilblained. She and the baby were alone until, too late, the carter came along. In our case, carriages and riders were passing every few minutes, people raising hands and wishing us good afternoon. If we'd needed help at all, either kindness or the sovereigns in my saddle bag would have guaranteed it. She might as well have been a lost traveller in Arctic wasteland for all the help she could expect. And yet she'd walked on, hoping for something better that never happened. When we came to a milestone, I suggested that Tabby should get up on Rancie.

'Don't you want to as well?'

I shook my head. She settled, holding on to the pommel of the saddle as I told her, while I led Rancie along, the sun dipping to the west in front of us, shining in our eyes and throwing long shadows back along the road. When the tower of Gloucester cathedral came in sight, we were passing a grove of withies, with a deep ditch between trees and road. Irrationally, I was sure this was where the baby had drowned and I shuddered.

'What's up?' Tabby asked, missing nothing.

'Just a horsefly. We'll stop at the next milestone and I'll get up with you.'

Gloucester was busy. The broad river Severn takes quite large ships down from there to Bristol, so timber and coal carts were going backwards and forwards from the docks. We found a small but respectable hotel – of the temperance persuasion as it happened – and I negotiated stabling and a feed for Rancie and a room each for Tabby and me. After two weeks of sleeping on Suzie's floor, I thought she deserved a little comfort. The hotel keeper promised chops, potatoes and tea in an hour and cans of hot water in our rooms for washing. I said I had an errand to do first and left Tabby to carry up our saddlebag while I took a short walk to the cathedral. A verger was checking candles, ready for evensong. When I asked him where I might find St Luke's, he seemed surprised that anybody should want it rather than his fine cathedral.

'A little new place, down by the docks.'

'So near the prison, too?'

'Yes.'

'Would it take an interest in prison charities?'

'I think it might.'

I walked back to the hotel, knowing that my guess had been right. All the guests ate dinner at a common table. There were twelve of them, including three clergymen. Over teacups after the meal, I managed to get into conversation with the most amiable of them. He wasn't surprised by my interest.

'Yes, indeed; I know the vicar there. He runs a charity which does what it can for these unfortunate people. If you like, I'll write you a note of introduction.'

I thanked him and he wrote the note there and then, on hotel notepaper at the table.

'What's that about, then?' said Tabby later, with her usual suspicion of the written word.

'A vicar we'll be calling on first thing tomorrow.'

The vicar was quite a young man, but almost completely bald with only a tonsure of sparse hair. His voice was deep, his eyes kind but weary. His small church and vicarage, both of raw-looking brick, in a poor area near the docks, was not the most desirable of livings. The plain curtains and modest furnishings in his study at the vicarage where we talked suggested that he was a bachelor who

didn't spend much thought or money on his own comforts. Judging
by the notices in his church porch, the Prisoners' Gospel Mission
was only one of several charities his parish supported, along with
Indigent Seaman and Relief of Dock Labourers' Widows. It seemed
close to his heart, though, and he was happy to tell me about the
work he and his volunteers did – mostly prison visiting. He showed
no surprise when I said my interest was in a prisoner who'd been
deported.

'Yes, they're heart-rending cases. We're allowed to see them as
they're taken away and give them a small parcel of comforts for
the voyage – a blanket, a cake of soap, a Bible. I've seen hardened
sinners crying like children when they're put into the coaches to be
driven off to the hulks. Even men who've been sentenced only to
seven years away know they might not see their homes and families
again. As for the poor wretches who are transported for life, I've
had some of them say to me that they wished they'd been hanged
instead.'

'The person I'm interested in was for life, and she was a young
woman,' I said.

A pained look came over his face. 'Joanna Picton?'

'You know about the case?'

'Of course. It was notorious here. And there aren't so many
women deported.'

'When was she sent away?'

'The end of May this year. The men, they're sent down to the
hulks at Woolwich to wait for the deportation ships. The hulks have
no accommodation for women, so they're conveyed to Woolwich
just before the ships are due to sail. Joanna was the only woman
this time. They sent her off on the London coach, wrist-shackled
to a warder.'

'Shackled?'

He looked down at the table, obviously uneasy with what he was
telling me.

'We did suggest that it was hardly necessary in Joanna's case.
The poor girl was sobbing and so distressed she could hardly walk
to the coach. But the prison governor insisted it was the rule. I think
up to the last minute they feared there'd be some desperate attempt
to rescue her.'

'We? There was somebody with you?'

'A woman. A remarkably good-hearted and determined woman.'

'Was her name Mary Marsh?' I said.

'I never knew her name. She said Joanna Picton had been employed in a household where she lived.'

'You thought her remarkable?'

'Decidedly. She came to me the day before Joanna was to be taken away and asked if there would be any chance to speak to her. I explained that the authorities would be unlikely to allow it and that in any case the scene was likely to be too distressing for somebody not used to such things.'

'But Miss Marsh wasn't convinced?' I said.

'She was immovable. If her motives had not been so kindly, I might even have said stubborn. She said she had a message for the unfortunate girl from her brother. I offered to deliver it, if I could, but that didn't do. Nothing would satisfy her but she should be there when Joanna was put on the coach. For better or worse, I gave in.'

'And did she talk to Joanna Picton?' I asked.

'She did, but for no more than a minute or two. I wouldn't want to impute any wrongdoing to your friend, but I think it possible that she even passed some money to a gaoler to look the other way while he was sorting out the shackles.'

'Do you know what they talked about?'

'No. I stood quite close, so that I could protect your friend in case of any difficulty, but not so close as to overhear. I presume the message from the brother was passed on. As I say, the girl was distressed and crying.'

'Crying too much to talk?'

'Not entirely. There were several occasions when your friend had clearly asked her something and she lifted up her head and spoke quite sharply. I thought perhaps your friend was asking her if she repented of that she'd done, which would have been quite understandable. If so, I'm afraid she didn't get the answer her kindness deserved.'

'Joanna spoke sharply? Angrily?'

'From the expression on her face, I think so.'

'Angry with Miss Marsh?'

'In my opinion, no. When the men came to put the girl on the coach, she clung to your friend and buried her face on her shoulder. They had to drag her away.'

'Miss Marsh must have found that distressing.'

'That's what I thought. When the coach had driven away, she

seemed dazed, not speaking, I supposed from shock at what she'd
witnessed and I regretted having given in to her. I brought her back
here and some of our ladies brewed tea. After a while she seemed
to recover and I realized I'd been wrong. She'd been simply dazed
with anger.'

He stared at me, eyes as puzzled as they'd probably been at the
time. I thought that anybody of feeling might be angry at what she'd
seen, but I guessed there was more to it than that.

'Why was she angry?'

'I don't know. But I do remember what she said to me. "Hypocrisy
should be one of the deadly sins." She said it very decisively, as if
it were somehow my fault as a man of the church that it weren't.
I began explaining to her that it was bound up with other sins, like
pride and bearing false witness, but she interrupted me, almost
rudely. "It seems to me that it's the one thing that should be unforgivable." I tried to remind her that nothing is unforgivable to our
Saviour, but I think she was sunk in her own mind, not hearing.
She was like a person who'd received a bad shock, almost stunned
by it.'

'A shock from what Joanna Picton had said?'

'It must have been. Perhaps it was the girl's lack of repentance
that shocked her.'

I didn't believe that for a moment. I don't think he did.

'And she didn't explain what she meant?'

'No. After a while she recovered and apologized for being sharp
with me. She said hastiness was a great fault. I said it was indeed,
but it was often a fault of generous natures. Like hers, I meant,
wanting her to feel better. She said she'd wronged somebody by
being hasty. I asked her what she meant, thinking she might want
to confide in me, but she shook her head and said it was up to her
to put it right. I said I'd pray for her. Then she thanked me and left.
I often think of her. I hope she's well.'

That came as a cold blast to me. Mary Marsh had seemed so
alive when he talked about her that I'd forgotten he didn't know.

'I'm very sorry to tell you she's dead,' I said.

He rocked back in his chair.

'When?'

'Just over a month ago.'

'Was it sudden?'

'Very sudden.'

He looked so shocked that I couldn't bring myself to tell him she'd been murdered. He might find out for himself in time.

'And you . . . why . . .?'

'I suppose when somebody dies suddenly, you think of all the things she might have told you and didn't,' I said. 'Finding out things you didn't know is a way of coming closer to the person.'

It was true enough, but I was still deceiving him, letting him think she'd been my friend. I wished she had been. I wished too that I could tell him more, but I didn't know where that would end. Mary Marsh had made a deep impression on him. Perhaps he'd hoped to meet her again in happier circumstances. I thanked him and said I must go, uncomfortable at receiving his condolences. The couple of half-crowns I dropped into one of the many collecting boxes on his window sill did nothing to ease my conscience. He showed me out and said I'd be welcome to call again. I knew I wouldn't call again.

Tabby was waiting outside. As we walked back to the hotel together, I gave her a pretty full account of what the vicar had told me.

'What's hypocrisy?' she said.

'Wanting people to think you're good when you aren't.'

'Nearly everyone, then.'

'The question is: what can Joanna have said to her to shock her so much? Mary knew the whole story already – the fair, the work-house, the baby dying. How could there be anything worse for Joanna to tell her?'

Just a few sharp words, almost certainly the last Joanna would speak in her native county, before the coach took her southwards at the start of a journey that would convey her like cargo to the other side of the world. Somehow they'd turned Mary's whole view of the case upside down. She'd been hasty. She'd wronged somebody and must put it right.

'There's one thing Joanna hadn't told anyone,' Tabby said.

'Who the father was? Yes, that's what I'm thinking, too. Everything's lost, so she tells Mary the name at last. But why not before?'

'Because she was hoping he'd do something to help her, right up to the last. So when she finds he isn't going to, she might as well say it.'

It was always a good test of my ideas, trying them against Tabby's commonsense. Again, she and I had come to the same conclusion.

'So Joanna says a name, and Mary's angry and shocked by it,' I said. 'We at least know what the name *wasn't*, don't we?'

'Paley.'

'Yes. Everybody suspected Peter Paley was the father, including Mary and Jack Picton. So if Joanna had simply confirmed it, Mary wouldn't have been so shocked. Then there's this hypocrisy word. Even people who don't like Peter Paley or his father admit they're not hypocrites. So neither of them was the father.'

'Who was, then?'

I didn't answer at first. A name was in my mind and I didn't want to say it. Tabby started scuffing her feet as she walked, which meant she was puzzled.

'It has to be somebody with a good reputation,' I prompted. 'Somebody Mary respected.'

'Colonel Kemble?'

We were about to cross a road at the time and I nearly stepped in front of an oncoming donkey cart in sheer surprise.

'*Colonel* Kemble?'

'Why not? He's rich, he was in the army and goes to church and so on. Is that what you call a good reputation?'

'It was the son I was thinking of, not the father.'

'Rodney again?'

'Yes. Imagine how angry she'd be. When she first finds out about Joanna, she wants him to help her, but he won't. If he were the father, naturally he wouldn't want to do anything in case it started tongues wagging. But Mary doesn't know that and thinks he's just being cowardly. Then, at the very last minute, she finds out the truth.'

'So she tells him what she's found out and he kills her – is that it?'

'What do you think?'

'Yes,' Tabby said. 'But it would work the same with his father.'

'I don't think so. She really cared for Rodney, in spite of the quarrel. That would make it worse.'

Tabby didn't look entirely convinced.

'There's a problem of time, though,' I said. 'She finds out the day Joanna's sent away, in late May. But she's not killed until July, six weeks later.'

'Perhaps he was trying to screw himself up to do it.'

'But if he intended to kill her, he'd have to do it before she had a chance to tell anybody else. In six weeks she could have told the whole world if she'd wanted.'

'Perhaps she didn't go and tell him straight away. She wanted to find out if Joanna was telling the truth.'

'But she believed Joanna; otherwise, she wouldn't have been so angry and shocked,' I said.

'She believed her at first; then she started wondering if it was true.'

That made some sense. In talking to the vicar, Mary had accused herself of being hasty. Perhaps she'd gone to the other extreme and looked for more proof before speaking out. But where would she have gone for proof? In any case, could she have lived under the same roof as Rodney for six weeks, knowing what she knew, and not speak out? We discussed those two questions for the rest of the way back to the hotel but came up with no answers.

SEVENTEEN

I paid our bill and collected Rancie from the stables. As I intended to get all the way back to Mr Godwit's house that day, we gave her an easy time on the return from Gloucester to Cheltenham. By early afternoon we were on the outskirts of the town. We found a trough for Rancie to drink and I burrowed in the saddlebag for a comb and a clothes brush to tidy myself up. We had no mirror, so I asked Tabby if I looked fairly presentable.

'You've got a smudge on your cheek.' I dipped my handkerchief in the trough and gave it to her to wipe it off. 'But I don't know why you're bothering,' she said. 'We'll only get all dusty again on the way back.'

'I'm paying a call first.'

'Who on?'

'Can't you guess? The same gentleman Mary Marsh would have called on.'

'Mr Paley?'

'That's right. The old one, not the young one.'

'Am I coming with you?'

'No. Go and find something to eat and drink. I'll meet you back here at three o'clock.'

She held Rancie while I used the edge of the trough to remount. I knew the Paleys' house – an imposing one behind a high wall on this side of town – and could easily have walked there, but both Paleys had an eye for a good horse. I'd need any advantage I could get to persuade Colum Paley to talk to me. The gates at the top of the drive were open. I rode straight through and round the side of the house to a stable yard large enough for an important coaching inn, but more orderly and restful. A dozen or more thoroughbred heads looked out from the boxes that surrounded it. A lad was sweeping up the few straw wisps that spoiled the perfection of the flagstones. When I asked him where I might find Mr Paley, he propped the broom against the wall and bolted into a room at the end of a row of loose boxes. I stayed in the saddle as Colum Paley strolled out, taking his time, wiping his mouth on the back of his hand. From the way he was dressed, he might have been mistaken for one of his own grooms, in gaiters, moleskin waistcoat and jacket, although clean and tidy like the rest of his yard. He was saying something to the lad behind him and didn't look pleased to be interrupted, but his face changed when he saw Rancie.

'Oh, so you're the one, are you?' he said.

I wasn't sure if he was speaking to my mare or to me, so I thought I'd better introduce her. I gave him her full name, Esperance, and a summary of her pedigree. He listened, giving a few quick little nods, approving her.

'She's the one that was giving a race to the lads up on the course?' he said.

'Only a pipe-opener,' I said. 'She's not in training for racing.'

'How old is she?'

'Eight.'

'You should be breeding from her. I've got a stallion might suit, Whalebone line, not great lookers but the speed's there.'

This talk of breeding, from a gentleman to a lady when we hadn't even been introduced, was hardly delicate, but his manner was direct and unembarrassed. Even at a disadvantage, on foot when I was on horseback, there was a presence about him. My only sight of him so far had been outside the assembly rooms. Seen close to, he was as broad-shouldered as Amos, though not quite as tall, with a good, squarish head and dark hair worn long enough to show the slight wave in it, giving him the air of a person who followed his own tastes. He was probably in his fifties, but with the energy of a man twenty years younger. I said that I hadn't thought of breeding from Esperance yet, making a mental note that if and when I did, I'd find something more amiable and better-looking than Whalebone's bloodline.

'Shouldn't leave it till too late,' he said. 'So, have they found the girl?'

He must have recognized me and heard of my connection with Barbara Kemble's disappearance. It was a reminder not to under-estimate Colum Paley.

'Not as far as I know, but I've only just got back from Gloucester. I want to talk to you about Mary Marsh.'

From his face, it took him a moment or two to remember who she was.

'The governess?'

'Yes.'

He'd been relaxed when we'd been talking about horses; now his voice and face were hard.

'You'd better get down, then.'

He helped me down without fuss, called to the stable boy to look after Rancie and led the way to the room at the end of the row. He opened the door to let me in first. It was a plain room with whitewashed walls and looked like a combination of a gentleman's study and a head groom's quarters. A reproduction of Stubbs's painting of Eclipse was the only picture, with various bits and bridles hanging from pegs on either side. Under it, a pine table crowded with feed bills and race schedules and an inkwell made from a horse's hoof. A sagging armchair containing a dozing spaniel stood by the fireplace. The smell was masculine: leather and brandy. A smaller table with two plain wooden chairs drawn up to it supported a decanter of brandy and several glasses, one of them half full.

'You'd better sit down, I suppose,' he said in that same hard voice.

Not wanting to disturb the spaniel, I took one of the wooden chairs. Colum Paley sat down in the other and glanced from the decanter to me.

'Like a drink?'

The tone seemed deliberately coarse now – a gentleman jockey's drawl. After the ride I'd have been grateful for a cup of tea or even a glass of hock, but brandy was the only thing on offer. I shook my head.

'Mary Marsh came to see you,' I said. 'It was earlier this year, sometime between May and when she died in July. She came to apologize.'

He took a slow mouthful of brandy, looking at me all the while, and didn't speak until he'd swallowed it.

'And what business is it of yours, Miss Lane?'

In every interview a time comes when you must decide whether to lie and, if so, how much. I looked into his brown, unblinking eyes and decided that lying was unjustifiable, not necessary and probably wouldn't work in any case.

'I became interested in the case of Miss Marsh, through an acquaintance. I'm almost certain that the man who'll appear at the assizes next week accused of murdering her is innocent. I think her death had something to do with the case of Joanna Picton. She was trying to discover the father of Joanna's child.'

'And she and the girl's brother were hell-bent on pinning that on my son. You saw a sample of it for yourself, outside the assembly rooms. The Lord knows what you were doing there with Barty Jones's ruffians.'

And I thought he hadn't noticed me in the hail of pennies. 'If Mary Marsh had lived, she'd have told Jack Picton's friends that they were wrong,' I said. 'Just minutes before Joanna Picton was deported, she told Mary who the father was. Sometime after that, Mary Marsh came to apologize to you and, through you, to your son.'

'And I told her she needn't have bothered.'

I had to hide my feeling of triumph at making a right guess. 'When was that?'

'If you think I'd write it down in a diary, I didn't. But I can tell you it was the week after the Derby.'

Late May, then. Soon after she'd seen Joanna.

'Did she just call and see you out of the blue?'

'No. She sent me a governessy little note, introducing herself and saying she'd take the liberty of calling on me on a date she named to discuss a matter of importance to both of us. I guessed it would be some church business, like closing down beer houses or sending missionaries to pester poor heathens, so I didn't reply and forgot about it until she arrived early one morning when we'd just got in from the gallops.'

He took another slow drink of brandy. He didn't seem drunk or anywhere near it, so probably it was as customary as coffee for him.

'Did she just come out with it?'

'Pretty nearly. I was quite short with her when I found out who she was. I told her I hadn't any money for church hypocrites . . .'

'You used that word – hypocrites?'

'Why not? So she'd better get out of the way of the horses and stop wasting my time, I told her. But she stood her ground – I'll say that for her – although she seemed nervous of the horses. And I'll give her credit for plain speaking too because she said to me, in front of the grooms and the boys and all of them, "Don't you want to know that your son wasn't the father of Joanna Picton's child?" I said to her, also in front of all of them, "I knew that

already, but thank you for taking the trouble to come and tell me."
She saw I was being sarcastic and some of the men were sniggering
at her. Well, I didn't care for that, even if she'd asked for it. So I
told them to get on with their work, took her in here and sat her
down, just as you're sitting now. And I asked her, just as I asked
you, what business it was of hers.'

'What did she say?'

'That she knew the girl and was sorry for her. So I asked her
how she'd come to the conclusion that my son was the father of
the brat in the first place. I said I supposed it was because of what
Rodney Kemble had told her after he and Peter nearly came to
blows at the races. She blushed a bit at that and wouldn't answer
directly, but I knew I was right. I said she shouldn't believe everything she heard, and she looked me in the face and said yes, she'd
been wrong, very wrong, and she was going to do her best to make
amends for it.'

He took another swallow of brandy.

'Did she say how?' I said.

'I didn't give her the chance. I gave her some good advice
instead, and it's much the same as I'm giving you now. Don't do
anything. When people try to interfere in what other people are
doing, it's usually for their own selfish reasons, even when they
pretend otherwise. Save men from gambling. Save labourers from
drinking. Save pretty girls from being looked at by young lads.
Save us all from this and that, but most of the time it's only
because they want to be looked up to as great men when they're
as miserable sinners as the rest of us, and probably more so. I
expected her to come back at me with some preaching, but she
didn't. She thanked me for my advice – though I could see from
her face she didn't intend to take it – apologized again and wished
me good morning.'

'And that was all?'

'Pretty nearly. I walked her to the gates because she'd shown a
bit of spirit and I didn't want the men making remarks at her. I
asked her how she was so sure now that Peter wasn't the father.
She said because the Picton girl had told her who it really was.'

'Did she say who?'

'No, and I didn't ask her. Not my business.'

'Isn't justice anybody's business?'

'I don't set myself up in judgement over people, like some.'

Was this a hit at Mr Godwit and his fellow magistrates? Colum Paley would certainly know I was staying with him.

'In any case, what difference would it make now? The baby's dead and the girl's transported,' he said.

'And her brother will soon be on trial for his life.'

'Serves him right, if half I've heard of that one is true. Want to save him, do you?'

'I don't want to see an innocent man hanged.'

He sighed. 'Giving good advice to a woman is like feeding beefsteak to a horse,' he said.

That seemed to be the end of it and I expected him to get up and escort me out, but he didn't.

'I suppose the Kembles are putting it about that my son has carried their girl off somewhere,' he said.

His voice wasn't so hard now, with something close to a note of appeal in it. I might have information he needed, after all.

'There's some evidence that Miss Kemble went of her own accord,' I said.

I couldn't see any harm in telling him and I owed no particular loyalty to the Kembles. He nodded as if he'd guessed that.

'To find Peter, do you think?'

'I doubt if Miss Kemble would do anything so desperate on her own,' I said. 'If she went, it means he managed somehow to send a message to her and make the arrangements.'

'Where do you think he is, then?' he said, looking sidelong at me.

'I have no notion. Have you?'

He shook his head. 'When he went like that, I guessed he was going to stay away for long enough to have me worried and then come back expecting me to slaughter the fatted calf for him. But he's been gone more than a month now.'

'Have you heard anything at all from him?'

He took his time about deciding to answer. 'Last week, a man came to me who'd found his horse right over west in Herefordshire.'

'I know the man,' I said. 'His name's Amos Legge.'

His head came up, surprised.

'Yes, that's the name. He's honest?'

'As the day.'

'That's how he struck me. He reckoned if we followed the trail of the horse back, we'd find out what had happened to Peter.'

'Yes, that's how he works. Have you seen him since?'

'No. He said he'd come back to me when there was any news. Then yesterday a note arrived.'

He took a piece of paper, much folded, out of his pocket and handed it to me. The paper was rough and smelled of saddle soap, the words few and direct:

> Mr Paley,
> To let you know your son is as well as can be expected and being looked after.
> Yours with Respect,
>   A. Legge

'Is that the man's handwriting?' Paley asked.

'Yes. Amos Legge beyond a doubt.' I couldn't help smiling because it was so typical of him. 'Did he deliver it?'

'No. Somebody who doesn't sound like Legge rode into the yard yesterday, gave it to my training groom and went off before anybody could ask questions. But what does it mean? Is it some kind of kidnap demand?'

'Amos is no kidnapper. It will mean exactly what it says.'

'*As well as can be expected* sounds as if something's happened to him. And why didn't Legge just tell me where he is? Does he want money from me?'

'No. I don't know the reason, but I'm sure there'll be one.'

Amos must have arranged for the note to be delivered when he was in the area collecting Barbara's trunk, but it wasn't my place to tell Colum Paley about that. There'd been a change in his attitude when he found I knew Amos. The hostility had gone, but he was looking at me in a puzzled way, as if revising some of his ideas.

'How did you come to know him, then?'

I told him only a little of the story, but enough to make his eyes widen. At the end, he laughed and poured brandy into a clean glass.

'You won't refuse to have a drink with me a second time, will you?'

I sipped. It was good brandy.

'So, he's found my son but won't say where.'

'I'm sure he will in his own good time.'

He laughed again. 'Do you think the girl's with him? It'll be a good joke if the Kembles have to welcome Peter into the family as a brother and son-in-law.'

I thought that Rodney Kemble might have a lot more than that to worry about. But it was an opportunity to get him to talk about what I wanted.

'Did the bad blood between Rodney Kemble and your son date from the business at the races?'

'They'd never been great friends. He and his father run some horses in a small way. Young Kemble's not a bad rider but a stickler for the rules – rather win on a technicality than breakneck over the fences. But they'd never been near coming to blows.'

'But at the fair at the races they did, over Joanna Picton.'

'Back to that, are we? Lot of nonsense.'

'But something did happen to Joanna at the races, and your son and his friends were there.'

'I was there too, so I can tell you exactly what happened. Yes, we were all of us playing a hand of cards and having a drink or two in one of the booths. And yes, there were some wenches there the lads were giving drinks to, taking kisses and so on, and believe me those girls weren't objecting to it – quite the reverse. And yes, one of them was your Joanna girl, though I wouldn't have known her from Eve at the time. They were playing forfeits with the boys and she grabbed Peter's cap and ran out of the booth with it. He ran after her, laughing, to get it back and that was when young Kemble saw them and decided Peter was taking advantage of her. That's as far as it went between Peter and the Picton girl, and if you think a man gets a wench with child just by kissing her, then I'm not going to be the one who tells you otherwise.'

'Joanna wasn't laughing when she got back to the Kembles' house that evening. She was scared and distressed.'

'Well, that wasn't Peter's doing or any of his friends'. It wasn't until young Kemble appeared and she knew she'd be in trouble back home that she sobered up and looked worried.'

If this was true, the case was looking black against Rodney Kemble.

'So did he take Joanna away with him?' I said.

'He never had the chance. Just as Peter and young Kemble were squaring up to fight, Holy Fanny and the magistrates appear like genies coming out of a bottle and constables start breaking up booths and arresting people right, left and centre.'

'Not including Rodney Kemble and your son, of course.'

'No. The constables had more sense than to take on young

gentlemen who might be handy with their fists. It was mostly the
booth keepers they arrested, and the girls, including the Picton girl.'

'You're sure of that?'

'Yes. The constables herded about a dozen of them up together
in a wagon. Some were like her, drunken skivvies on a day out,
and some were what you might call the professionals from the town,
but that didn't make any odds.'

'What were the women charged with?'

He shrugged. 'Being drunk in a public place, disorderly conduct,
resisting arrest. The magistrates always find some reason when they
want to.'

'Who was giving the orders?'

'Some high-up from the county constabulary and the chairman
of the magistrates, Penbrake, with Holy Fanny and his party cheering
them on.'

'Joanna must have been released,' I said. 'She was back at her
work place that evening. If she'd been up before the magistrates,
she'd certainly have been dismissed out of hand.'

A picture was forming. Rodney Kemble finds the family kitchen-
maid drunk and disorderly on the racecourse, but before he can drag
her home she is arrested. He manages to secure her release, possibly
by overawing or bribing a not very bright constable, leaving him
with a scared and miserable scullery-maid on his hands. In his eyes,
the girl has no reputation worth worrying about. Did he take his
reward for freeing her in a very direct and brutal way? If so, she'd
have been too scared and miserable to accuse her employer's son.
Some threat or promise from him might have kept her silent to the
very last. If Mary Marsh had discovered all that, she wouldn't have
let things rest. She'd have thought about it for a long time – no
hastiness now – and perhaps looked for more evidence, just as I
was doing. Then, when she was quite sure of her ground, she'd
asked Rodney Kemble to meet her in the glade in the woods. Colum
Paley was saying something. I tried to listen.

'. . . can ask anybody who was there. Half the town will have
seen it. I'm not saying my son behaved like a choirboy or even how
I'd have liked him to behave. Perhaps I should have stopped what
was going on, if I'd paid more attention. What I am saying is if
you think he got a child on the girl, then you're wrong. But as I
told you, I don't see how it matters now.'

This time he did stand up, discussion over, and escorted me to a loosebox where Rancie was nibbling delicately at a net of hay. He led her out himself and then whistled up one of the boys to hold her while he cupped his hands to throw me into the saddle. As I settled myself, I was aware that he was giving both Rancie and me a long look.

'Shouldn't leave it until too late,' he said again. Then, as he walked beside us to the gate: 'And if you see your friend, tell him to come and see me.'

I said I would, not admitting I had no notion where Amos was and what he was doing. For all his hardness, Colum Paley was a worried man.

EIGHTEEN

When we got back, Mr Godwit was worried too – in his case about almost everything. Where had I been for so long? Had I eaten dinner? Was there any news from town about Barbara? I avoided the first question and said no to the other two. I hoped he couldn't smell the brandy on my breath. Tabby helped me untack Rancie and turn her out to graze in the evening sun and then disappeared to the back door for supper in the kitchen. Mr Godwit conjured up hot soup, cold salmon and hock for me and sat anxiously while I ate and drank. As soon as the plates were cleared, he asked another question.

'You've remembered the assizes start on Saturday?'

That gave me a jolt – only two and a half days away.

'I thought it was Monday.'

'Monday's when the court proceedings begin, but the judges and their party make their formal entrance to the city on Saturday evening. We magistrates have to be there to welcome them.'

I breathed again. Four and a half days at least.

'How soon is Picton's case to come up?'

'It's listed first, for the Monday morning. When I see the others on Saturday, I'd like . . .' He paused, swallowed. 'I'd like at least to have some idea if there's any new evidence.'

He said it quite humbly and I felt ashamed of myself. He'd taken an amazingly bold step, by his standards, in asking me to investigate. He'd given me hospitality and coped as calmly as he could with my comings and goings. He might even pay me, though with so many complications I couldn't depend on that. He was owed an explanation and, if my suspicions turned out to be right, it would come as a bad shock. The least I could do was prepare him for it, even if I wasn't ready to mention a name yet.

'It's to do with Joanna and the baby,' I said. 'A man respected in the community and known to you was the father of the child. Mary Marsh found out who it was. Whether she told Jack Picton, I don't know. I think not. I'm sure she intended to tell him at some point, but she decided to make sure by confronting the father of the child first. She arranged a secret meeting with him, told him what she suspected, and he killed her, to stop her telling people.'

Mr Godwit had closed his eyes when I started speaking. Now the lids were clamped tight shut.

'Young Paley?' he murmured.

'No, and not his father either; I'm sure of that. But it's probably one of the Paleys that Jack Picton will try to accuse in court on Monday. If so, it will damage his case, just as you thought.'

Mr Godwit opened his eyes, but only after he'd clasped his palms over his nose and mouth, so that he looked like a nervous lady peering over a fan.

'So we're back where we started?' he said, only just audibly.

'Worse in one way. When we started, we weren't sure if he was innocent or not. Now I'm certain he *is* innocent. Innocent of murdering Mary Marsh at any rate.'

Guilty, I thought, of being a rabble-rouser, a rick burner, a neglectful son and uncaring brother until it was too late to matter. But none of those deserved the gallows.

'But can you prove it?' Mr Godwit asked, from behind his fan of fingers.

'Not yet, no.'

'Not yet? But by Monday night . . .'

His voice trailed away, but it was a fair point he was making. By Monday night Jack Picton would be taken back into Gloucester prison as a man condemned to death. Any new evidence would have to be watertight to overturn a verdict once given.

'So I've only four days to find proof,' I said. 'Or, if not proof, at least something strong enough to persuade a jury to acquit him.'

'Can you do it?'

The true answer was that I didn't know, but I said I hoped so. He nodded, but didn't ask how I intended to set about it, which was just as well. When I said I had a note to write, he offered me the use of his study. I sat at his desk and wrote a couple of lines. When I looked out of the window, he was standing in his garden in the twilight, waiting for his old spaniel to do its business in the shrubbery. I folded the note, addressed it and took it up to bed with me.

It didn't seem any better a plan in the morning than it had the night before, but it was the only one I had. It was no surprise to find Tabby down by the paddock at first light.

'We going somewhere?'

'Cheltenham again, but I want you to do something first.' I gave her the note and a shilling. 'Take this over and give it to the vicar's boy. He's sure to be up early. Tell him it must be delivered today, as soon as possible. Then come back here and I'll tell you what next.'

While she was gone, I brought in Rancie and gave her a small feed while I did my best with tack cleaning. I couldn't find sponge or saddle soap and the leather of the saddle flap was stiff and beginning to crack. Amos would be annoyed when he saw it, but that was the least of my worries. Tabby was back before I finished and helped me tack up. We went at a walk for the first mile, with Tabby on foot alongside, to give Rancie time to digest her breakfast. Then I hoisted Tabby up behind and we were in Cheltenham before the invalids had even left their hotels. I dismounted and helped her down.

'The business of today is to find Amos Legge,' I said. 'I'm going to ride round all the livery stables and coaching inns I can manage on both sides of town. I want you to stay in town and ask at the hotel stables and anywhere else you can think of. But whatever happens, meet me back here at four by the church clock.'

She nodded.

'Another thing, keep your ears open for anything to do with Barbara Kemble,' I said. 'It seems strange that nobody has found any trace of her going out of town. I'm beginning to wonder if she ever left town at all. You might have a look at that dressmaker's house I showed you.'

Another nod. I gave her some money, remounted and rode out of town on the road westwards, for no better reason than that way I shouldn't have the sun in my eyes. In the next hour and a half, I inquired at three inns, two livery stables and a tollgate, with no useful result. One of the inns remembered a man of Amos's description from two or three days ago, but that was no help because I knew he must have been in the area then, in any case. I went back through the town and rode out for nearly two hours in the other direction towards the Cotswolds, with only one doubtful sighting and that on Tuesday, two days ago. I began to wonder whether he'd ridden back home to Herefordshire and his fiancée, but why would he go without seeing me? More to the point, why hadn't he told Colum Paley where to find his son? It wasn't like Amos to leave a job undone. With no answers, I turned back towards Cheltenham, hot, dusty and worried. I'd made my plan relying on finding Amos. Without his swiftness and physical strength, it would involve much more risk and might not work at all. I realized now that I'd relied on him too much. I'd assumed, wrongly, that he'd somehow manage to appear when I needed him. Amos, the married man, wouldn't be there in future and I'd have to become accustomed to a large empty space. I only wished it hadn't been today.

I arrived back in town with time to give Rancie a long drink at the water trough before meeting Tabby. There was another thing to consider. Without Amos, I'd have to take Tabby as a hidden witness when I kept the appointment I'd made. The problem was she wouldn't stay hidden if she thought I was being threatened. She'd be out of hiding and fighting like a terrier, whatever the odds. I rode on to the place where I'd told her to meet me, wondering how to prevent that happening and finding no answer. I arrived a few minutes before four. No Tabby. Four o'clock struck. No Tabby. Half past four. No Tabby. By now I was annoyed. In spite of Tabby's refusal to learn reading and writing, she was capable of telling the hours and reasonably punctual. The exception was when she was on the trail of something or somebody. If she'd picked up a scent of where Barbara might be, she'd follow it, oblivious of what the church clock said. My fault. I should have impressed on her how important it was to be here. Even more important now there was no Amos, although she couldn't have known that. I asked some loitering lads if they'd seen her. Not since she was with me in the morning, they said. At half past five, I distributed small change and a message to give to her if they saw her.

'Tell her I can't wait and I'm going home. She's to catch up with me if she can.'

Time was pressing, but I rode as slowly as I dared, turning in the saddle every few minutes in the hope of seeing a small figure in a dust cloud behind me. Mr Godwit was away on some errand to a neighbour when I arrived and he had left a message saying he'd be back in time for dinner. I was glad of his absence. I left Rancie in the gardener's care, fetched pen and ink from the study, and spent some time in my room writing a note, using the marble top of the washstand for a desk. It was quite short, addressed to Mr Godwit, and told him where I was going, whom I was seeing and why. I left it on my pillow, where it was unlikely to be found until tomorrow morning. If I came back in time to reclaim it, so much

the better. Mrs Wood was surprised to hear I shouldn't be joining
Mr Godwit for dinner. She offered tea and cake instead and I ate
and drank sitting at the kitchen table in my riding clothes, suddenly
hungry.

'If Tabby comes back, tell her to wait for me here,' I said.

The problem of how to prevent her from trying to rescue me if
it came to it had solved itself, though not the way I wanted. I walked
along the now familiar road, the sun low in the west and stretching
my shadow out across the fields. It looked as lonely as I felt. If
there'd been more time, even a day or two more, I shouldn't have
kept the appointment. Perhaps the other party wouldn't be there.
That thought was comforting, even though it would mean that my
plan had fallen at the first hurdle and Jack Picton would probably
hang. Let him. He was an ungrateful man at best. Innocent men
were hanged quite often and I couldn't worry about all of them. A
sudden incongruous memory came to me of Mr Disraeli in his
evening finery sitting by the fish pond, and I was angry with him
for his part in setting me swimming in these waters. I was angry
with everybody, myself included for not managing things better. I
was walking too fast. Half past eight, I'd written in my note. That
would be just as the light was going. No point in being there too
early.

I took the first turning off the road, the way to the servants'
entrance. They'd all be occupied now, clearing up after dinner. From
the side of the house, a smaller track to the left led towards the
woods. Still no sign of anybody, but the other party might be
watching me from the house. I walked quickly along the woodland
track, determined that our meeting should be at the time and place
I'd chosen. When I reached the shelter of the trees, there was no
sign of anybody following me. My heart was thumping as I followed
the faint track. When it came on to a wider path, with deep ruts
where timber had been drawn out, I turned right. There was mud
in some of the ruts from Monday's rain. It squelched into my left
boot through a split I hadn't known was there, sliming my stocking
and toes.

Through a space where a big oak had fallen, I could make out
the back of the house – a solid block against the dusk, a few lights
in the windows. A dog barked from the stable block, too far away
to be anything to do with me. Mary Marsh would have come this
way forty-four days ago. I was walking in her footsteps and the

thoughts in my mind were her thoughts. Being the person she was, she'd have worked out in advance what she was going to say. The word 'hypocrite' would be in there somewhere. It had been the main thing on her mind after that last meeting with Joanna. And at some point she'd have asked, as I intended to ask: 'So, what do you intend to do about it?' If she'd been allowed to get that far. Perhaps she had – and then received her answer in a blow to the skull with a lump of iron. The difference between us was that she wasn't expecting it. I hoped that would be enough.

In the glade the weeds seemed to have grown taller. The willow-herb was going to seed, streaks of white fluff and a few faded pink flowers. The birds had gone quiet and not so much as a field mouse rustled last year's leaves. I took out my watch, with just enough light coming through the branches to see the time. Twenty-three minutes past eight. I'd decided that I'd behave as if Amos was really where I wanted him to be, behind the oak at the far side of the clearing. I'd say my piece, and if the other party tried to attack me, I'd shout out and then run towards the house. I thought he wouldn't attack. Everything I'd seen of Rodney Kemble suggested a man under almost intolerable strain, with no savagery left in him. When I next looked at my watch, only three minutes had passed. I wondered if there was time to take my boot off and twist the stocking round so that my toes weren't sliding on mud. Odd, the tricks the mind plays. I counted slowly to two hundred, to keep my breathing steady. It must be time now. Perhaps he wasn't coming. Then I was annoyed with myself for feeling so relieved. I wanted him to come, didn't I?

Nearer dark than twilight now. He wasn't coming. I'd give it five minutes more and then walk back. But something would have to be done about the stocking. I sat on a tree trunk, pulled my boot off, loosened my garter and eased the stocking round. Then the footsteps came. In the few seconds it took to get my breathing back under control, I lost the sound and thought I must have imagined it. Then they started again, faint as if from several hundred yards away. They weren't coming from the house as I expected, but from further away behind the stable block. Something about them was wrong. They were coming in my direction, quite rapidly judging by the sound. It was the rhythm that was wrong. Somebody was taking long strides, too long for what I remembered of the way Rodney Kemble walked and too urgent. Why should he hurry to a meeting that he'd have wanted to avoid if he could? The only explanation was that he'd screwed his courage to the sticking point and was coming to deal with me before it deserted him. These weren't the steps of a man who'd stand and listen to reason. I fumbled at the garter and struggled to push my foot back into my boot, cursing my stupidity. I wanted to run now, but he'd hear me, even see me in the last of the light. All I could do was stand up and keep in my mind what I'd intended to say to him – if I had the chance.

I still couldn't see him, but I could hear his breathing, steady in spite of his hurry. Then suddenly I could see him, much closer than I'd thought. He'd been invisible against the darkness of the trees until he moved into the glade. I gasped, both from the closeness and the height of him. I hadn't remembered Rodney so tall. The words I'd prepared wouldn't come. He spoke first, stopping suddenly a few yards away.

'Well, I'm duthered! How come you knew I'd be here?'

The voice and the hay-and-leather smell of Amos Legge were so unexpected that I thought I'd imagined him. Even now, I couldn't find words.

'You gone lame, then?' His voice was concerned. Even in the near dark, he could sense that I was standing awkwardly, boot half on. 'I'll carry you, only we'll have to hurry because he's chasing after me.' He jerked a thumb back in the direction he'd come.

'Who's chasing you?' I got words out at last, even though my brain was buzzing like a disturbed bee hive.

'The brother.'

'Rodney Kemble? But he's the one I'm waiting for.'

'I wouldn't, if I were you. He's not in the best of tempers.'

'Why? Have you told him . . .?' I couldn't grasp what Amos knew or didn't know, but there was no time to think about it because he was bending, ready to pick me up.

'Amos, there's no need. It's only my boot. Just give me a moment.' I bent and wrenched it straight.

'I could wait and fight him,' Amos said. 'Only if I did, I'd have to knock him down and I reckon he's got enough troubles without that.' Then, as an afterthought: 'And he's carrying a shotgun.'

'He killed Mary Marsh,' I said.

'We can sort that out later.' Amos made it sound like a matter of course. 'Only, if you're sound on your legs, we'd better move.'

There were other steps now, distant but determined ones coming quite rapidly along the path from the stable block. Rodney Kemble knew his woods. I might have insisted on standing our ground and having it out with him after all, but that would have made a fight inevitable and even Amos was not shotgun-proof. I took the arm that he offered, hitched my skirts up with the other hand and we moved rapidly back along the path. As soon as we'd cleared the back of the house, Amos steered us aside under the trees. He gripped my arm as a warning to keep quiet and we stood listening. After some time we heard the footsteps again. Rodney Kemble came striding past us, only yards away, making for the side entrance of the house. It was too dark to see his face, but his whole posture was jagged with anger and hurry. Instead of going back on the track, Amos found a way through the trees and back on to the road. As we walked towards the village, my heartbeats steadied enough to make talking possible.

'Amos, what had you said to Rodney Kemble?'

'I didn't get much chance to say anything. I was in their stables, talking to a man I knew, when he came in and saw me. From what he said, he reckons you've made off with his sister and I've been helping you. He doesn't seem to like you very much. I thought if I stayed, it would only lead to unpleasantness, so I went.'

'But what were you doing in the Kembles' stable yard in the first place?'

It was too dark to see Amos's face, but I sensed an awkwardness.

'The lass wanted a few little things she'd forgotten – bracelets, something with feathers. Then there was a note to be delivered to her maid. I was coming out this way anyhow to see you, so I said I'd do it.'

'Lass? You mean you were running an errand for Barbara Kemble?'

'That's about the size of it.'

'Amos, what have you been doing?'

He took a few steps before answering. 'Well, it's a little bit of a story.'

NINETEEN

I heard most of it next morning, when we were riding back down-hill towards Cheltenham, Tabby perched behind Amos on the big skewbald cob he'd borrowed from somewhere. The night before he'd had supper in the kitchen and slept in the hayloft, another puzzle for Mr Godwit, who by now was dazed almost beyond questions and harassed by preparations for the formal opening of Gloucester assizes next day. The three of us set out after breakfast on a fine morning.

'So, it was follow the horse,' Amos said. 'I came back on Monday by way of Ledbury and had another little talk with the man who was trying to use Paley's thoroughbred to pull a cart. As I guessed, he knew the fellow he'd had it off better than he wanted me to think he did, in payment of a debt for some weaners he'd had off him, and, as it turned out, the other fellow had a half-brother who worked at a farm not far off the racecourse here, so that begged the question of why he'd gone all the way out to Ledbury to sell a good horse, but then the brother's not what you'd call a full peal of bells . . .'

I rode close and half listened, knowing Amos wouldn't be hurried and we'd have to go through this trail of doubtful horse dealing until we came to what mattered. It had a calming effect after the alarms of the night before, like the buzzing of the bees in the traveller's joy that looped the hedges we rode past.

'Any road, I came back here and went to the farm where the brother worked, and got the story out of him, promising I wouldn't make trouble for him if he told me. He and a friend were out poaching rabbits early one morning, middle of last month, and there's this horse grazing by a path, reins broken and saddle gone. I daresay the horse had rolled until the girth buckles broke. Some of them will. He had enough sense to realize it must belong to somebody, but he says the friend persuaded him to take it over to his brother to sell and split the money. Which they did, though there wasn't a lot left to split after the cut the brother took out of it. So I say goodbye and thank you to my man and start thinking. The only reason for a good horse like that to be wandering on its own is that the rider's come to harm. And the most likely way for a rider to come to harm is by falling off at a jump.'

'The reapers saw him galloping across a stubble field half a mile from the racecourse,' I said.

'Some fields have stone walls in these parts and a half-mile is a long way for a horse to gallop that's already had a race.'

'So young Paley came a cropper?' I said.

'Must have. But all he remembers of it is waking up with his head against the wall, sun high up in the sky, bird shit on his face and no horse.'

'He told you this himself?'

'He did. He says he was lying there for a long time even after he came to, not capable of moving. He'd hit his head a right crack, broken a leg and a few ribs for good measure, plus his nose had bled and there were bramble scratches all over his face. As the sun starts to go down, it occurs to him that he'll be dead if he spends the night outside as he is, so he manages to get himself upright against the wall and then drags himself along to a farm track, with his nose starting to bleed again. By the time the old fellow found him, he must have looked like something escaped from the slaughterhouse.'

Even though I had no particular feeling for young Paley, I couldn't help wincing at Amos's breezy account of it.

'So he was found. Why didn't he get word to his father?'

'From what he says, and I'm inclined to believe him, he wasn't capable of anything for a week or more. The old fellow manages to get him along to the cottage where he lives – more of a hovel by the sound of it – and then Paley passes out again. He comes to, lying on an old sheepskin on a plank with a sheepdog licking his face. His leg's been put in a splint, quite handily all things considered, and he feels as if he's been asleep for a hundred years, though it probably wasn't more than a few days. He's still not capable of doing anything, but he says the old fellow looks after him as well as he can, considering he must be around eighty years old, bent double with arthritis, and a cleft palate so Paley can't make out half the things he's saying. Not that he says a lot. He feeds Paley on oatmeal porridge and boiled turnips, which is all he has to eat himself, and slowly but surely he returns to the land of the living. By then he's had the chance to do some thinking.'

'Not before time,' I said.

'You could say so. He works out that half of his plan's gone pretty well right, though not the way he intended it. He's disappeared and his father will be starting to get worried about him. But the other half of it's not going well at all.'

'You mean eloping with Barbara Kemble?'

He glanced sideways at me. 'You knew about that, then?'

'Yes, but too late. So the plan from the start was that she should join him?'

'Yes. He was going to ride the horse to London, sell it, arrange the special licence, the clergyman and so on, and then send word for her to come and meet him.'

'To London, on her own?'

'There was a friend of his supposed to be bringing her.'

'Name of Postboy?'

'That's the one. The idea was that his father would be pleased when he heard about the marriage, because the girl's a good match, all things considered, and her father would just have to put up with it. So there he'd be, blushing bride on his arm, debts paid off by dad, all songbirds and rose petals. And thinking it over, it still seemed to him a good idea in spite of what had happened. The problem was letting his friend know where he was. There was nothing like pen and ink available, and in any case the old fellow never went more than three fields away from where he lived, so it was no use asking him to carry a message. So that was the state of affairs when I found him.'

'And how exactly did you manage that?'

He smiled, not trying to hide the fact that he was pleased with himself. 'Wasn't difficult, once I'd worked back to where the horse had been found in the first place. I got the lad to take me to exactly where they'd first seen him, and stood there for a bit to get my mind on how a horse would see things. Once you've done that, you can take a fair guess at where he'd have to have been to get to where he was. I'd guessed by then that the rider must have taken a pretty bad tumble, so I walked round the fields, having a look where it might have happened. There was a wall with hoofprints on the take-off side, a bit smudged but you could see where he'd skidded going into it. Then there were a couple of stone blocks on the other side he'd dislodged and the brambles flattened down from a man and a horse landing on top of them. From there it was just a matter of looking round to see where a badly hurt man might have been taken, and there weren't many houses in that part of the country.'

All this a month after it happened. Amos had reason to be pleased with himself, but he still had some explaining to do.

'So you found Peter Paley,' I said. 'Why didn't you tell his father? Why didn't you tell me?'

'I sent a message to his father as soon as I found him, letting him know he was all right. I couldn't do more than that without breaking my word.'

'And what about me?'

He seemed surprised at the hurt in my voice. 'I thought you'd have worked it out. Then, when I saw you talking to Postboy and his friends, I was sure you had.'

I thought sadly that this was a measure of the distance that had already grown between us.

'And you gave your word to Peter Paley to say nothing. You've even been helping him with his plans to elope. Why?'

He was crestfallen now. He'd brought his triumph to me and I was spoiling it.

'I was sorry for him, I suppose. He was so pleased to see me, after all that time on his own with the old fellow. And he was worried about his horse and his young lady.'

'Was he now? Which of them did he ask after first?'

Amos looked away. 'I can't rightly remember.'

So I had my answer. Not that Amos would have thought any the worse of him for it.

'He asked you to help him, and you agreed?'

'Not straight away. My first idea was to get him back home. Then he told me the story of how he'd let his young lady down and she'd be mad with worry, not knowing if he was dead or alive. So, in the end, I agreed I'd fetch his friend, the one they call Postboy. He and young Paley and I talked it over. Paley was dead against going straight home before the business with the young lady was settled. Postboy knew of this old farmhouse up in the hills where he'd camped out sometimes when he needed to get away from the duns. Paley's leg was set enough to be moved by now, so we fetched a cart and took him over there.'

'I hope he said thank you to the old man.'

'He did, fair enough, and left him the money he had in his pocket. It wasn't a lot, and from the look on the old fellow's face it was as much use to him as teacups to a camel. Still, it showed willing.'

We were close to Cheltenham by now, the horses walking out

easily, Tabby leaning forward round Amos's back, so as not to miss a word of the conversation.

'And you agreed to collect Barbara Kemble's trunk,' I said. 'Weren't they lucky, having you to help with their elopement plans?'

I knew I sounded bitter, but I couldn't forget the long hours of panic and the useless search for Barbara. I thought I could guess why Amos had fallen in with the plan so readily. The prospect of his marriage had made a romantic of him.

'The fact is we did get galloped away with,' Amos said defensively.

'Oh?'

'The arrangement was that Postboy should carry a letter to Miss Kemble from young Paley, letting her know the situation. We'd agreed that he'd wait until he heard back from her and then let his father know what was happening. Only she didn't wait. She wrote straight back to Postboy, saying she was running away and to meet her at a certain house in town on Monday. It was the Sunday by the time we got the message and there was no stopping her.'

'The house?'

'Where one of her friends lives.'

Near her dressmaker, I guessed. And the comings and goings of Postboy in a variety of vehicles would have caused no comment in Cheltenham. Had Barbara been hiding under a rug on the back seat of a carriage? No matter. She'd thoroughly outmanoeuvred me.

'So, where is Barbara Kemble now?' I said.

'Up in the old farmhouse, with young Paley.'

I said nothing to that. Her reputation was well and truly gone now.

'Respectable, like,' Amos said. 'She sleeps upstairs; he's downstairs on account of the leg.'

'The perfect knight,' I said sarcastically. 'His drawn sword between them.'

'And me sleeping on the landing,' Amos said.

I said things couldn't go on as they were and we'd have to let both fathers know, whether the two young troublemakers liked it or not. Amos didn't argue. You could see that the responsibility had been weighing on him. In Peter Paley's case, there'd be little harm done. His father seemed prepared to accept things. Barbara was another matter. I supposed she'd have to marry Paley, which was what she'd wanted all along – or perhaps only convinced herself she wanted. But it was too late to worry about that now. The problem was that there might be yet another family grief confronting her.

'We have to decide what to do about her brother,' I said.

'He'll calm down in the end,' Amos said.

He sounded remarkably tolerant about a man who'd recently been chasing him with a shotgun, but then he didn't know the full story. I told him as concisely as I could, but even so we'd reached the town centre by the time I'd finished.

'So you think he killed the governess. What are you going to do about it?'

'I don't know. In all honesty, I just don't know. When I asked him to meet me where she died, I hoped I might jolt him into admitting it.'

'Not likely, was it?'

'What else was I to do? The trial's three days away. There's no hope of getting convincing evidence in that time.'

'Even if you could, would you want to hang the poor lass's brother?'

Clearly, Barbara had been working her charms on this newly susceptible Amos. The misfortune of Joanna Picton and the bravery of Mary Marsh weren't as stark in his mind as in mine.

'If I could only get him to admit to fathering Joanna's child, it might be something,' I said. 'At least we might be able to stop Picton damaging his case in court even more by naming the wrong man.'

I could see from Amos's expression that he thought it was a faint hope, and he was right. His mind was still on the eloping couple. We'd agreed that we should go straight up to the farmhouse and talk sense to them. It was up a track just past the beer house where Amos had collected the trunk, so we turned on to the road out of town.

'Whatever they decide to do, I want a chance to talk to Peter Paley,' I said. 'He was right at the centre of what happened at the fair. He might have some idea of what became of Joanna after she was arrested. He has no reason to like Rodney Kemble. If he'd seen him taking Joanna off on her own, he'd surely say so.'

'He hasn't up to now.'

'Because nobody's asked him up to now. Nobody in all this has cared enough about Joanna to worry, except Mary Marsh.'

'She'll be nearly there by now,' Amos said. 'Three months, it takes them.' I glanced at him, surprised he should know. Three months to Van Diemen's Land. 'I've heard some people do all right there.' He was looking between the ears of the skewbald cob as he spoke. 'New country, good climate. She might even find somebody and marry.'

He was trying to console me and, by implication, telling me to stop worrying about something I could do nothing to alter. It was good advice. I might have no choice but to take it.

We said nothing else until we came within sight of the farmhouse, a tumbledown place in a dip, with a wavering line of smoke rising from the chimney.

Amos slid off the cob and helped Tabby and me down.

'I'd best go in first and warn them they've got visitors.'

We gave him a few minutes and followed. Peter Paley was on a bed by the wall. The bedstead was carved oak and might have been handsome a hundred years ago, before the woodworm got to it. The man lying on it, propped up on one elbow against a rough pillow, might have been handsome more recently. He had the same square head and dark hair as his father, but his hair was dull and dusty, his skin tightly stretched over the bones with a greyish look. Weeks of confinement indoors and a diet of oatmeal and turnips do nothing for a person's complexion. He'd been shaved quite recently – by Amos perhaps – but bristles were beginning to show. Somebody had managed to find him a shirt that was still reasonably clean and a pair of old loose trousers, slit up to the knee on the left leg to accommodate the splint. He made some effort to stand up when I came in, reaching for an ash stick propped beside the bed.

'It's all right,' I said. 'How is your leg?'

I hadn't intended to show any sympathy, but he looked so thin and apprehensive. I guessed Amos had told him who I was, so he'd know about my connection with Barbara.

'Mending, I think. But I suppose I'll always walk with a limp now.'

I think he was trying to be stoic, but he sounded like a regretful boy, aware for the first time in his life that some things went wrong that could never be put right.

'Where's Miss Kemble?' I said.

'Upstairs.'

'She bolted up there when she knew you were here,' Amos said.

He'd stoked up the fire and was bending to tidy the grate. 'I don't think she wants to face you.'

'I'll go up to her later,' I said. 'I want to talk to Mr Paley first.'

'Miss Lane, will you please do something for me?' Peter Paley said. He spoke urgently, like a man galloping too fast at a fence. 'Will you go to Barbara's father and tell him that he has nothing to reproach her for? She is still exactly the virtuous and dutiful daughter that she was when she left his house.'

He must have spent the last few minutes working out a delicate way to put it.

'We'll discuss all that later,' I said. 'There are some things I want to ask you first.'

Peter Paley subsided back on the bed. Amos glanced at me and the open door, asking if I wanted him to leave us alone. I shook my head. Tabby would be listening outside, in any case. There was a rough stool by the wall. I pulled it up and sat beside the bed.

'I'd like you to think back two years,' I said. 'To the Cheltenham race fair the year before last.'

His face twisted and he groaned, possibly from pain in his leg because he'd moved sharply. 'Not that again. It's poisonous gossip from people who hate my father and me.'

'I know,' I said. 'I've spoken to your father. He's quite certain you did not father Joanna Picton's child.'

His mouth opened and he looked up at the ceiling, panic-stricken, though I was speaking quite softly.

'You haven't discussed all that with Barbara, then?' I said.

'She knows there have been unjust rumours. She believes in me.'

'All the same, she might not like to hear you were kissing and playing forfeits with a drunk scullery-maid.'

He glanced at Amos's back, as if appealing man to man for help, but Amos was busy with brush and pan.

'I was much younger then. There were a lot of us. It wasn't only me.'

I took pity on him. 'It's not that I want to talk about. It's what happened afterwards.'

'Squaring up to Kemble, you mean?'

'That for a start. Why?'

'It . . . it was about the girl. He got the wrong idea. I should have tried to explain, I suppose, but the others were cheering me on and before I knew it . . . well, you can't back down, can you?'

'But you didn't fight.'

'We didn't get the chance. Police, magistrates and clergymen all over the place.'

'And Joanna Picton was arrested.'

'That wasn't my fault. They rounded up everybody who couldn't run fast enough.'

'But you could run fast enough. So, I suppose, could Rodney Kemble. He wasn't arrested either.'

He smiled for the first time. The smile had a touch of malice in it. I waited till it faded, knowing the next answer might go a long way towards proving my theory.

'Did you happen to notice which way Rodney Kemble went?'

This time he actually laughed. 'Did I notice? We all noticed. Back to his daddy, fast as a ferret down a rabbit hole.'

'What do you mean?'

'After we'd all got back together and found none of us had been picked up, some of them were egging me on to find Kemble and have the fight elsewhere. There were quite a few bets riding on it. All for me to win, of course; it was just a question of what round I floored him in. Only he didn't wait. We spotted him at the bottom of the hill, riding at a good canter for home.'

Confidence had come back in his voice as he was telling the story, making him the swaggering boy again.

'You're sure it was him?'

'Certain. He was riding a showy grey you'd spot three fields away, and in his shirtsleeves because he'd taken off his jacket when he thought he was going to fight me and he'd not stopped to pick it up again. He must have lit off the first instant he got a whiff of Holy Fanny and the rest. We hallooed after him, but he was too far away to hear.'

'And the women and the others who'd been arrested, where were they at the time?' I said.

He had to think about that, puzzled as to why I should want to know. 'They'd got them herded into two carts by then – men in one, women in the other. Then they rolled away downhill into town. I remember somebody saying there'd never be room in the lock-up for the lot of them.'

'Was Joanna in the women's cart when it went away?'

'Yes. She . . . she was being sick over the side. Some of the other women were laughing at her.'

Perhaps there was the slightest hint of shame in the way he said it, or more likely I imagined it because I wanted it to be there. The man who'd kissed and laughed with her wanted nothing more to do with her. Her employer's son had ridden off and left her as soon as his blood cooled and he realized he'd made a fool of himself in public. To be honest, though, my sorrow at that moment was less for Joanna than for the collapse of my theory. Rodney Kemble had not rescued Joanna from arrest and then brutally claimed his reward. She was in the cart under police guard when it rolled away. Some hours later she'd arrived back at her place of work, exhausted and distressed. In the last few minutes before she began her journey to the other side of the world, she'd told one person what had happened in those hours, and that person was dead.

I probably sat there, saying nothing, for some time, because Amos broke the silence.

'Are you thinking of going upstairs and seeing the lass?'

I climbed a flight of stairs so steep that it was more like a ladder and pushed open the one door leading off the landing. The room inside was so steeply triangular that it was just possible to stand upright on one side of it, and the opposite side had space for a window no more than eighteen inches high. It had so many timbers that it was like being on board a ship. Within it, Barbara had made a kind of disorderly cave of the things from her trunk, with dresses in a rainbow of colours hanging from nails in the walls, shawls heaped on the low pallet bed. A bonnet was tied round one beam by its green ribbons. A range of cut-glass jars and small silver containers, including the toilet water flask, ran along the top of another beam. The contrast between the things Barbara had thought she'd need on her elopement and the place where they'd ended up was pitiful. She sat on the bed, face pale among all the colours, looking at me with an expression halfway between defiance and tears. I waited for her to speak.

'Is my father very angry?'

'What do you think?'

'I had no choice. They shouldn't have tried to keep me away from Peter.'

'So, what do you intend to do now?' I said.

Her mouth opened but she said nothing. She hadn't expected the question. She hadn't thought beyond her great romantic decision to all the lesser ones that would follow. There were round red marks on her arms that looked like flea bites. She started scratching, looked at me and then let her hand drop.

'Do?' she said at last.

'Are you planning to set up house here?'

The look she gave me was answer enough.

'Well, then?' I said.

'Are you going to tell my father where I am?' From her voice, she more than half wanted that. When I nodded, the look on her face was first relief, then apprehension.

'It's only fair to him,' I said. 'He's at least as much worried as angry.'

'What about Peter?'

'He'll have to go back to his father, too. Apart from anything else, he needs a doctor.'

'They can't keep us apart. We love each other.'

She looked me in the eye. It had been a simple statement, with none of the drama or attitudinizing I'd have expected from her. For once she wasn't concerned with the impression she was making.

'Yes, I believe you do,' I said.

If love had survived seeing Peter as he looked now, and three or four days without a maid, warm water and a looking glass, then it was more than a passing fancy.

'My father must accept that we're engaged or I'm not going back. You'll tell him?'

'I'll tell him.'

I didn't add that there'd be no choice about it. After what had happened, she'd have been forced to marry Peter even if they fought like Kilkenny cats all the way to the altar.

I suggested that we should join the others. As I was turning towards the stairs, I noticed a book on the beam, among the toiletries. I looked more closely, curious to know what Barbara had chosen to bring with her. No visible title, but something familiar about it. It took me some moments to realize that it was similar to the letter books I'd found in Mary Marsh's desk. I picked it up and opened it. There were no letters pasted inside, but pages covered with Mary's handwriting and some rough sketches. Barbara's eyes were on it when I looked up.

'She wouldn't have minded. She wrote it for me.' She stood up, took the book from me and opened it. 'There. Read it if you want to.'

It was a poem, spread across a double page, headed 'On a Young Lady's Engagement to be Married' – a clever epithalamium in the Elizabethan style, witty and tender, butterflies and swallows sketched in the margins.

'She wrote it for me when Peter and I were first engaged,' Barbara said. 'She copied it out on a scroll tied with pink and white ribbons. I wanted to bring it with me, but in the hurry of packing I couldn't find it. I knew she always kept a copy of things, so I went and took the book from her room. She'd have wanted me to have it.'

'May I borrow this, please?' I said.

Barbara was torn. She wanted to please me, but the poem was clearly precious to her.

'I'll be very careful of it,' I promised.

She nodded reluctantly.

We went downstairs and she sat by Peter's bed as if he needed protecting. He took her hand and smiled at her, trying to be reassuring. When I said that Barbara's father must be told, he accepted it without question. Amos had probably been saying much the same to him while we were upstairs. It was settled that I should ride Rancie to the Kembles with the news. Amos would come with me as far as the Paleys' house with a similar message for Peter's father. We anticipated that both parties would come and collect their elopers as soon as horses could be harnessed. Tabby would stay at the farmhouse with them until we came back, an arrangement that didn't please her at all.

'What am I supposed to do here?'

My suggestion that she might help Barbara with her packing received the reception I'd expected.

Amos and I rode back down to the main road, with Mary Marsh's book tucked into my saddle bag.

'So it wasn't the lass's brother, after all,' Amos said. He sounded glad about it.

'No. There's not a doubt about Peter's story. He doesn't like Rodney Kemble and he had no notion that he was helping him when he told it. Whatever happened to Joanna Picton after the fair had nothing to do with Rodney Kemble.'

A cart crowded with women had rolled away, downhill to the

town gaol. Some of the women would have been drunk, some defiant, one at least physically sick. Around them, all the apparatus of authority – police, church, magistrates. Mary Marsh had come away from her last meeting with Joanna with one word on her mind. Hypocrisy. It had even more force now.

TWENTY

Once we were down the hill and on the more level road back into town, I took out the book. Rancie's walking pace was so smooth that there was no difficulty in reading as we went along. It wasn't a letter book like the others, rather a place where she made random notes or drafted things that she'd later write out as fair copies, like the poem for Barbara. I skimmed through, looking for references to Joanna or Jack Picton, but had found none by the time we came to the Paleys' house.

'Will you be all right on your own?' Amos said. 'If you wanted to wait, we could ride out together – just in case the brother gets okkerd again.'

'I don't think he will. We've found his sister for him, after all. You'll be needed back at the farmhouse, seeing the two of them on their ways.'

He nodded. One of the many good things about Amos was that he didn't fuss. We agreed to meet later at the Star. I put the letter book back in my saddlebag as Rancie and I rode through the town, but took it out again when we were on the road back to the village. For the first mile or so, we ambled along and I read without result to what looked like the last jottings in the book, with nothing but blank pages behind. I was closing it to put in my saddlebag when something caught my eye. It started several pages after what had looked like the last entry, which was why I'd almost missed it. It was unmistakably Mary Marsh's hand, though not her usual writing. Normally, even in the jottings, she was neat. This was not neat at all. Two facing pages were seamed with crossings-out, like a badly darned stocking, measled with small ink spots where her pen nib had sputtered from being pressed too hard. Sometimes the words were thickly inked, sometimes so thin that they were scarcely readable, as if she'd grudged the time needed to put pen to inkwell. It was so difficult to read that I brought Rancie to a halt. Then, once I'd made sense of it, we were away at a pace that must have delighted her heart, making for the Kembles' house. The hedges passed in a blur and the rhythm of her hooves kept a drumbeat accompaniment to my anger.

We walked the last mile, to cool Rancie down and for me to get my thoughts in order. The first thing was to deliver the news about Barbara, and it was a relief when Colonel Kemble appeared on the steps so promptly that he must have been watching from a window. I tried to report as factually and unemotionally as I could, like a junior officer with dispatches, repeating word for word what Peter Paley had said. He responded in kind, nodding quickly now and then, giving nothing away by his expression. When I'd finished, he said: 'Well, we'd better go and fetch her, hadn't we?'

He was speaking to his son as well as to me, because by then Rodney was standing in the hallway behind him.

'I'll go,' Rodney said. 'I'll take the brougham.' He was trying to seem as much in control as his father, but less successfully.

The colonel nodded. If Barbara could be brought home without attracting too much attention, then the damage might be limited. Some story might be concocted that she'd gone to stay with friends and a message telling her father had been unaccountably lost. Nobody would believe it, but the decencies would be preserved. If that was in the colonel's mind, he gave no sign of it. He even remembered to thank me and ask if I'd care to come in.

'I think I should go with the brougham,' I said. 'Barbara might like to have another woman there.'

He nodded again. By now Rodney had disappeared, presumably for the stable block by way of a back door. I rode Rancie in the same direction, rein loose and at a walk. The stable yard was in confusion. The horse that drew the brougham was out at pasture and a groom had been sent running for it. Another groom and a boy were dragging the brougham out of the carriage house, with Rodney looking on impatiently. I slid off Rancie and walked over to him, leading her.

'I need to talk to you,' I said. 'About Mary Marsh.'

He turned, looking furious. 'Not now.'

'It won't wait. I have a letter to you from her.'

'A letter?'

It unbalanced him. There was more fear than anger in his face now.

'Her last letter.'

'Where did you get it?'

I opened the saddlebag and gave him her book, open at the right pages. He glanced from it to me, seeming reluctant to look at it.

Then he looked down at last and read, standing as still as the mounting block beside us.

'It's not addressed to me,' he said at last, sounding dazed.

'Not by name, no. But who else could it be?'

He nodded.

By now the groom was back with the horse, but it had been rolling and its flanks were clotted with dried mud. One man started on it with the dandy brush while another picked out its hooves.

'It will take them a while,' I said. 'Is there somewhere else we can talk?'

He led the way into an empty loose box. Since there was nobody free to hold Rancie, we both followed him. He leaned against the hay manger and read the letter again, squinting in the dim light.

'I never saw it. Not until now,' he said.

'No. She didn't send it. You can see what an effort it was for her to write the draft. In the end she decided it would do no good.'

The reasons for that decision were in the letter that she'd never sent. She wrote that she'd asked him for help once before and he'd felt unable to give it. She'd been angry and she was sorry for that. It was as painful for her as it must be for him to revisit something that had hurt them both so deeply, and it was only under the harshest necessity that she did so now.

'It is to you, isn't it?' I said.

His reluctant nod confirmed it. 'She didn't send it because she thought I wouldn't help her,' he said.

His voice was as flat and level as a slab on a grave. I could have recited by heart the passage in her letter which he was probably rereading now:

> There are two things which I must tell you now. The first is that your caution when I first spoke to you on this subject – a caution which I so much derided at the time – has been proved right. The gentleman I named to you then is entirely innocent of the cruelty of which I accused him. I now know *for certain* the father of Joanna's child. I had it from her own lips. She never spoke until the last because he had convinced her that her only hope of rescue lay in keeping silent. When she discovered that he'd never intended help at all, she broke that silence. The second thing I must tell you is his name. He thinks the respect in which he is held and his high place in

the community protects him from exposure. I am determined
to prove him wrong. I know that I have forfeited any personal
claim on your help in this by my previous hastiness and my
unkindness to you. So what I may not ask you for my sake, I
can only ask in the name of justice.

He looked up at me. Something had changed in his eyes.
'So she accused him to his face and he killed her?' he said.
'Yes.'
I waited. Rancie nuzzled at my shoulder. The voices and shifting
hooves from the yard seemed to be coming from another world. I
thought: 'Suppose she had sent it, what would you have done?' I
wouldn't ask him.
'So what are we going to do?' he said.
I told him the outlines of what I was planning. He asked if I
needed him to be there. I said no, but afterwards there would be a
time when he'd need to speak out, in court even. He nodded,
accepting it. At some point he closed the book and handed it back
to me. The head groom came and looked over the door.
'Brougham ready when you are, Mr Kemble.'
Rodney was all activity, arranging for a groom to come and look
after Rancie, springing on to the driving seat of the brougham.
'Are you coming with me, Miss Lane?'
When I said yes, one groom opened the door and another helped
me in, though I didn't need it. No question of riding beside Mr
Kemble in the driving seat. To his credit, he drove well into town
and through it, though fast. I had to lean out of the window to direct
him to the old farmhouse. When we got there, I jumped out as soon
as the wheels stopped turning and went inside to warn Barbara that
we were there. The reunion between brother and sister was witnessed
by me inside the room and Tabby listening at the door. Amos was
keeping Peter Paley company in the garden, since his last meeting
with Rodney Kemble had not been on cordial terms. Rodney and
Barbara were as formal as a pair of ambassadors sealing an uneasy
truce.
'I'm taking you home,' he said.
'For now,' she said.
As arranged, Peter Paley limped in from the garden, leaning
heavily on his ash stick.
'Hello, Kemble,' he said, not very hopefully.

Rodney ignored him and spoke to his sister.

'Have you got your things?'

'It's only for a few weeks,' Barbara informed her brother. 'Peter and I are going to be married very soon.'

'Are you coming back with us, Miss Lane?' Rodney said to me.

Barbara ran to me and took my hand. 'Do, please.'

So we all went back together, Barbara and me inside, her trunk strapped on the back and Tabby sitting on the trunk. When we drew up outside the Kembles' house, Barbara clung to me, wanting me to go in with her and face her father. When I told her he wouldn't want a stranger there, she accepted it, rearranged her hair and bonnet and went up the steps and inside with the air of a young aristocrat going to the guillotine. Tabby and I stayed on board until we reached the stable yard and Rodney got down. He still had the look of a man picked up by a whirlwind and set down again.

'You'll tell me what happens?' he said.

I promised. Rancie was well rested by now and Tabby rode behind me the short distance back to Mr Godwit's house. It was almost dinner time, so I washed, changed, ate steak and kidney pie and raspberries and cream, discussed his theories about the migrations of birds. It was only fair to give him one calm hour, because after dinner I was going to do something that would shatter his peace more thoroughly than anything that had gone before. He'd introduced himself to me as a coward. Now I was going to ask him to be a hero.

TWENTY-ONE

The start of the assizes is like some pilgrimage in the Middle Ages, with people converging from all directions on a cathedral city. The two judges – on a circuit of the shires to try cases too serious for the local magistrates – had started from Oxford and travelled westwards over the Cotswolds, into Wales and back to Gloucester, with their entourage of clerks, chaplain, valets and servants. From various points in the county, the high sheriff and his party, senior officers of the constabulary, mayors, magistrates and beadles shook mothballs out of their ceremonial robes, burnished maces and chains of office and came to the city to welcome the judges. The reasons for all this pageantry – ninety-three reasons – did not have so far to travel. They were where they'd been for weeks or months past, in the prison between the cathedral and the river, waiting for their few hours at the assizes. Our part in the pilgrimage was small and nervous. Even at the best of times, a journey away from home to stay overnight was a serious undertaking for Mr Godwit. As it was, with the burden he now carried and his apprehension about what he had to do at the journey's end, he delayed our start by an hour or more.

The judges were to make their formal entrance to the city on Saturday evening, and Mr Godwit was obliged to be there with his fellow magistrates in good time for their arrival. Well after midday on Saturday, the gig was still waiting outside his house, with the cob in the shafts and the driver in his seat. Three or four times Mr Godwit had put his foot on the step to get in but then remembered something important he must tell his housekeeper or gardener. After issuing detailed instructions on the spaniel's supper, he caught my eye.

'We should be going, I suppose.'

If I'd been a gaoler escorting him to the dock, the look he gave me would have been much the same. I said I'd meet him at the hotel in Gloucester and went over to where Rancie was waiting in the shade of a tree. By now Tabby was well gone. I'd sent her down to Cheltenham straight after breakfast, to deliver a note to Amos at the Star. I hoped she'd still find him there, even though I hadn't kept my appointment with him the day before. The note said simply that there had been developments in the case and I needed to talk to him. Tabby was to wait, and I'd be with them as soon as I could. For the last hour I'd been almost mad with impatience, but I had to make sure that Mr Godwit was launched on his journey with no chance of retreat.

Once the gig had rolled out of the gate and into the road, it was an easy matter to pass it and we made the journey to town in about half the time Mr Godwit would take. As I hoped, Amos and Tabby were waiting in the yard at the Star. They were both drinking beer. Tabby preferred gin and hot water but would make do with what was offered. I dismounted and, while Rancie drank at the trough, I told Amos how things stood and what I proposed to do about them.

'We'll be getting started, then,' he said.

'You'll be needed back home, won't you?'

'Nothing that won't keep.'

I decided not to ask questions, more relieved than I cared to show that he'd be with me this last time. The skewbald cob was already tacked up in one of the boxes. We both mounted, Tabby hopped up behind Amos and we joined the pilgrimage to the assizes. The road was busy, but we managed to ride side by side for long enough to discuss the plan. Amos was worried that so much of it relied on Mr Godwit.

'He's a nice enough old gentleman, but no fighting cock.'

'He doesn't need to be, especially now you'll be here, too. All he has to do is keep his nerve.'

'And what if your man doesn't take the bait?'

'Then it will be my own fault for not placing it properly.'

But in truth that was what worried me most, especially since the details couldn't be planned in advance. We came to Gloucester well ahead of Mr Godwit and found the hotel in Southgate where the Cheltenham contingent would be staying. The first problem was persuading them to find me a room. They were full almost to the rafters, but eventually an attic chamber at the back was offered. My maid would have to share a double bed in an even smaller room with two others. I nodded to that, knowing that Tabby would choose to sleep on the floor of my room. It didn't matter greatly since neither of us was likely to spend much time asleep. Amos had disappeared by then. He'd be finding somebody he knew in the stable yard to ensure accommodation for the horses and himself.

I washed in the grudging pint of lukewarm water that was all the
hotel would provide, changed into the dull but respectable blue
cotton twill I'd brought along in my saddle bag and went down to
meet Mr Godwit. He arrived two hours later and in a flurry, with
little time to change before the ceremony of welcome for the judges.
I waited and walked with him the short distance to the Shirehall.
A small crowd had gathered outside, watching the worthies assembling on the steps in front of the Ionic columns that made the
building look like a cramped Greek temple. The high sheriff and
his party were at the centre, flanked by the city mayor and a platoon
of clergymen, sleek as magpies in their black cassocks and white
neckbands. A court usher waited beside the mayor, clutching two
incongruous posies of rosebuds, lad's love and sprigs of rosemary.
They were for the judges – a relict of the days when they held
bunches of herbs in front of their noses to keep off the plague germs
that showed no respect for anybody. A large group of magistrates
stood to one side of the clergymen. Mr Crow noticed us, gave a
cheery wave quite out of keeping with the dignity of the occasion
and signed to Mr Godwit that he should come and stand between
himself and Penbrake.

'I'll see you later, back at the hotel,' I said to Mr Godwit.

He walked towards the others steadily enough and took his place
with his fellow magistrates. That much achieved, at least. As it
turned out, only one judge arrived to be welcomed. The other had
been detained by business left over from last week's assizes in
Monmouth. Speeches were made, a posy presented and then they
all went inside for the official opening of the session.

I stayed outside, with an errand to do. I'd managed to find out
from Mr Godwit that the lawyers, regular as house martins in their
roosting habits, usually stayed at the Booth Hall Hotel, conveniently
close to the Shirehall. A polite inquiry to the first legal-looking
gentleman I saw in the lobby produced the name of the barrister
who'd be defending Jack Picton on Monday. I found out later that
his nickname on the circuit was St Jude, from his habit of repre-
senting hopeless cases. In spite of that, he was a pleasant and
humorous man, with the long face and ruminative eyes of a moorland
sheep. If he'd been wearing his wig, the resemblance would have
been complete. We talked in the hotel's coffee room. He hadn't yet
met Picton but knew from the papers on the case that he'd be dealing
with a more than usually awkward client. I explained my interest

as briefly as I could, without bringing Mr Godwit into it by name, and asked when he planned to see Picton.

'I'm hoping they'll let me talk to him early tomorrow, before the prisoners go in to chapel. If not, it will be in the court cells on Monday.'

'There's something I'd be grateful if you'd put to him,' I said. 'It explains why he won't talk about what happened on the night of the murder, and why he's sure somebody was trying to trap him.'

The lawyer sighed. 'I shall try to discourage him from talking about this trap idea. It sounds too much like flailing around in desperation.'

'There was no trap,' I said. 'But there was a good reason why he thought there was. He had probably received a note from Mary Marsh asking him to meet her in the woods that night.'

'Probably, you say. But I gather there's no proof of that. He didn't keep the note.'

'No. Trust him not to do anything so useful. But let's take this as a hypothesis. He goes to meet her. He probably gets there early. While he's hidden and waiting, he sees somebody else near the house, behaving furtively. That man is so well connected in the local community that Picton concludes that he's part of a plot to trap him in some illegality. He runs away and hides.'

The lawyer looked at me like a sheep at a patch of moss where it had half hoped to find grass.

'Leaving Miss Marsh to be murdered?'

'He had no idea she was in danger. By then he'd probably convinced himself that she was part of the plot.'

'Giving him a motive to kill her?'

'Somebody else had a much better motive. Mary Marsh knew something that the other person wanted to conceal at all costs.'

'Hypothesis,' he said wearily. 'No proof. The jury won't like it.'

I'd decided in advance not to tell him the whole story yet. Lawyers were discreet, but, in a city surging with them, gossip would circulate.

'There's a way of testing it,' I said. 'If you see Picton tomorrow, I'd like you to tell him what I've just told you and then mention a name to him. See how he reacts.'

'The name?'

I told him. It meant nothing to him, but then he wasn't from this part of the world. He agreed to mention it, but I could tell he was only doing it to avoid an argument, not from conviction.

'May I meet you here this time tomorrow?' I said. 'I hope to have more to tell you.'

He said, gallantly, that it would be a pleasure, but I could see he expected nothing from it. Another assizes, another hopeless case.

Back at our hotel, the party from Cheltenham was sitting down to a late supper in the dining room. Voices grew louder as the gentlemen relaxed from formality and moved rapidly through roast beef and claret to dessert and then port. I didn't join them. I'd have been the only woman in the room and didn't want to be conspicuous. It was a different matter when they moved to the room next door to take coffee. A distant female relative of one of their number might properly join them there. Mr Crow noticed me first and roared out a welcome in a voice that would have carried over a battle at sea. His invitation, 'Come and sit beside me, my dear,' must have been heard by everybody in the room. He gestured with his ear trumpet at the space next to him on the sofa, stood up to welcome me and then sat down beside me.

'So, what is a lovely young lady like you doing with tedious old gentlemen like us?'

That brought glares from several gentlemen around him, but he couldn't be quelled or ignored.

'Business at court,' I said, smiling at him.

He laughed as if it were an excellent joke and repeated it at the top of his voice, just in case anybody in the room had missed it.

'Business at court. Are you going to dress yourself up as a barrister, like whatsername in that play?'

'Do you think I'd make a good one?' I said.

'Sure of it. With you pleading for him, there's not a juryman in the land wouldn't find Cain himself not guilty.' He repeated 'Cain himself' several times, chuckling.

A couple of the clergymen were looking shocked, but the other men seemed to have decided that since there was no competing with Crow, they might as well get what entertainment they could out of him.

'Jack Picton, too?' I said.

A sudden silence in the room. Only Mr Crow seemed unaware of it.

'You're not worrying your head about that rogue, are you? He'll be dancing a jig over the gatehouse before the month's out.'

It wasn't only the clergymen who looked shocked at that.

Hanging people was all very well, but you shouldn't be indelicate about it.

'Ten to one he's found not guilty,' I said.

Jaws dropped all round us, at a lady talking like a leg. Anybody not listening to us before was listening now. Even Mr Crow looked surprised, but he recovered quickly.

'Ten to one. In pennies.' He wasn't being miserly. This was all still a joke to him and he didn't want to take my money.

'Guineas,' I said.

He took the trumpet out of his ear, shook it and put it back in again.

'Guineas?'

I moved closer to him and dropped my voice, but not too much. 'On second thoughts, I can't take your money,' I said. 'It wouldn't be sporting. You see, I know he didn't kill Mary Marsh and there's evidence to prove who did.'

'Evidence? What evidence?' Even Mr Crow had to take that seriously.

A small crowd was forming round our sofa. I pretended to be aware for the first time of the attention we were attracting and belatedly struck by discretion.

'I shouldn't be talking about it, should I? Mr Godwit has it. He's taking it to Picton's barrister tomorrow, after church. I expect he'll tell you.'

I stood up, wished Mr Crow goodnight and left with all eyes in the room on me. Only one pair mattered. I waited in the hotel lobby. After a few minutes Mr Godwit joined me, looking worried. I suggested we should talk outside, so we went into the warm darkness and stood on the pavement. Tabby was loitering not far away.

'Well, that's the bait,' I said. 'From now until it's over, you mustn't be on your own. If you'll give me your room key, I'll wait for you up there.'

'In my room?' He sounded more alarmed at that than anything that had gone so far.

'Don't worry; you'll hardly know I'm there. I'll be on a chair by the door. You can even put a screen across if you like.'

'But what will people think?'

'If this goes as we hope, they'll have a lot more to think about tomorrow than where I spent the night. If you think we need a chaperone, Tabby will be there.'

That did not comfort him. He'd ventured a long way – further than in his worst nightmares – but on this point he was immoveable. At some point in the discussion, Tabby disappeared. She came back with a tall figure beside her.

'I'm as good a watchdog as you'll need,' Amos said out of the darkness.

Mr Godwit spun round and gasped, not recognizing his voice at first, aware only of his size.

'It's all right. I don't snore,' said Amos reassuringly.

'But . . . but where will you sleep?'

'On a rug across the inside of your door. Don't worry; I've spent many a night in the straw waiting for a mare to foal. This won't be any worse.'

So it was settled. Amos was to take off his boots and go up the servants' stairs and wait by Mr Godwit's room. Mr Godwit and I would go up the main stairs together; I'd wish him goodnight and go up a floor to the room that Tabby and I would be sharing. That arrangement meant he wasn't a moment alone. With that achieved, Tabby and I made a nest for her on the floor of our room with the counterpane and bolster from the bed and she curled up in it, fully clothed except for her shoes. I took off my dress and petticoats but kept them ready on a chair by the bed and left a candle burning on the washstand. I slept fitfully, and although Tabby didn't stir, having a cat's ability to doze anywhere as long as she was left alone, I guessed she was more awake than asleep, waiting for the outcry from downstairs that would surely come if anybody tried to get past Amos. But by the time the sky through our small window had turned from dark to grey, nothing had happened.

'He didn't come, then,' Tabby said, turning towards me.

'No. So he'll have to take his chance this morning.'

The servants were already stirring. Soon everybody would be assembling again for the morning service at the cathedral, which was the other part of the assizes opening ritual. After that we'd all be going home.

Just before eight o'clock I went down and knocked on Mr Godwit's door. It was opened by Amos, looking as spruce as if he'd slept on goose feathers and been dressed by a valet.

'Slept well, did you?' he said.

'No. I don't suppose you did, either.'

'Well enough,' Amos said.

'Not a wink,' Mr Godwit said from behind him.

I believed him. He was fully dressed for church, neat enough, but his face was pale and he'd cut his chin shaving. He and I went down to the dining room together, leaving Amos on guard in the room and Tabby foraging for breakfast for them both. Quite a few of the party from the night before were in the dining room and Mr Godwit and I received some curious looks, though nobody said anything beyond normal morning politenesses. With breakfast over, people began collecting hats, coats and gloves and strolling towards the cathedral. Bells were already pealing from its tower, over the sunlit streets and the river and the prison in between. Mr Godwit and I waited in the lobby until almost everybody had gone and then went in the same direction. Mr Godwit wanted to hurry, but I kept us to a steady walk. The peals of bells had changed to one summoning note when we reached the cathedral close and the assizes judge and his procession had just gone in as we reached the doors. The cathedral was crowded, but an usher managed to find us places on the end of a pew near the back, as I'd hoped.

It was, if you managed to concentrate on it, a splendid service. The choir and organist were as good as I'd heard anywhere. I was just aware of that, but most of my attention was elsewhere. It was hard to pick out one person from another because, apart from those in robes of office, all the men, both clergy and laity, were in various forms of black and merged together. I thought I'd identified our man near the end of a pew but couldn't be sure from the back. I kept my eyes on him, waiting for any movement. An anthem, a reading, a hymn all passed. We knelt to pray, a long list of prayers, including several for the judges, justice in general, repentance on the part of sinners. We finished praying and sat for the sermon, to be given by the high sheriff's chaplain. He mounted the pulpit and read out his chosen text slowly and sonorously. It echoed round the cathedral like a voice from a sea cave.

Proverbs chapter four, verses fourteen and fifteen. Enter not into the path of the wicked, and go not in the way of evil men. Avoid it, pass not by it, turn from it and pass away.

A shuffle of approval at the appropriate choice of text went through the congregation, but I didn't share it. It was hard to be certain in the ranks of black backs, but I thought our man wasn't there any more. While we were praying, he'd disappeared. I got up and signed to Mr Godwit to come with me. He looked horrified but followed. As I went out of the door, I heard him explaining to the usher that his niece had been taken ill. Evidently, I'd been promoted up the family tree. He caught up with me in the close and I hurried him back down towards the hotel.

'Him?'

'Yes.'

My doubts had left me now we were out and moving. When we got to the hotel, I practically ran upstairs to Mr Godwit's room, with him not far behind. We found the door shut and nothing looking out of the way. I thought I'd been wrong after all, until Amos's voice came from inside.

'That you, Miss Lane?'

'Yes.'

'Hold on a minute.'

Scuffling came from inside and a man's voice, slurred but protesting. Mr Godwit recognized the voice and so did I. He looked at me, his expression saying that I was right, but he still didn't want to believe it. Tabby opened the door just enough to let us in. A man in black was slumped in a chair, his nose bleeding, Amos standing beside him. The man raised his head, another gout of red jerking from his nose on to his shirt front.

'Penbrake?' Mr Godwit said to his fellow magistrate.

What he intended by making it a question, I don't know. Perhaps, what are we going to do about it? If so, Penbrake gave him an answer by jumping up suddenly and making for the door. Amos and Tabby moved in front of him. Penbrake turned, swerved past me and Mr Godwit and went straight out of the window, through frame, glass and all. A woman's scream sounded from the pavement. When Amos and I reached the window, Penbrake was already on his feet. He lurched away, across the road into a narrow street leading downhill. For a moment it looked as if Amos intended to vault across the sill through jagged glass and follow him the most direct way.

'Don't,' I said. 'He can't get far like that.'

Far enough, as it happened. We lost the trail because when Amos ran down the stairs to the hotel lobby, the hotel manager and two porters tried to stop him, assuming that the fracas upstairs had been his fault. Even when I arrived and explained as best I could, they were slow in understanding. Looking back, maybe I can't blame them. But it meant that by the time Amos, Tabby and I were across the road, all we had to follow was a trail of bloodspots and eventually we lost even those in a maze of small streets leading down to the docks. If it hadn't been a Sunday morning, there would have been more people on the streets to see him or even stop him.

As it was, they didn't find him until well into the afternoon, floating in the arm of the docks where the barges tie up, close to the canal entrance and almost within sight of the prison where Joanna Picton had spent her last few weeks in her native country. I wished there was some way of letting her know that, but by then the ship that carried her would be near the other side of the world.

TWENTY-TWO

Later that afternoon, Mr Godwit and I took our story and the book with Mary's letter to St Jude. He'd managed to have a meeting with his client, and Jack Picton's reaction to Penbrake's name had been much as I expected. Yes, he had seen Penbrake when he waited in the woods at the back of the Kembles' house. That was the name he'd intended to spring on the court in the morning. By then rumours were flying around the town and some of them weren't far from the truth. Now Penbrake was dead in such strange circumstances, his old associates were remembering stories about his ways with women that they'd chosen to disregard when he was their colleague and dining companion.

When Picton's barrister stopped doubting our sanity and realized what we were bringing him, he practically ran off to arrange meetings with the prosecution and possibly a judge in chambers. We decided to stay an extra night in Gloucester to hear the result, and he came to see us after dinner, looking like a man who'd put his money on an outsider and seen it romp home.

'Case adjourned.'

'Only adjourned?' I said. 'Why aren't they releasing him?'

Shocked at such impatience, Mr Godwit and the barrister explained that the law did not work like that. There must be more legal discussion and, at some future point, an appearance before the judges when the prosecution would state that they were presenting no evidence.

'A few more weeks in prison won't make much difference to Jack Picton,' Mr Godwit said cheerfully. 'As soon as they let him out, he'll probably do something to get himself put back in again. And it's better than being hanged.'

'What about Penbrake?' I said. 'Will it come out in court that he killed Mary Marsh?'

That depended on a lot of things, it seemed, but the answer was 'Not necessarily'. I had to accept that, but resolved that I'd do all I could to make sure the facts were publicly known. Telling Mr Crow would be a good start.

* * *

Early next morning we set out towards Cheltenham as we'd come, myself on Rancie, Amos and Tabby on the skewbald cob, Mr Godwit some way behind in the gig. He'd invited me to stay for a few days longer and I'd decided to accept, mainly to get Rancie well rested for the ride back to London. I wasn't looking forward to it on my own and wondered whether I should ask Amos, as a final kindness, to find a sturdy pony for me to buy so that Tabby could ride with me. I could afford it. Mr Godwit had agreed to pay my fee, plus a generous amount for travelling expenses. The darkness of the cloud that the case had cast over his contented life was obvious now from his relief when it was lifted. When we came to Mr Godwit's house, Amos dismounted to help me down.

'There's something I should do first,' I said. 'It won't take long. Can you wait here until I get back?'

He nodded and I rode to the Kembles' house, turning off the drive towards the stable yard. As I'd hoped, I found Rodney Kemble there, talking to the head groom. He looked at me, told the groom to take Rancie and then led the way to a place where we could talk. As it happened, it was under the tree where Mary Marsh had sketched him from her window. The news of Penbrake's death hadn't travelled this far. I told him about it as simply as I could.

For a long time he said nothing. Then: 'I wish she'd told me what she was going to do. I wish she'd sent that letter.'

'At least it's done something that she'd have wanted,' I said.

The letter that she'd never sent to him, now in the hands of the lawyers, had given every last detail of Joanna's story: how, on the day of the fair, Penbrake had taken her from the cell where she was locked up with the other women and offered her freedom in exchange for what he wanted. Confused and terrified of the consequences if she had to appear in court, she'd given in to him. Later, when she knew she was expecting his child, she'd gone to him, but he'd threatened her with even worse consequences if she told anybody. When she faced hanging, he'd had to change tactics. He managed to see her in prison and promise to save her, provided she kept quiet. If the sentence hadn't been commuted, she'd have found out how worthless his promise was on the gallows.

'Mary should never have gone to face him on her own,' Rodney Kemble said. 'It was madness.' He was trying to shift his anger against himself on to Mary.

'Brave madness,' I said. 'And maybe not madness. Perhaps she was going to offer him a bargain: she'd keep quiet about what he'd done if he'd help get Joanna Picton back from transportation.'

I guessed that she'd have hated having to make any kind of bargain with Penbrake, but she was a practical woman, using what resources she had.

'She must have known she was putting herself in danger,' he said.

'People don't expect to be murdered.'

There was nothing I could say to console him. Time might do that, or perhaps another woman as remarkable as Mary, if he happened to be lucky enough to meet one. As we walked back to the yard, I risked asking after his sister.

'She's marrying Paley in October.'

He said it through gritted teeth. I smiled inwardly to think that Barbara had got what she wanted. I could understand her brother's anger. Although Peter Paley had not been as guilty towards Joanna as Rodney had believed, his record was not the sort that a brother would welcome. I thought, but didn't say, that married happiness was an unpredictable affair and the union might well turn out better than he expected. Barbara and Peter loved each other, were young enough to learn some sense, and both families had plenty of money. The omens could be worse, though it might be some time before Barbara got back the book with the engagement ode.

As Rodney Kemble and I parted, he said, 'I wish you could have met Mary. I think you would have liked each other.'

'I think so, too,' I said.

Back at Mr Godwit's house, Amos was waiting for me at the paddock gate. He helped me dismount and then untacked Rancie and turned her out. We watched as she rolled like a puppy in the grass. There was so much I wanted to say to him, but I didn't want to speak because that would be the beginning of goodbye. He broke the silence.

'Well, I suppose I should be going.'

'Yes, if you're planning to get home to Herefordshire tonight.'

'Not that far. Just down to the town to take back the cob.'

Then on home tomorrow, I supposed. After all that had happened to us together, he deserved more than my silence.

'Amos, with all my heart I wish you and your bride my very best. I'm sure you'll be happy. You deserve to be. Write when you can and let me know you're well.'

But he'd never been a great man for writing. Rancie was on her feet now, shaking herself and making that contented 'hrrrr' sound. Amos was looking at her, not at me.

'So we're not going back together?' he said at last.

I tried to laugh. Had it just occurred to him? 'I don't think your wife-to-be would like that,' I said.

'I don't reckon she's got a lot to say in the matter, considering she's not my wife-to-be any more.'

I stared at him. 'What do you mean?'

He looked back at me, his expression unreadable. 'Elopement seems to be the fashion. I had a message from home a couple of days ago to say she's gone off with my cousin. I always knew she liked him best, any road.'

Relief and pity for his loss hit me together. I'd like to say pity was the greater, but I don't know.

'Amos, I'm so sorry.'

'Need a good horse when you're eloping,' Amos said. 'Has to carry the pair of you.' His face was still expressionless, so I thought the remarks were just his way of hiding his hurt, until he suddenly grinned at me. 'So I made sure they had one – my wedding present to them.'

My laughter made Rancie turn and stare and set the spaniel barking and the white ducks quacking in Mr Godwit's quiet pond.

Lightning Source UK Ltd.
Milton Keynes UK
UKOW01f2358020318
318822UK00001B/9/P